"He had always liked to be left alone when he didn't feel well, but lately he found he hated it. Maybe, he thought, I'm afraid I may die alone, but what of it? Animals are supposed to prefer to die alone; why not man? It was bound to be a lonely business, any way you did it."

"One will long remember . . . Jordan Phillips, his courage and love of life . . ."   —*Commonweal*

". . . at an age when the whole concept seems impossibly abstract, Jordan doesn't do badly at all and anyone who's just begun to realize his own mortality will probably find Jordan a comforting intercessor."   —*Kirkus Reviews*

About the Author

Paige Dixon also writes under her real name, Barbara Corcoran, and another pseudonym, Gail Hamilton. Ms. Dixon grew up in New England and has lived in Montana, Key West, Florida, and England. She believes that having lived in many different places has given her much inspiration for her writing.

Other VAGABOND BOOKS you will also enjoy:

Blackbriar
  by William Sleator
Dear Lovey Hart, I Am Desperate
  by Ellen Conford
Gimme an H, Gimme an E, Gimme an L, Gimme a P
  by Frank Bonham
Sometimes I Don't Love My Mother
  by Hila Colman

A Time to Love
A Time to Mourn

(hardcover title: May I Cross Your Golden River?)

A novel by
Paige Dixon

Copyright © 1975 by Paige Dixon. This edition is published by Vagabond Books, a division of Scholastic Magazines, Inc., by arrangement with Atheneum Publishers.

Vagabond Books

SCHOLASTIC BOOK SERVICES
New York Toronto London Auckland Sydney Tokyo

for Gertrude Gilbert
and in memory of
Vedder Gilbert

ISBN 0-590-32396-2

12 11 10 9 8 7 6 5 4 3 2 1   10   1 2 3 4 5 6/8

Printed in the U. S. A.   06

First

Jordan opened his eyes and saw his mother smiling down at him.

"Happy birthday," she said.

"Thank you," he said sleepily. "Is it a good day?"

"Beautiful day."

He and his brothers teased her because she set such store by the weather as an omen. She claimed to remember what the weather had been like on all the important days of her life, including the days that each of her five children were born. On the day of Jordan's birth it had been sunny and bright in the morning, with a violent thunderstorm at night.

Jordan punched the mattress of the bunk above him, and his youngest brother Skipper (born in a blizzard) protested with a sleepy growl. "You'd think," Jordan said, "when a man gets to be eighteen, he could have a room of his own."

His mother opened the shutters and looked

1

out at the peaks of the Flatiron Mountains. "Cheer up. A year from now Alex will be in medical school and Tony will have his doctorate. You'll have more rooms than you need."

"A year from now," Jordan said, bunching up the pillow under his head. "A year is forever."

"When you're my age, it's five minutes. Skipper, get up. I'm starting breakfast."

Skipper groaned. "It's Saturday."

"I know, and you're due at the market in exactly fifty minutes."

"Skip hasn't gotten used to work," Jordan said. "It's come as a terrible shock to him. Carrying all those sacks of groceries . . ."

"Ah, come on," Skipper said.

"Skip thought only the big boys had to work, not Mama's little lamb." He ducked as Skipper leaned down and aimed a wild punch at him.

"Don't start roughhousing now," their mother said. "Downstairs in twenty minutes, on the double."

"Aye, aye, sir." Skipper swung his feet over the edge of the bunk and slid to the floor. At fourteen he was still short and wiry, unlike his three six-feet-tall brothers. "Come on, Jordan, on your feet. You think you can loll in bed just because it's your birthday?" He snatched off Jordan's blanket. "Think you're the king, huh?" He laughed and scrambled out of the way as Jordan pretended to lunge at him.

"Eighteen minutes." Their mother went out of the room.

Skipper grabbed his jeans and danced down the hall toward the bathroom, feinting and jabbing at an imaginary foe.

2

"Don't use up all the hot water," Jordan called after him. "I want a shower."

Jordan's older brother Alex appeared in the doorway, carrying a white laboratory jacket. "Happy birthday, Number Three Son."

"Thank you, Herr Doktor," Jordan said. "You working at the hospital today?"

"Till four."

Jordan yawned. "What do you do anyway?"

Alex shrugged. "Push gurneys. Help old ladies in and out of bed. Get coffee for the nurses."

"Tough life. You bringing Jenifer to the party tonight?"

"Sure. Wait till you see the present she got you."

"Yeah? Is it good?"

"I like it."

"Well, you can't borrow it."

Alex laughed and went downstairs.

Jordan was the last one to come to the breakfast table. He had dressed carefully in his new white tennis shorts and cricket sweater, and his curly, dark red hair was damp from the shower. He grinned as Skipper rose elaborately and bowed him to the table.

"This way, Your Highness," Skipper said. "This way, sire. Let me seat you."

"Seat him on the chair, Skip," said Tony, the oldest, "not on the floor."

"How you talk!" Skipper said. He shoved the chair to catch Jordan at the knees, but Jordan was too quick for him.

"Sit down, Skipper," his mother said. "You're joggling the table."

"Happy birthday, Jordie," Tony said in his

3

quiet voice. He was thinner than the other two older boys, and he stooped a little.

Jordan nodded his thanks.

"Why are you all dolled up?" Alex asked. I know it's the great day, but I mean . . . Aren't you working?"

Jordan shook his head. "Mr. Parsons had to go to Denver. He gave me the day off."

"When Jordie is a great trial lawyer and I am a great trial," Skipper said, "he will defend me and I will go scot-free, and all the world will marvel at the great bond that ties us. Please pass the marmalade, Tony."

Tony leaned forward to give him the marmalade jar. "It'll rot your teeth."

"And when you're a great author, Tony, you'll write a prize-winning series exposing marmalade."

"I wish you wouldn't wave your arms around, Skipper," his mother said. "You'll knock over your milk."

"Skipper is irrepressible this morning," Alex said drily.

"And when Skipper is irrepressible," Jordan said, "everybody duck."

"Now, how many will be at the party?" his mother asked. "I need to know about the food."

Jordan counted them off on his fingers. "You and me, these three. Jenifer, Susan, Em . . . Is Bitsy coming, Tony?"

"No. She's gone to Aspen with her folks."

Jordan looked at his mother. "Eight, and Terry . . ." He paused. "And I suppose Pat?"

"Of course Pat," his mother said.

4

The boys groaned.

"Why do we always have to have Pat?" Skipper said.

"Because your sister married him," his mother said sharply, "and I hope you will all treat him decently."

"Have we ever been rude to him?" Alex said. "Since Terry married him, I mean."

"Not outright rude," she said, "but try to treat him like a human being."

"But Mom, he isn't a human being," Skipper said.

"Knock it off, Skip," Tony said. "Don't worry, Mom. We'll treat him all right."

She sighed. "I know he's a trial sometimes. But you must remember, you probably wouldn't have liked anybody Terry married."

"But Pat . . ." Jordan said.

"Just remember, each one of you, that the rest of your family may not be one hundred percent in favor of whomever you marry, either, and how would you feel if we weren't nice to her?" She looked at Jordan and looked away again.

"She means Susan," Skipper said. "She thinks Susan is too old for Jordie."

"Oh, do shut up, Skipper," Alex said.

Jordan pushed his plate away, frowning. "If you all find Susan so repulsive, we'd better call off the party and I'll take Susan out."

"Don't be absurd, Jordan," his mother said. "You know we like Susan. I'm not sure I want you to marry her, but that's hardly the issue, is it, when you're only in your first year at the uni-

5

versity." She got up and found a memo pad. "I'm going to be reading themes most of the day, so I'll have to count on you all to help for the party."

"Did you assign themes to those poor creatures already?" Tony said.

"I always do, right from the first week, one a week."

"You're a masochist."

"You mean 'sadist,'" Alex said.

"No, masochist. She has to read them."

Ignoring them, she put on her glasses and made notes. "Tony, you get the ice cream, will you? What kind do you want, Jordan?"

"Coffee," Jordan said.

"Half coffee, half chocolate, I think. Two quarts of each."

"Three quarts of each," Jordan said.

"All right, get it at Mr. Tripps'." She looked over her glasses at Tony. He nodded. "I'm giving you a ten-dollar bill. Don't forget my change. Alex, on your way home please stop at the Mexican place and get three dozen taco shells."

"Oh, good," Jordan said. "You're going to make those avocado things."

"What about the cake?" Skipper said. "I've always wanted to make a cake with diagonal stripes . . ."

"I'll make the cake," his mother said.

"With fifty-two candles," Skipper said, "one for every maiden who's thrown herself off the Flatirons in hopeless love for old Jordan."

"You never stop talking," Jordan said. He gave Skipper a light punch in the biceps. Skipper returned the punch.

"Watch the milk!" their mother cried, but it was too late. The half-full glass went over. She sat back in her chair, looking discouraged. "If just once we could get through a meal without Skipper knocking something over."

Chastened, he got up and found a dishcloth. "I'll clean it up." He looked at his brothers. "Oh, be quiet. You probably knocked over plenty of milk in your time."

"Nobody's said a word," Alex said.

"Well, I can read your minds." Skipper scrubbed the tablecloth. "If you'd only get plastic tablecloths, we wouldn't have this problem."

"I hate plastic tablecloths," his mother said.

"The mailman's here." Tony started to get up, but Jordan got up ahead of him and went for the mail. He came back, sorting through the letters. He gave several envelopes to his mother.

"Bills," she said.

He handed a large manila envelope to Tony.

"Rejection," Tony said.

"I've got a card and a check from the old man," Jordan said.

His mother looked up quickly, but she said nothing.

"How much?" Alex said.

"The usual ten."

"I hope you'll write and thank him," his mother said.

"Oh, Ma, we always do," Tony said.

"He's moved," Jordan said. "He's in Bangor, Maine."

"A safe distance," Tony said.

Alex picked up the card and looked at it. "I wonder why he bothers."

"He's a sentimental man," his mother said.

"I hardly remember what he looks like," Jordan said.

"He looks rather like you, as a matter of fact," Tony said. "Doesn't he, Ma?"

"Perhaps a little. The same coloring."

"I never saw him at all," Skipper said. "I don't believe in him. He's like the Tooth Fairy."

"You're the one who drove him away," Alex said. "You were the straw that broke the camel's back, Skip."

"Don't talk like that," his mother said.

"Why did he leave?" Skipper asked. "Nobody ever really told me."

His mother took off her glasses. "He was never really a family man."

Jordan laughed. "If you weren't a family man, I can see it would be a shock to find yourself with five kids."

"He meant well," his mother said. "It was just too much for him."

Tony pushed back his chair. "The Boulder Florist Shop is getting impatient. See you later." He got a white jacket from a hook in the hall.

"Are you taking the VW?" Jordan said.

"I was. I can take the motorbike if you want it."

"If you don't care."

"Sure."

"Don't forget the ice cream," his mother said.

"Are you taking the Volvo, Alex?" Skipper asked.

"Yeah. You want to be dropped off?"

8

"He'd better take his bike," his mother said, "in case no one is available to bring him home."

"Oh, I'll bring him home," Alex said. "What time are you off, Skip?"

"Four-thirty."

"What about you, Ma?" Jordan said. "You want a ride to campus? I'm going out the Baseline first but I can drop you off."

"I'll walk," she said. "It's a nice day."

"Sometimes this house sounds like a dispatcher's office." Alex said. "Hurry up, Skip."

"Right on." Skipper grabbed a last piece of toast and followed his brother out the door.

"Remember your lunch," his mother called after him. "In the refrigerator."

"Got it."

The back door slammed, and in a minute the old Volvo wagon roared.

Jordan looked at his mother and smiled. "It's like a morgue around here when everybody clears out."

She nodded. "Are you playing tennis with Susan?"

"Yes." Jordan got up. "Anything you want me to do for the party?"

"No. It's your party. You get to relax."

"Going to have any 3.2?" He said it with careful casualness.

"No, I am not. Just because you're eighteen doesn't mean we have to start serving beer."

"I just asked." He got his tennis racket and a can of balls. "See you later."

"Jordan . . ." When he looked back, she said, "Don't be huffy about the beer."

"Who's huffy?" He took the keys to the Volks-

9

wagen from the nail by the kitchen door and went out.

"Put some oil in the car," she called after him, but he didn't answer.

As he walked toward the garage, Emily Faulkner leaned on the wooden fence that separated the Faulkner place from the Phillips'. She was just Jordan's age, a pretty girl with freckles and a ponytail. She had her jeans tucked inside boots.

"Hey, man," she said, "happy birthday."

Jordan brightened. "Hi. Thanks." He came over to the fence. "Do I get a birthday kiss?"

"Nope. You're too big."

"Remember how you used to kiss me on my birthday when we were little?"

"Yes. I usually had to rassle you to the ground to do it."

"You wouldn't have to rassle me now."

She looked disconcerted for a moment, but then she laughed and said, "You're practicing. How's Susan?"

"Okay. The party's at 8:00 tonight. I suppose you've heard."

She nodded. "I'll be there if I don't break my neck. I'm riding in the rodeo today."

"Barrel-racing?"

"Yes. I don't know what I do it for. It's silly."

"You do it because you're competitive."

"I don't know. What were you looking so crabby about when you came out just now?"

"Ma won't let me have beer at my party."

She laughed. "You're jealous because Alex had it for his."

"Well, it isn't fair."

"He's two years older."

"Oh, you always stick up for Ma."

"Us girls stick together." She saw him glance toward the garage, and she said quickly, "I've got to go. Have a good day."

He waved and ran to the garage. He was going to be late, and Susan got mad when he was late. It took a minute to warm up the car. He glanced in the back to see if the charcoal was there. He had it in mind to take Susan up in the hills for a picnic lunch after the tennis match — if she would go. She was not the world's greatest outdoorsman.

He pushed in the choke and backed the old car carefully out the narrow drive. "All right, World," he said aloud, as he swung around and headed out toward the Baseline Road, "today I am a man. Watch out!"

Second

Jordan played tennis well. For the last three years he had reached the semifinals in the county tournament, and next year he was determined to make the finals. But lately he had run into an odd problem. His hand would unexpectedly start to tremble, sometimes quite violently, and his wrists seemed weak. Today, in the games with Susan, he had more trouble than he had ever had before. Once, in a perfectly simple lob, he drove the ball clear out of the court because his wrist jerked. And another time, at the net, he dropped his racket. Susan, who was only an average player, almost beat him. It took him three sets to beat her.

He took a little run as if to jump over the net, then walked around it. "After three sets with you I can't make it."

She smiled. "You were really off your game today, old boy, or else I'm getting good." She pulled a comb from her pocket and combed back her long golden hair. She was almost as tall as Jordan.

"Did I ever tell you you're the prettiest girl in the Rocky Mountain West?"

"You've mentioned it."

"*And* the world. *And* the universe." He took her hand, and they walked away from the courts along one of the paths that crisscrossed the big campus. "How do you feel about a picnic? I know a super place."

"With ants?"

"I will personally dispose of any ants."

"Aren't we headed away from the car?"

"I just want to see my mother for a minute." He led her through the ivy-covered arch to the front of the Liberal Arts building.

"You and your mother." Her voice had a trace of annoyance.

He looked at her quickly. "I was kind of teed off at her this morning. I want to make up."

"You're a mama's boy."

He laughed. "No. She isn't that kind of a mother."

"I'll wait for you." She held back at the door.

"Oh, come on in and say hello."

But she shook her head and sat down on the stone steps.

Jordan's mother looked pleased to see him. She shoved her glasses up on her forehead. "How was the match?"

"Lousy. I had to fight to win. Hey, Susan and

13

I are going on a picnic. I'll be back in the late afternoon. Need anything?"

"No. Have a nice time." She looked at the stack of papers on her desk and sighed. "I'll get home sometime, I guess."

"Make 'em wait for their themes. Other instructors don't get them right back."

"But then one gets so far behind. I'll leave pretty soon. I want to make the cake so it will have time to cool properly."

He gave her shoulder a quick squeeze. "Sorry I was so crabby about the beer."

She patted his hand. "You do understand? I hate to start it before we have to. Skipper will be there, and Em . . ."

"I know. It's okay. See you."

She smiled at him. "Thanks for coming by."

Outside on the steps Susan was talking to an undergraduate, who left when Jordan came out. Susan stood up. "Sometimes I think I should have gone to college. All these cute men."

Jordan made a face.

"How is your mother?"

"All right." They cut across the grass toward the parking lot. The maples on the campus had already turned scarlet, and in the distance the lower slopes of the mountains were golden with aspen.

"She doesn't like me."

Jordan looked at her sharply. "Don't be ridiculous."

"She thinks I'm a clod because I didn't go to college. And I'm too old for you, she thinks."

"You're talking like some nut. My mother

doesn't care whether people went to college or not."

"She looks down on secretaries."

"Cut it out, Sue. Don't talk that way."

She laughed and ran ahead of him, skipping a few steps. "I don't care. They can't take you away from me."

He caught up with her. "So who wants to? Come on, I'll race you to the car."

When they got to the Volkswagen, he leaned against it, holding on to the door.

Susan laughed again. "Wore you out, didn't I?"

"The funny thing is, you did. Or something did." He leaned down and rubbed his ankle. "I didn't know senility set in this soon." He got into the car and sat still for a minute. "I must have done something to my ankle on the court."

"Excuses, excuses," Susan said. "You're just a tired old man." She leaned against him.

Jordan rumpled her hair gently. She sat up and combed it again.

"Sorry," he said. He drove out of the lot and in a few minutes he stopped at the market to buy hot dogs and buns, mustard, piccalilli, some onions, and a huge bag of potato chips. Skipper, who was wheeling a cart very full of groceries to some woman's car, waved at them as they drove off.

"That Skipper is cute," Susan said, snuggling up to Jordan again.

"I'm glad there's one of my family you approve of." He said it lightly.

"Oh, your other brothers are so superior," she said. "That Alex, just because he's a premed

15

student . . . and Tony — he never even knows I'm alive. He looks right through me."

"He's probably writing a poem in his head about you."

"That'll be the day. Does he really write poems?"

"Sure. He's even sold a few. He writes plays, too. He's good."

"And your sister and that creepy husband of hers . . ."

"Couldn't we talk about something else?" Jordan said. "Like what do you suppose those things hear when they listen to outer space?" He pointed to the enormous metal discs near the side of the road.

"I don't even know what they are."

"Project Ozma. They listen for communications from space."

"I don't believe in all that stuff."

Jordan laughed. "Do you believe in the moon?"

"Well, I can *see* that."

After a while he turned left and drove up a narrow road that led into the hills. He turned again into a graveled parking area. The land sloped sharply down toward a rushing stream, where there were picnic tables among the trees, and a stone fireplace. Jordan unloaded the food and carried the charcoal briquets down to the fireplace.

"One picnic lunch coming up," he said. "Sit down and enjoy Mother Nature."

Susan found a relatively clean bench, dusted it off with a Kleenex, and sat down. "I'm starved."

"I won't be long." He got the fire going and

came to sit on the pine needles at her feet while the briquets burned down to coals. "I forgot to get Cokes or anything."

"I wish we'd brought beer."

"So do I. I didn't think. And hey, you don't have to buy it any more. I can buy it myself now."

"On the way home we'll stop at The Cave and celebrate your liberation," she said. She leaned down and kissed him.

When they had finished lunch, they sat on a boulder at the edge of the creek and dangled their bare feet in the cold water. They watched a water ouzel strutting along under water, seeking out grubs with his beak. He flew up from the stream in a shower of tiny drops and sang his clear song.

Jordan watched him. "I hope I never have to live anywhere but Colorado."

Susan looked shocked. "You don't mean that."

"I do."

"I thought you were going to be a Washington attorney. Supreme Court and all that."

He laughed. "Honey, you don't start with the Supreme Court. I'm aiming for that when I'm an old man. Maybe by that time I won't mind so much if I have to leave here."

"I can't wait to get out of Colorado," she said in a low, intense voice. "I hate it."

"How can you hate it? It's so beautiful, and so . . . I don't know . . . clean and everything."

"I hate it. I want to live in New York or Chicago . . . or . . ." Her tone changed and she smiled at him . . . "Washington."

He looked concerned. "That's going to make a problem, isn't it?"

"Oh, no," she said lightly. "I'll just have to convert you."

He didn't answer. After a few minutes he got up and said, "I'm thirsty. Let's drive up to Ward and get a Coke or a beer or something."

"I thought Ward was a ghost town."

"No, there are still a few people there. There's a little store."

They drove up the mountain road, spinning gravel under the wheels. The car gave a few sharp pings when the going got steep, but it still took the hills pretty well for an old car, Jordan thought.

They came upon the little town gradually, driving past abandoned mine shafts and cabins that were falling in on themselves. The cabins that were still standing were clustered along the sides of the steep road, most of them empty, like old gravestones marking lives that were gone.

"It's a spooky place," Susan said.

Jordan accelerated as they came up the last pitched stretch of road into what was left of the town. He pulled off in front of the tiny general store and went inside. In a few minutes he came out grinning, with two tall cans of beer and some cookies.

"Didn't even have to show my ID," he said. "Already I look like a Supreme Court justice. Come on, I want to show you a neat place." Overriding her objections to the steep and rubbly path, he led her up a sharp ascent to the

18

ruins of a small hotel. He put down the beer cans and lifted her up onto the wide, columned porch. "Sorry about the steps. They've been gone a long time." He flung out his arm. "Look at that view!"

Below them the small mountain they were on plunged down through thickly wooded canyons to the valley below. All around them the Rockies thrust snow-clad peaks into the vivid blue sky. On the lower slopes of the mountains the aspen and the evergreens made designs of gold and dark green.

"It's pretty," Susan said. She kicked aside some of the broken glass that covered the porch. Vandals and wind and hail had broken all the big windows. "I mean the view is pretty. This place is a mess."

"But think what it must have been like in the old days," Jordan said. "Can't you see us sitting in comfortable rockers on this porch, looking out at all that?" He grabbed her hand. "We're on our honeymoon, you see, and we like it quiet. There's a very good waiter in a white starched jacket who brings us tall iced drinks whenever we want them . . ."

"Mint juleps," she said.

"Well, it's the wrong part of the country, but never mind. Let's say this waiter is from Kentucky or Georgia or someplace, and he loves to make mint juleps. In the cool of the evening we walk along that path . . ." He pointed to the far side of the hotel where the land rose again. "We see deer coming out for a drink in the twilight, and off in the woods an elk bugles . . ."

He did an imitation of a bugling elk. "Ducks are flying over, going south for the winter. In the morning while you're still asleep I go fishing, and we get the chef to broil my trout for our dinner . . ."

"And what do we do in the evening?" Susan said. "There's not even a movie house."

"Honey! We're on our honeymoon. Who needs movies?"

She giggled. "Jordan, you're a disgrace."

"No," he said, "I'm happy and I'm eighteen. Wow!" He gave her a quick hug. "Come on, I'll show you the inside." He took her in through the door, which hung askew on its hinges. "Watch that floorboard; it's rotting."

She followed him, stepping gingerly and clinging to his arm. "This is spooky. Do we have to go in?"

"Oh, come on, it's interesting. Look, there's the desk where you would check in. Imagine I own a lot of very productive silver mines — that's before silver collapsed, of course — and I'm very rich . . ."

"I thought we were newlyweds."

"Time flies. It's our silver anniversary and I've just been appointed to serve out the term of a congressman who's died. After that, I'll be reelected, of course, and I may go on to be president. Would you fancy the White House, my love?"

"You bet."

"Very well. You shall have it." He prowled around the remains of the lobby. "People have really stripped this place. When I first found it, there was still some nice paneling left and wrought iron hinges. They're all gone." He disappeared for a moment.

"Jordan?"

"I'm out here. Come on out. This was the dining room. And look, what a small kitchen. Well, there weren't more than a dozen rooms, I guess." His voice echoed in the empty room.

"Let's go," she said.

"Man, what a neat fireplace," he said. "I suppose somebody will swipe that mantelpiece one of these days. Want to see the bedrooms?"

"No," she called back. She flicked a Kleenex over a dusty windowsill and sat down. "Hurry up. It's cold in here."

He came back in a minute. "It must have been really neat. Nothing in the bedrooms now, though, except some torn mattresses. I think people have been camping out in here."

"I think it's a horrible place," she said. "I'm leaving." She went out onto the porch, picking her way disapprovingly through the debris. "And what about the beer? I thought you were thirsty."

"Oh, sorry. I forgot." He picked up the cans from the porch and opened them. "There you are." He lifted his can. "Here's to Oliver Wendell Holmes, Junior, Clarence Darrow, William O. Douglas, and all the other likely lads."

"Including Jordan Phillips, I suppose."

"Naturally." He laughed and drank his beer. "Want to sit?"

"Not here. I don't like this place. It's too dead."

He found her a flat boulder a little distance from the inn. "There. You can see the view and turn your back on my hotel." He sat down beside her.

"Jordan," she began, in a tentative voice.

"Yeah?"

"I was talking to my boss. He needs somebody part-time in the stock room."

He looked at her. "So?"

"He'd pay you quite a lot more than old Parsons gives you."

He didn't speak for a moment. "Sue," he said finally, "we've talked about this before. It isn't so much what Mr. Parsons pays me. Mr. Parsons is a first-rate lawyer, and he's teaching me. By the time I get to law school, I'm going to have a good start." He ran his hand through his hair. "Besides, he depends on me for a lot of little things."

"Well, whose career are we talking about, yours or Mr. Parsons'?"

"That's a silly question. Mr. Parsons has his career, a very solid one. He can teach me an awful lot, Sue. That's how young guys used to learn the law, you know — Lincoln, for instance — working in some established lawyer's office as a clerk."

"But he pays you peanuts." She was exasperated.

"In cash, maybe."

"Jordan, cash is the only kind of pay there is."

"No, you're wrong." He took her hand between both of his. "Hey, let's don't fight on my birthday, all right? Believe me, Sue, I am right about this. Have a little faith."

She pulled her hand loose and got up. "Let's go. I've got a lot of things to do."

Feeling hurt, he watched her for a moment as she climbed carefully down the path. Then he got up and followed her.

When they got back to town, he said, "You still want that beer at The Cave?"

"No," she said coolly. "I've got to do my laundry this afternoon. It's the only time I have." She paused and then added pointedly, "I work for a living."

When he got home, his mother had just come in. "Did you have a nice picnic?" she asked.

"Great," he said abruptly. He went up to his room and shut the door.

Third

When Alex and Tony had both come home from work, Alex knocked on Jordan's door. "Pull yourself together, man. Tony and I are taking you to The Cave for a beer in twenty minutes."

Jordan opened the door. He had been sleeping and he was still in his tennis clothes. "You're kidding."

"Certainly not. Get dressed."

In fifteen minutes Jordan came downstairs. Skipper, who was decorating the big birthday cake, whistled. "Ladies and gentlemen, right out of the pages of *Playboy* we present that walking fashion plate, Mr. Jordan Phillips, Esquire."

Jordan was wearing light gray denims, a gray turtleneck, and a plum-colored velvet blazer. His mother smiled at him. "You do look nice."

"The guys are taking me to The Cave."

"I know. I'm not fixing dinner. There are roast beef sandwiches and salad in the refrigerator. You can all help yourselves. But do come home in time to eat something before the party."

Alex and Tony came into the kitchen.

Their mother shook her head. "Why anyone would want to go to The Cave, of all places . . ."

"Rites of passage, Mom," Tony said.

They went in the VW, Alex driving. He parked a couple of blocks from The Cave. The street was crowded with students celebrating Colorado's victory in the day's football game.

It was the first time Jordan had been inside The Cave. It was a big, barny place, with tables along the walls. Students with schooners of beer in their hands milled around or found a seat somewhere. Alex rushed for a table where people were leaving, but another group got there first.

Above the din Jordan said in Tony's ear, "Now I understand the sign over the door. ABANDON HOPE ALL YE WHO ENTER HERE."

Alex pounced on another table and waved his brothers in. They slid along the benches just ahead of a couple. "Squeeze in," Alex said to them. "Always room for ten or twenty more."

Tony came back from the bar balancing three schooners of beer. He slid two along the wet surface of the table to Alex and Jordan, and he lifted his own. "To Jordan."

Alex lifted his glass. "To Jordan."

The girl at the end of the table said, "To who?"

Tony pointed to Jordan. "Kid brother. Eighteen today."

The couple toasted Jordan.

Jordan laughed. He felt happy. "Hey, will you guys stop toasting me so I can drink this stuff?" He took a long swallow and wiped the foam from his lip. "Here's to Coors. Best beer in America."

"Made with Rocky Mountain spring water," Tony said.

"By mermaids," Alex said.

A girl who was in Jordan's sociology class waved to him, and a few minutes later his English instructor nodded. Everyone was excited about the game, and Jordan thought he had never in his life heard such a bedlam of voices. He hadn't realized The Cave would be so great. He liked being one of the three older brothers instead of one of the two younger ones. When Skipper is eighteen, he thought, I'll bring him here.

All too soon Tony looked at his watch and said that it was time to go. It seemed to Jordan as if they had just come. Out on the street the daylight was dazzling and the crowd denser than ever. A long line snake-danced down the sidewalk, chanting. The end person grabbed at Jordan to get him into the line, but regretfully he ducked away. It would have been fun. He was eighteen, he had just had his first public drink, he was a university student, and his team had won a game. It was a good day.

And in the evening it got still better, except that for a while he worried that Susan wasn't going to show up. He had offered to go and get her, but she had refused because she wanted to be able to leave when she was ready. Twice Jordan went into the kitchen and called her apartment, but there was no answer.

She came at last, looking beautiful in a dress

he hadn't seen before, a floor-length blue-and-lavender-patterned dress with puffed sleeves that made her look almost demure. Except for her eyes, she was wearing no makeup. Jordan saw his sister Terry look her over when she thought no one noticed. Terry, who was pregnant, looked pretty but not exactly glamorous in a maternity dress. Em, who was not much interested in clothes, looked well-groomed as she always did, in one of her pantsuits. Alex's girl, Jenifer, was the only one, Jordan thought, who could offer Susan any competition, and in his opinion Susan won hands down, although Jenifer was very pretty in her small, dark way, and Jordan liked her.

Susan sat on the floor beside him. "Never mind all those other girls," she said. "Pay attention to me." She smiled up at him, her most beguiling smile.

"I was just thinking," he said, "that you don't have any competition."

"But they're all so useful." She watched Jenifer and Em bringing in plates of sandwiches and tacos from the kitchen. "Little women at work. I'm lousy at that. I never know what to do in another woman's house."

"All you have to do is sit where I can look at you. After all, it's my birthday."

"Your friend Em is madly in love with you," she said, as Em went past them and smiled at Jordan.

He laughed. "You're out of your mind. We've known each other since the cradle. Besides, all Em's affections are for horses."

Jordan's brother-in-law, Pat, came over and

sat in the chair next to them. He was a minister in a small parish church, and although he was not quite thirty, he already had the plump look, the bulging stomach, of a much older man. He folded his hands over his stomach in a complacent way that always made Jordan wince. He had tried hard to like Pat because he loved his sister, but he found it difficult. Pat treated them all like wayward children.

"Well, Jordan," he said, "is the eighteenth turning out to be memorable?"

"Very," Jordan said. He was determined to be agreeable. "You know Susan, don't you, Pat?"

Pat looked her over in his slow, appraising way, and nodded. "I believe we have met."

"Five or six times, I think," Susan said brightly.

Jordan crossed his fingers. "Did you go to the game, Pat?" He knew his brother-in-law's fondness for spectator sports.

"Oh, yes. It was a great game." He launched into a long description of some of the tenser moments.

Seeing Susan's look of boredom, Jordan glanced around for help, but everyone was busy. Tony was going through a stack of records for the stereo, Alex and Jenifer were setting out punch bowl and cups, Em and Terry had disappeared into the kitchen, and Skipper was wandering around the room with a trayful of sandwiches, offering them to the others. Pat went on and on about a blocked punt.

"It sounds like a good game all right," Jordan said, seizing a moment's pause for breath in Pat's account. "I wish I'd seen it."

Pat leveled a disapproving look at him, his round, jowly face seeming to squeeze itself up like one of those rubber faces children play with. "None of you went."

"No. Well, Alex and Tony were working, and I..."

Pat interrupted him. "You were going through your dusty briefs, I presume." To Susan he said, with a perceptible touch of sarcasm, "A remarkable lot, these young fellows. Author, doctor, lawyer . . ." He glanced up at Skipper who stood patiently beside them, waiting for them to take a sandwich. "And what are you going to be, Skipper?"

"Indian chief," Skipper said. "What else is left?" He leaned past Pat to offer a sandwich to Susan.

Susan burst out laughing and Pat heaved himself to his feet, smiling with the smile of one who feels he has been put down.

"It is a fortunate thing," he said, "that the Church managed to get in, even if by the back door." He sailed away in search of his wife.

Susan rolled her eyes upward. "He is really, really too much."

"Have another sandwich," Skipper said. "Have two. I sliced those cucumbers with my own lily-white hands."

Jordan smiled his approval at Skipper. As a family they had always protected each other from outsiders, and now they would protect Terry's husband, even if they were not fond of him. He was glad Skipper reacted that way, changing the subject like that. He got to his feet.

"When do I get to open my presents?"

His mother came in with a big silver urn full of coffee. It was her wedding present from her mother, that silver service, and she only brought it out on festive occasions. "Right after the cake, Jordie," she said. "Tony dear, turn down the stereo just a touch, will you? Nobody can hear himself think."

Tony turned it down, saying, "You're not supposed to think at parties, Mom."

When it came time to bring in the cake, Terry came to her brother and turned him around. "You're not supposed to see until it bursts upon us in all its glory."

Jordan grinned at her. During the hard years when their father was gone and their mother worked during the day and took classes at night to finish her M.A., Terry had been like another mother to them. Jordan hadn't been happy when she had married Pat, but maybe Pat had something that Terry saw and her brothers couldn't see. Anyway, she seemed happy.

"Turn around." Terry took his elbows and turned him.

His mother was carrying the cake ablaze with its eighteen candles, gorgeous in the decorations Skipper had given it. They all sang "Happy Birthday" and Jordan grinned, both embarrassed and pleased. He liked the idea that his family always celebrated birthdays and Christmas and Thanksgiving in more or less the same way. It made him feel as if things would go on like that forever, although of course they couldn't.

"Blow!" they chanted, and he blew hard.

"Blow!"

All but seven candles went out. "He's going to have seven children," Skipper said, blowing out the remaining candles.

"He'd better make it to the Supreme Court in a hurry, then," Terry said. "Children are expensive." She flashed a warm smile at Pat.

After the cake came the presents. A set of law books from Tony, an oxford gray pullover that Em had knitted, lamb's wool slippers from Skipper, a jacket from his mother, a braided leather wristband from Jenifer, money from Alex. But best of all was the sterling pen and pencil set from Susan.

"It's a terrific birthday," he said. "Everything's super."

Terry and Em knelt to gather up the presents and the wrapping paper. He got up to help them, and without warning his left knee buckled and he fell forward. There was an instant of shocked hush, and then they all pressed forward to help him up. He felt like a fool. But when he began to put his weight on his left leg, it folded again like the leg of his old childhood Raggedy Andy. Alex put Jordan's arm around his neck.

"Take it easy," Alex said. He held him up.

"What's wrong with it?" Jordan felt bewildered and vaguely scared. He made another try but the same thing happened.

"What is it?" his mother cried out sharply.

"Don't worry, Ma. Probably tennis knee," Alex said. "Let's get you on the sofa, old boy, where you can be comfortable." He and Tony lifted Jordan onto the sofa.

"I feel like an idiot," Jordan said.

31

"It's just too much excitement," Skipper said. "It's gone to your knees." They all laughed, in relief.

"Shouldn't he go to bed?" their mother said. "I think he's tired."

Alex held up his hands. "He can go to bed in a minute, Ma. First I have a piece of news that can't wait." He glanced at Jenifer. "I know it's a dirty trick to use Jordan's party for my own news, but I can't wait another damned minute." He paused dramatically. "Ladies and gents, Miss Jenifer Bates has agreed to marry . . . guess who? . . . *me!*"

For a moment the only sound was his mother's gasp. Then she said, "Oh, Alex, I'm glad!" and the whole room broke into a clamor of congratulations.

Later, when the guests had gone, Alex said, "It was dirty, wasn't it, to grab your party like that? Maybe we should have waited." He sat beside Jordan, poking gently at his knees. "Does that hurt?"

"No, nothing hurts. It just doesn't work. Alex, I'm really glad about you and Jenifer."

Alex's dark blue eyes were almost black as he smiled. "Thanks, chum. She likes you guys. I think it's going to be good. Of course we can't get married for a while, what with no money and all that, and me with med school still to go . . ."

"Alex, don't wait too long," Jordan said. "There's always a way to figure out the money. We'll all help."

Alex patted Jordan's knee. "I know you would.

But you've got Ma and Skip to help, not to mention yourself. Don't worry, we won't wait too long. Let's get you up to bed. Hey, Tony, let's make a cradle for him."

When they got him to bed, Jordan said, "What's wrong with my leg anyway?"

"I don't know," Alex said. "We'll get Dr. Parkhurst over here tomorrow if it isn't better, but it'll probably be okay by then, maybe a little stiff. How much tennis did you play?"

"Three sets. I often play that much or more."

"Tell you what you do, Jordie," Tony said. "You put that sterling pen and pencil set under your pillow and by morning I guarantee you'll be fit as a fiddle."

Jordan smiled. "I'll try it."

His mother leaned over and kissed him. "Susan looked awfully pretty tonight."

Pleased, he said, "Yes, didn't she?"

"She's a beautiful girl," Tony said.

Skipper came in with a cup of coffee. "Here, drink yourself into oblivion."

"Thanks, Skip. That's just what I feel like, some of Ma's good coffee."

"I hate to tell you," Skipper said, "but I made this coffee."

"That's just what I need," Jordan said, "some of Skip's good coffee."

His mother put out the light, and they left him alone.

"When I come up to bed, after washing all the dishes, cleaning up the debris, vacuuming the rugs, and returning in my pumpkin," Skipper said, sticking his head in the door, "I will try to get into my bunk without putting my foot in your face."

"I will be grateful." When Skipper had gone, Jordan sipped the good, strong coffee. It had been a funny way for the day to end. But certainly by morning he would be all right again. He put down the cup and slid down under the covers.

Fourth

Jordan slept late. When he awoke, the sun was streaming in the east windows and Skipper was combing his hair in front of the mirror.

"How do you feel?" Skipper said, looking at him in the mirror.

"I don't know. I haven't had time to find out."

"Well, you'd better check. There's been a steady stream of faces peering in at the door to see how your Majesty is."

"What faces?"

"Your devoted mother, your devoted brothers, even your devoted sister on her way to church."

Jordan sat up and stretched his legs cautiously. "That's just because I never have anything the matter with me. Pull a muscle and they think I'm gone for good." He swung his legs to the floor and stood up, holding to the top bunk. He took a careful step and then another. "Everything's a-okay."

Alex came to the door and looked at him. "All right?"

35

"Sure. A little shaky, that's all."

"You look tired."

"Well, it was a busy day."

"Susan called."

"Any message?"

"Call back when you're up."

Jordan went down the hall to take a shower, whistling. It had been a little scary, his leg giving out like that, and that shaky business in his arm. Too much tennis. I'm getting to be an old man, he thought — got to watch it. He laughed aloud from the sheer pleasure of being alive. And there was still hot water for his shower. He sang lustily, splashing the water and getting soap in his eyes. He had to wash his hair with his left hand though, because his right arm wouldn't lift that high. He turned up the water as hot as he could stand it and let the tiny needles beat against his shoulders. He'd get out the old handball later and do some exercises to strengthen his hand muscles.

After breakfast he called Susan. "Let's go for a ride. Tony says I can use the VW. He's working on his dissertation. Eleven o'clock? . . . Right. See you."

"Eat a good breakfast," his mother said. "Don't rush."

"When did I ever not eat a good breakfast? That was a nice party, Ma."

"I'm glad you enjoyed it." She looked at him searchingly. "Take it easy today, will you?"

"Sure. We're just going to ride up north to look at the foliage and listen for the elks bugling."

36

Tony looked up from his book. "Does Susan like to hear elks bugle?"

"She's never heard them. Are you being snide about Susan?"

"No, I'm not being snide about Susan. Don't be touchy."

"She's not an outdoor type like Bitsy, except for tennis. She doesn't ski and go camping and all, but that's not all there is in the world."

Tony held up his hands. "I never said it was. I have nothing against Susan."

"That's called damning with faint praise, isn't it?"

Tony got up with his book and his cup of coffee and went into the living room.

"Why are you taking out after Tony?" his mother said.

Jordan frowned. "I'm not."

She took a little envelope from her pocket and put it beside Jordan's plate. "This is a little extra birthday present. I didn't get a chance to give it to you last night."

"Something else? You already gave me that neat jacket . . ." He opened the envelope and took out two tickets. His face lit up. "Ma! Tickets for the Thanksgiving ball!"

"I thought you and Susan would enjoy it."

"Oh, she's dying to go, but I didn't think I could afford it." He got up and kissed his mother's cheek. "You're a real, living, breathing doll."

"Thank you. Maybe Tony can get you a good price on a corsage for Susan."

"Corsage? I've never given a girl a corsage.

In fact, I've never been to a real ball before."

"I hope you'll enjoy it."

"Oh, man, you know I will! Hey, Tony!" He went into the other room to show Tony the tickets and to discuss the corsage. "Are you and Bitsy going?"

"I guess so," Tony said. "I'm not much of a guy for dances, but Bitsy likes it."

"Is Alex going?"

"I don't know. They're feeling so married now, they're on this kick about economizing." Tony grinned. "Jen bought a big pink pig that they put all their spare change into."

"Pig?"

"Yeah, piggy bank. A big pink pig with flowers painted all over it. Can you see Alex?" They both laughed.

Jordan combed his hair again, stooping a little to see himself in the oval mirror behind the sofa.

Tony took the keys to the Volkswagen out of his pocket. "She knocks a little on hills as you may have discovered, but she always makes it."

Later Jordan shifted into first gear as the little car began to *ping-ping-ping* on the steep road outside Estes Park. He pulled off the road onto a pine-needle-covered trail and stopped. "Let's walk up a little way. I heard elk here a couple of weeks ago."

"Will they attack us?" Susan asked.

"We aren't going that close." He got his .22 rifle from the trunk.

Susan gasped. "What's that for?"

"I just wanted to do a little target shooting. There's a place up here we use." He laughed. "Don't look so scared."

"I'm terrified of guns."

"It's just a .22 I want to show off, so you'll see what a good shot I am. I'm the best shot in the family." He took her hand and they walked up the trail, Susan looking fearfully into the woods on both sides of the road.

"We should have brought something to put chokecherries in," he said, breaking off a branch. "Ma makes wonderful chokecherry jelly." He led her into a little clearing where there were several empty beer cans lined up, some of them with bullet holes in them. He set one up on a stump. She watched him nervously, keeping behind him.

He turned to her and held up his hand. "Listen."

From some distance away came the bawling sound of an elk.

"What is it?" She grabbed his arm.

"Elk." He put his arm around her protectively. "They're pretty far off. And don't worry — we won't go any closer. You don't fool with any wild animal in the mating season."

"I don't like it," she said. "Let's go."

"Can I have a couple of shots first? What letter on the beer can do you want me to shoot out?"

"Oh, I don't know. The S."

"Top half or lower half?"

"Top."

He lifted the gun and aimed, hoping his hand wouldn't jerk. The bullet knocked the can off the stump. When he brought it to her, grinning, the top loop of the S had been shot out.

"All right," she said. "You're a good shot. I'm impressed. Now let's go."

They had lunch at a little café in Estes Park. Most of the shops along the main street were closed, now that the tourist season was over. They walked over to the lake. The water reflected the colors of the foliage near it. The sky was intensely blue, and the air was so clear it seemed to sparkle.

When they sat down on a wooden bench, Jordan asked Susan to go with him to the Thanksgiving ball. The boredom and restlessness that she had shown in the woods vanished. Her eyes shone.

"Oh, Jordan, I'd love to go! My roommate says it's a marvelous ball. I'd adore to go."

He showed her the tickets. "Tell me what color dress you'll wear, so I can get the right corsage. Tony says . . ."

But she wasn't listening to what Tony said. She was thinking intently about her wardrobe. "I don't know. I might get a new dress. Yes, I think I will. I'll let you know about the color." She squeezed his arm. "Oh, Jordie, you really are a love." But when he started to kiss her, she put him off as she often did. "People will see us."

"There's nobody around."

"Somebody might come along."

Frustrated and annoyed, he stood up. "Let's go then."

"All right, but don't sulk."

"I'm not sulking."

"If we were about to get married, like Alex and Jenifer, it would be different. But a girl has to look after herself. I mean, you have to look after number one, right? Nobody takes care of you if you don't take care of yourself."

He strode along ahead of her. "I was only trying to kiss you; anybody'd think I was trying to rape you or something."

Wheedling, she caught his arm. "Oh, Jordie, don't be mad." She pulled him to a stop and gave him a long kiss. "There. Satisfied?" She got into the VW, smiling at him.

He shook his head, half-pleased, half-exasperated. "I don't understand you."

"That's my charm. I'm the Mona Lisa. Let's drive fast all the way home."

"Why? Have you got a date?"

"Oh, Jordan, you are impossible."

He started the car and pushed the clutch pedal in. But the leg muscles wouldn't respond. The knee jerked and trembled. He sat clutching the steering wheel, trying to will his muscles to react. His forehead was damp with the effort.

"What are we waiting for?" she said. "Are you brooding?"

He clenched his hands on the wheel hard to steady his shaking fingers. He felt frightened. What was the matter with him? With a great effort he spoke calmly. "You'll have to drive. My knee's gone out again."

"Oh, no!" She hated to drive.

"I'm sorry."

She looked at him and spoke more gently. "That's all right, Jordie. I'm sorry." She got out

41

and came around to the driver's seat.

With difficulty he swung his legs out of the car. "I'll have to lean on you, I guess." He said it tightly, feeling scared and humiliated. "The right leg is working, but not the left." Leaning on her he hopped around the car, using his other hand to brace himself on the hood and the side. He lowered himself into the passenger seat and let out his breath. "Thanks."

"Does it hurt?"

"No. Just won't work."

"What you need is a good rest." She got into the driver's seat and started down the road. She stripped the gears and said, "Oh, sorry."

Jordan closed his eyes. Susan was not the world's greatest driver. He hoped she wouldn't ruin the VW.

"You ought to see the doctor. He'll probably strap up that knee for you. You've got tennis knee, that's what you've got." She drove too fast, and she talked all the way. Jordan sat with his head back against the head-brace, silent most of the time. She was probably right, he was thinking. Tennis knee. He didn't know why he felt so frightened.

No one was home but Tony. He came out and helped Jordan into the house and then he drove Susan home. When he got back, he said, "I'm going to call Dr. Parkhurst."

Jordan protested. It was Sunday; no need to get the man out on a Sunday.

"I'll just ask him what he thinks," Tony said, "if he's home."

"He'll stop by," Tony said when he came back.

Jordan tried to sound casual. "Does he have any ideas?"

"Oh, you know how they are. They won't commit themselves till they've had a look. You'll be all right, won't you, if I go back to work? Want anything to eat or anything?"

"No, I'm all right." Jordan leaned back and closed his eyes. He felt tired.

Dr. Parkhurst came in a few minutes. He was a tall, athletic-looking man, who seemed much younger than he was. Jordan noticed how fit he looked in his off-duty clothes, a pair of jeans and a sweatshirt. He can't be very young, he thought; he delivered all of us.

"Hi," the doctor said. "Excuse the clothes. I was raking leaves."

"I'm the one to say 'excuse me,' getting you out on Sunday, and it's probably for nothing."

"Well, let's take a look." He spent a long time poking and prodding and asking questions. "Any pain in your arm?"

"No, it just doesn't always work too well."

"How about your hands? Have trouble buttoning your shirt, things like that?"

"Yes, sometimes I do."

The doctor picked up a tennis ball from the table. "Catch." He tossed it to Jordan. Jordan dropped it.

Several times the doctor tested Jordan's knee reflexes, and each time Jordan's leg jerked up violently. "Notice any hoarseness? Any trouble swallowing?"

"No."

"Let's look at your eyes. Keep looking at this

43

spot on my forehead." He moved his small light slowly, close to Jordan's eyes. He sat back and studied Jordan. "How's your sex life? Any chance of syphilis?"

"Good God! I hope not." Jordan laughed uneasily. "You're kidding, I hope."

"It always pays to check. No leg pain, you say."

"No. It just gave way, as if the muscles weren't working. My girl says it's tennis knee. Plus tennis shoulder."

"I hate to contradict the lady, but she's wrong. It would hurt here." He tapped Jordan's knee. He opened his black bag and put back the little silver hammer. "I don't really know what it is, Jordan. I want you to stay off it tonight, and in the morning have somebody bring you over to the office. I'd like to get some blood tests and so on." He stood up, looking very big. "Ask your mother to let my secretary know when you can come in, all right?"

"Sure. You don't . . ." Jordan felt silly asking the question. "You don't think it's serious, do you? I mean I'd take a dim view of going through life in a wheelchair or something." He tried to make it sound like a joke.

Dr. Parkhurst didn't laugh. "I honestly don't know what it is. It may be nothing, just some strain of some kind. We won't cross bridges."

Jordan tried another joke. "Maybe it's all in my mind."

"It's possible."

"You're kidding."

"Not necessarily. Such things do happen."

"But there has to be some reason, doesn't there? I mean like if I was scared I was going to get drafted or something like that, if there was a war on."

"A lot goes on in the subconscious that we'd be amazed at. But I'm not saying it's psychosomatic; you were the one who brought that up. How is your mother?"

"Fine. She's on campus doing some work."

The doctor shook his head. "She works too hard."

"I know."

He snapped his bag shut. "All right, then, see you in the morning. Tony," he called into the other room, "keep your brother off his feet."

Tony came into the room, taking off his glasses. "All right. What is it? Do you know?"

"Nope. Not yet."

"Leave it to Jordie to have something exotic." Tony went out with the doctor to his car.

When Tony came back, Jordan said, "Was that on the level? Doesn't he really know?"

"No, he says he has no idea. He'd tell you if he knew. He's not a cagey-type doctor."

"X-rays and all that will cost money."

"I think your Blue Cross will cover it. Anyway, don't worry about that."

The phone rang. "If that's Susan," Jordan said, "tell her everything's all right."

But it was Em, who had seen the doctor drive away. When she heard what had happened, she came over and sat with Jordan until his mother came home at the end of the afternoon. Em talked to him, played records for him, made coffee. She was such good company that Jordan almost forgot to worry.

At dinner time his mother brought him a tray,

and Alex set up a card table so they could all eat with him.

"If I'd known I'd get all this attention," Jordan said, "I'd have whacked up my knees long ago."

"Don't think it's going to last, son," Skipper said. "One day is all you get. One to a customer."

Alex helped him up to bed in the evening.

"What's your diagnosis, Herr Doktor?" Jordan said.

"I don't have one, Jordie, but I don't imagine it's anything to worry about." He eased his brother carefully into the bunk. "We'll find out in the morning." He stood looking down at Jordan. "Anything you need?"

"Nothing but a little reassurance."

"You've got it. I'm not worried about you."

Jordan smiled. "All right, Doc. I'll take your word for it."

After Alex had gone and the light was out, Jordan lay very still for a long time, trying to hold off the feeling of dread that threatened him. It was just because he'd never had anything wrong with him, he told himself; he just wasn't used to it.

Long after Skipper had come up to bed, moving quietly in the dark in order not to wake Jordan, whom he thought was asleep, Jordan still lay awake. The house and the night outside grew still. Only Skipper's breathing kept him from feeling that he had fallen into some deserted planet.

Fifth

Dr. Parkhurst spun around in his swivel chair to face Jordan and his mother. "I'm stumped. I don't know what it is. I can't see a thing." He tilted Jordan's face toward the light and studied it. "You're better this morning. The pattern seems to be that when you've rested, it clears up; when you're active, you get problems. My suggestion is: stay home, off your feet, for three days. Then let me see you again. If things seem to be all right, then we'll let you out on a restricted basis. No tennis, no scrambling around in the mountains for a while. We'll just have to play it by ear, Jordan."

"Three days out of classes? I'll get behind."

"Yep. I'm sorry."

"I can get your assignments," his mother said. "It won't be the end of the world, three days."

"What if it keeps coming back?" Jordan said.

"Then we'll ship you up to Mayo Clinic and find out what in blazes it is."

47

On the way home Jordan said, "Mayo Clinic? I don't want to go to any Mayo Clinic."

"I don't think you'll have to. I think it will clear up."

She was right. On Thursday he went back to classes and to his part-time job in the lawyer's office. He felt tired but otherwise he was all right. He did as Dr. Parkhurst had told him. He played no tennis, did no climbing. Instead of walking to campus he rode the motorbike. For the next couple of weeks he stayed off his feet as much as he could. As a result, he got more serious studying done than he had since classes started. When he dated Susan on the weekends, they went to the movies, and once he persuaded her to go to the campus production of *King Lear*, but she found it depressing.

The first Sunday evening he and Susan went with Alex and Jenifer to dinner at the restaurant that clung to the side of Flagstaff Mountain. They stayed outside on the terrace waiting for their table. Below them in the valley the lights of the city twinkled.

"It's like looking at the sky upside down," Jordan said.

"I used to do that when I was a kid," Alex said. "I'd stand on my head and look at the sky."

Jenifer laughed and said to Susan, "The Phillips boys never do anything the way other people do."

"You're telling me!" Susan said.

"Speaking of doing things," Alex said with elaborate casualness, "we've set our wedding date."

48

Susan said, "Oh, you lucky dogs! When is it?"

"Christmas Sunday," Jenifer said. "Two o'clock."

"Did you tell Mom?" Jordan said.

"Not yet. We just decided it today. We haven't told anybody." Alex touched Jordan's shoulder. "Will you be best man?"

Pleased, Jordan said, "Sure. What does the best man do?"

"Oh, lose the ring and all that."

"What about Tony? Will he mind?"

"Tony and Skipper will be part of the service," Jenifer said. "They'll stand up with us."

"A church wedding?" Susan asked.

Alex made a face. "The works."

Jenifer shook his arm. "Hush. A girl only gets married once."

"We hope," Alex said.

"I want a church wedding, too." Susan looked at Jordan.

"How about a nice cathedral?" he said. "Something cozy." He looked at Alex. "I didn't know you were going to get married so soon."

"You're the one who told me not to waste time."

"That's right. It feels funny, though. My brother, married."

"Your sister's married," Susan said.

"That's different. She's a girl."

Alex laughed. "You're identifying, and it scares you. I know. All guys get scared. It's the girls who can't wait to get hitched."

"Don't be a male chauvinist," Jenifer said.

Over the loudspeaker a voice said, "Mr. Phillips, your table is ready. Mr. Phillips, please."

49

Alex made a sweeping gesture. "After you, Mr. Phillips."

"You first, my dear Mr. Phillips," Jordan said. He stepped back for Alex to precede him. He took one backward look at the lights of the valley. He felt lonesome somehow, Alex getting married.

"Come on," Susan said, "I'm starving."

The evening was so successful that three weeks later they went to Flagstaff House again, this time with Tony and his girl, whose family had saddled her with the nickname of "Bitsy." Bitsy was small but she had the strength and the willowy grace of a dancer. She was leaving the next day to ski in the early snow in Austria.

The night was not quite the success that the first one had been, because Susan and Bitsy had a tendency to antagonize each other. Susan didn't think much of athletic girls, and to Bitsy, Susan was empty-headed and frivolous. The brothers tried to smooth over the moments of hostility but it was Jenifer who was the real peacemaker. She managed to divert attention or change the subject whenever the conversation became uncomfortable.

When the brothers got home at the end of the evening, Jordan was feeling defensive. He waited for Tony to make some derogatory remark about Susan, and when he didn't, Jordan said, "Bitsy and Susan didn't exactly come off as kindred spirits, did they?"

Tony shrugged. "It doesn't matter."

"If they're ever sisters-in-law it would matter," Jordan said.

"Let's don't worry about that. You'll probably fall for at least ten other girls before you marry anybody, and I'm not going to get married for years."

"Does Bitsy know that?"

"Yes, she knows it. I want to give myself a chance to write before I take on a family. She understands that. If she finds some guy she wants to marry, she's perfectly free to do it."

"That's very broad-minded," Jordan said.

"No, it's selfish. I want to stay free."

Skipper was bouncing a Ping-Pong ball on the floor. "What noble brothers I've got," he said. "Oh, what noble fellows. Any girl in the world would feel proud to marry one of my noble brothers."

Alex laughed but Tony said, "Why don't you shut up for once, Skip?"

"Me?"

Jordan said, "You. The man is referring to you."

"Catch!" Skipper threw the Ping-Pong ball at Jordan, who was standing with one elbow leaning on the piano.

Jordan jerked his shoulders as if to raise his hand and intercept the ball, but his arm remained at his side and the ball hit him on the cheek. It fell to the floor and rolled under the piano, and he stared down at it with a look of surprise.

"Was that necessary?" Tony said to Skipper.

Skipper said, "I'm sorry. I thought Jordie would catch it. He just let it hit him."

Alex was looking at Jordan. "What's the matter?" he said.

Jordan raised his head and looked at him. "I couldn't lift my arm. It's bothered me some before but not that much." Frowning, he looked down at his arm. He moved his shoulder and lifted his arm two or three inches. "God! I wouldn't even be able to serve a ball."

Alex came over to him and felt his shoulder. "Does it hurt?"

"No. It's just the way my knees were. It just won't work." He searched Alex's face. "What is the matter with me?"

"You'd better see Parkhurst tomorrow," Tony said.

"I think he'd better make arrangements for you to go up to Rochester," Alex said. He put his arm around Jordan. "Come on up to bed. It's late."

"Jordie," Skipper said, "I didn't mean to hit you." He looked as if he might cry.

Jordan forced a smile. "I know it, Skip. It wasn't your fault."

"I'll tell Mom to call Parkhurst in the morning," Tony said.

As Jordon went up the stairs with Alex, he heard Skipper saying, "I really didn't mean to hit him, Tony. Tony, what is the matter with him?"

Sixth

The arrangements with the Mayo Clinic were made quickly. Jordan's mother wanted to go with him, but he protested so strongly that she gave in, and it was decided that Alex would go. At first Jordan had been determined to go alone, but his family persuaded him that that was not wise.

"Supposing your legs give out suddenly," Tony had said, "and you're all alone, on the street or somewhere, in a strange city?"

He did insist that his mother should not come to the airport to see them off, so Tony drove Alex and Jordan to Stapleton Field early one morning. Jordan had never flown, and he tried to keep his mind on that part of the trip. His shoulder had recovered from whatever had been the matter, and he was feeling quite well.

He was interested in the process of the electronic search at the airport and amused when Alex was held up because something metal showed up in his jacket. It took a bit of hunting to find the thing that had caused the *blip* on the electronic detector. It had slipped down through a tear in the pocket.

The inspector held it up and looked at it. "What is it?"

Alex looked embarrassed. "It's a buttonhook."

"A buttonhook." The man held it up, studying it. Some people behind Alex laughed.

Alex held out his hand. "It's my grandmother's buttonhook. You know — high-buttoned shoes?"

The man gave him a strange look. "Sure. Sure. High-buttoned shoes." He glanced at Alex's feet. Enjoying his audience he looked at the line of waiting people. "His grandmother's buttonhook." He handed it back to Alex. "Good luck, son, with all those buttons."

Jordan was laughing.

"Idiots," Alex said, striding along unnecessarily fast toward the plane gate.

"Why did you have it in your pocket?" Jordan said.

"I didn't know it was there. I lost it a long time ago." He pulled out his pocket and looked at the tear in the cloth. "I used it when I was making that radio for Skipper. You can get at things with it." He put it back in a different pocket. "Grandmother Jordan gave it to me when I was a little kid, because I liked it. I guess it belonged to her mother."

"It did look funny," Jordan said.

"I suppose so. But it makes me mad, the way a person can't do anything out of the ordinary anymore without everybody being suspicious of him or laughing at him — or both."

They came into the waiting area and showed the airline man their tickets. "We're all so regimented."

"But if it saves hijacking . . ."

"I know, I know. But I still don't like it." They sat down to wait for the plane. "Grandmother Jordan told me one time, when she was flying to the East Coast, at the time when people were very tense about hijacking, she dropped that little bottle of nitroglycerin pills she took for her heart, and she said to the stewardess, 'Oh dear, I've dropped my nitroglycerin.' The poor stewardess turned white. She thought Grandmother was going to blow up the plane."

Jordan laughed. Alex was the best one he could have come with. He acted as if everything were perfectly natural, and he was fun to talk to. He made a promise to himself not to depress Alex while they were on the trip. It was good of him to have come.

When they got to Rochester, the weather was much colder than it had been at home, and a few dry, light snowflakes were swirling in the wind.

They checked into the small hotel where Dr. Parkhurst had made reservations for them and then went to the clinic. Jordan filled out forms and was given an early morning appointment for tests. He was nervous, but the people he talked to were pleasant and so matter-of-fact that he felt reassured.

"After all," he said to Alex when they left, "I guess hundreds of people come here and find

55

out all the things they were scared of aren't true."

"Of course," Alex said. "As our mother is fond of saying, 'Never trouble trouble till trouble troubles you.'"

"Let's call home tonight," Jordan said.

"Yes, I told her we would."

They unpacked what little they had brought, and Jordan took a long, lazy bath. Worry had become suspended somehow, and all he felt was a kind of pleasant indolence. After they had called home and talked to their mother and to Skipper, they went down to the dining room for dinner. In the evening they watched television and chatted about inconsequential things. Jordan went to sleep early and slept better than he had for several nights.

The next few days fell into a pattern. While Jordan reported at the clinic for his various tests, Alex roamed around Rochester. In the late afternoon they met again at the hotel room and Jordan rested. They had dinner sometimes at the hotel, sometimes at a different restaurant, and in the evening they watched TV and went to bed early. Alex had brought books along and he sometimes studied late, after Jordan had gone to sleep. Once Jordan woke up and found Alex looking at him.

"What is it?" he said.

"Oh, nothing. I was just trying to think out a problem in anatomy. Go back to sleep."

When the tests were over at last, both Jordan and Alex were asked to meet with the doctor in charge of Jordan's case. He was waiting for them in his office. He looked very young, and he had an easy, informal manner.

"Jordan tells me you're premed," he said to Alex.

"Yes."

"That's fine. We need all the good doctors we can get." He picked up Jordan's chart, looked at it briefly, and put it down again. "Jordan, what you have is amyotrophic lateral sclerosis."

Jordan looked quickly at Alex and back to the doctor. "What's that?"

The doctor said to Alex, "Are you familiar with it?"

"Lou Gehrig's disease, isn't it?" Alex spoke quietly, but his face was white.

"It's called that. Actually it's a disease of the anterior horn cell and the pyramidal tract, involving the motor systems . . ."

"What does that mean?" Jordan said. Alex's face frightened him.

"It means a weakening and atrophy of the muscles."

Jordan was leaning forward tensely. "How do you cure it?"

The doctor hesitated. "We don't cure it."

Jordan stared at him almost angrily. "You *don't* cure it?"

"We don't know what causes it. We seldom see it in anyone as young as you. Usually people in their forties or fifties . . . One of the things we suspect as a possible cause . . . but we don't know . . . is the flu, yet everyone has flu. So who knows? For instance, it's prevalent in Guam. Why Guam?"

"You mean my muscles will just give out and there's nothing you can do?"

The doctor looked unhappy. "Plenty of rest. Preserve the strength that you have in your muscles as long as you can. I'll prescribe thiamine chloride to make you more comfortable . . . There should not be any pain, except possibly a little discomfort in your shoulders . . ." He looked at Alex. "Brewer's yeast after meals . . ."

Jordan interrupted him. "And how long does this go on?" He knew it was illogical to be angry with the doctor, but he was filled with rage.

"There's no way of telling. People have lived twenty years with it, but I must tell you that that is exceptional. It could be several years . . . or several months."

"Am I supposed to sit around in a wheelchair and wait for it to kill me?"

"Not necessarily, although a wheelchair would take some of the strain off your muscles."

"It sounds like a jolly life," Jordan said bitterly. "Or a jolly few months."

The doctor looked sad. "It won't be jolly. It will be damned difficult, and I'd give an awful lot to know how to stop it."

"I thought the Mayo Clinic could cure everything."

"Jordie . . ." Alex said.

The doctor shook his head at Alex, and to Jordan he said, "We wish that were true."

Jordan looked at Alex with a smile that pulled at the side of his face. "I guess the Supreme Court won't have to hold its breath waiting for me."

Alex said to the doctor, "With care and luck he could have quite a while, couldn't he?"

The doctor looked down at his desk. "With great care and phenomenal luck." He handed a typed sheet to Alex. "These are instructions. I'll be sending a report to Dr. Parkhurst today." He stood up and shook hands with Alex. "I'm sorry." He held out his hand to Jordan, but Jordan turned away.

"Jordan," Alex said.

"Let him be," the doctor said.

"We appreciate what you've done, Doctor," Alex said. "We're grateful to you . . ."

The doctor interrupted him almost fiercely. "For God's sake, don't be grateful. Remember, if you're going to be a doctor, all the times you have to be the voice of doom, and how hateful it is . . ." He broke off and went out of the office quickly.

"Let's go," Alex said gently.

The rage had faded out of Jordan's eyes. He looked tired enough to collapse.

In the taxi they sat silent. The wintry sky looked like blue-gray steel, and the bare black branches of the trees were splayed out against it in random patches.

"Looks like winter already," the taxi driver said.

In the hotel room Jordan threw himself on the bed and lay with an arm covering his face. Alex walked around aimlessly for a few minutes, as if he couldn't keep his mind on what needed to be done.

"I better pack some," he said. "We leave kind of early tomorrow." He glanced uneasily at

Jordan, but Jordan gave no sign of hearing. Alex opened the one suitcase they had brought and began to toss things into it.

After a while he said, "Are you hungry?"

"No." Jordan's voice was muffled.

"Well, I'll have some stuff sent up. If you want some later, it'll be here. Any choice?" When Jordan didn't answer, Alex sighed and rang room service. "Room 308. Will you send up . . . uh . . . two chicken sandwiches, two roast beef sandwiches, a pot of coffee . . ." He paused. "And a bottle of wine. Oh, claret, I guess. Thank you." He hung up and looked at the back of Jordan's head. "Jordie, I'm going to call Terry. She can talk to Mom."

"No," Jordan said.

"Jordie, we have to tell them."

Still not looking at him or uncovering his face, Jordan said, "We don't have to yet."

Alex persisted gently. "Jordie, they'd know something was wrong. Mom would know right away, and she'd worry herself sick. It wouldn't be fair."

Jordan turned his head. His eyes were unusually bright, as if he had a fever. "Make them understand, then, they are not to tell anyone outside the family. *Nobody.*"

"All right." Alex tried to call the number but the circuits were busy. In about ten minutes he opened the door for the room service waiter, who wheeled in the wagon and opened the wine bottle. The waiter glanced at Jordan's figure stretched out on the bed, his head buried in the pillow. Assuming he was asleep, he said, "If you will sign, sir," in a low voice, and left.

Alex took the silver cover off one of the plates and began to eat a chicken sandwich. "I feel as if I ought not to be hungry," he said, "but I'm starved." He poured a glass of wine from the bottle and drank it all at once. He refilled it and drank half of it and finished the sandwich. Then he called Terry again, and this time he got her.

"Terry, this is Alex . . . Yes, today . . . It's . . ." He hesitated, looking at Jordan's back. "Lou Gehrig's disease . . . Gehrig." He raised his voice as if he were angry. "Well, look it up then. . . . Sorry. I'm a little upset. You talk to Mom tonight, will you? I'm not going to call her." As Jordan turned to look at him, he said, "And listen, this is very important: Jordan doesn't want anyone outside the family told about it. Got that? Nobody at all. Be sure Pat understands that. . . . We get in at 10:40 tomorrow morning. Be sure somebody meets us. . . . All right . . ." His voice broke suddenly, and he hung up.

"Did she promise?" Jordan asked.

"Yes."

"If it gets around . . ."

"For God's sake, Jordan, you can count on us."

Jordan seemed to deflate suddenly. "I know, I know." He turned on his back and stared at the ceiling. The only light Alex had put on was a small table lamp, and now the darkness of the northern night soaked into the room. He had left the draperies open at the window. Every few minutes a neon sign across the street made a red smear in the dark.

"Want some wine?"

61

"Yeah." Jordan sat up and took the glass.

"Better have a sandwich."

"Later." Jordan got up and carried his glass to the window and stood looking out. "Who is this Lou Somebody anyway?"

"Gehrig? He was a baseball star. A pitcher, I think, in like the thirties or twenties."

"How did you know about him?" Jordan refilled his wine glass.

"Last year in anatomy, Miller showed us a film clip, where this Gehrig got some kind of huge ovation in Yankee Stadium."

"I thought that was Babe Ruth."

"Well, they both did."

Jordan picked up a sandwich. "I should have gone in for baseball."

"Miller showed us the Gehrig clip because he was talking about muscles and this disease that Gehrig had."

"Maybe they'll change the name to Phillips disease," Jordan said.

Alex winced but he didn't say anything.

"Did he have a lot of pain?" Jordan asked the question in an offhand way, as if he were not really interested.

"I don't think so. Mostly he got weaker and . . ." Alex turned away.

"And what?"

"Well, he couldn't make his muscles work right sometimes. I remember when it first came on he was in the locker room trying to untie his shoe-laces, and he couldn't. Something like that."

"In this film clip, was he in a wheelchair?"

"No. He was on his feet. I remember he thanked the people, and he . . . he cried because he was so touched. You know, all that . . . well, love, that people were giving him, you might say."

"This is a good sandwich."

"Yeah."

"We need another bottle of wine. I mean we're going to need it, Alex."

Alex called room service and ordered another bottle. He divided what was left in the first bottle between his own glass and Jordan's. "Try another sandwich."

"Why not?"

Jordan stretched out on his bed, punching a pillow up as a bolster behind his head. "And what did Babe Ruth have? Babe Ruth's disease?"

"He had cancer."

"They're a pretty unhealthy lot, aren't they? What's-his-name, Campanella, he was in a wheelchair. What did he have — Campanella's disease?"

"Cut it out, Jordan; It isn't a funny subject."

"No, I see that. I do see that it isn't funny."

Alex made a helpless gesture. "I know you do. I just . . . I don't know. I'm not making a lot of sense."

"Nothing makes sense, brother."

The waiter knocked and came in with the second bottle of wine. He smiled at Jordan. "Good evening, sir. You had a nice nap?"

"Beautiful nap, thank you."

When he had gone, Alex poured wine into the glasses. "We'd better slow down a little. We'll get smashed."

Jordan raised his glass. "Here's to smashed."

"No, that's stupid. You just feel rotten in the

morning." Alex sat down on the other bed. "Would you like some more lights on? It's dark in here."

"No."

They sat in silence for a while, sipping the wine. "This Gehrig person," Jordan said. "Do you picture him up there playing heavenly baseball, or how do you picture him? Is he just gone-gone-gone?"

"I don't know, Jordan."

"I thought you medical men had all the answers."

"Damn it, Jordie, don't take that bitter, wise guy tone with me," Alex said angrily. "That's not going to help."

"What *is* going to help?" Jordan's voice was angry, too, and close to tears. "I haven't had much experience with this scene. You'll have to excuse me if I don't know how to play it."

Alex got up and went to the window. He put his foot on the low sill and stared out into the darkness. After a while he said more calmly, "If you're asking me if I believe in life after death, I don't know. The only thing I feel sure of is that there is a tremendous lot going on that we have absolutely no idea of."

"Like what?"

"If I knew like what, I'd know. Haldane . . . you've heard of Haldane?"

"Slightly."

"Haldane said, 'The universe is not only queerer than we suppose, but queerer than we can suppose.' I believe that. When we try to imagine a hereafter, the best we can come up with is usually something like our life here. I think our imagination is very, very limited, really just to what we've experienced. And I think there's an awful lot more that we've never dreamed of." He came back to his bed and sat down. "It may turn out to be very exciting and wonderful."

"Or it may turn out to be nothing."

"Yes, it may. The only thing is, when you consider the earth, or the universe, it kind of looks as if things don't turn into 'nothing.' I mean the process is change, not extinction — or so it seems, anyway."

After a silence Jordan said, "It's a funny thing, but I don't believe I ever really thought about it, not in any serious way." He poured more wine for both of them.

"Listen," Alex said, "don't get sick on this stuff. A wine hangover is murder."

"I wonder how long I've got," Jordan said.

"Don't think about it that way. It's the quality of a life that counts, not the number of days. Get all you can while you can. I don't mean 'get' in a material way — there's no point to that — but get joy, get . . . oh, you know . . . love, kindness, that sort of stuff. Understanding. Enjoyment . . ." He lifted his glass to the light and looked at the wine. "For instance, did you notice how pretty the wine looks?"

Jordan held up his glass. "Very pretty."

"I'm feeling a bit squiffed."

"And you were worrying about *me* drinking too much."

"I'm a lousy drinker. Listen, Jordan, what about Keats?"

"What about him? Was he a lousy drinker?"

"No, I mean . . . he died when he was twenty-five or so, but look what he left the world."

"Poems."

"Some of the world's greatest poetry." He reached over and tapped Jordan's knee earnestly. "Look at Mozart."

"Just a broth of a lad when he died."

"Right. And look what *he* left the world."

"Music."

"Right. Glorious music."

"But I'm not a poet, and I can't carry a tune."

"We'll think of something." Alex put down his glass and leaned back on the pillows. Within a couple of minutes he was asleep.

When he awoke half an hour later, Jordan was kneeling by the window with his head on his arms. Alex jumped up. "Jordie! I didn't mean to go to sleep. Why didn't you wake me up?" He went over to his brother.

Jordan looked up at him. "Alex," he said in a low voice, "I'm so scared."

Alex knelt beside him and put his arm around his shoulders, rocking him a little as if he were a child. "I know," he said. "I know, I know."

Seventh

Jordan fastened his seat belt and looked at his brother's pale face. "You look terrible."

"I feel terrible. I should never drink more than one glass of wine. I suppose you're feeling fine?"

"Great. Never felt better." While the plane was taking off, he said, "You don't think Mom will make a fuss, do you?"

"Did she ever?"

"No. Anyway, Alex, I was thinking: that doctor could be wrong."

Alex glanced at him, but he didn't answer.

"I mean he *could* be. He admits they don't know anything about this disease."

"He said they didn't know *much*."

"All right. It could be a wrong diagnosis. Or even if I have it, I could be one of those people it doesn't develop with. Right?"

"If you have it, it will develop. I think you should keep your head on. I mean, be ready for whatever happens. Don't tell yourself fairy

67

stories and then have to be jolted out of them."

Jordan looked out the window as Rochester tilted away underneath the plane. "I'm going to live as if I never heard of it."

After a moment Alex said gently, "You can't quite do that, Jordie. Live the way the doctor said. Spare yourself, take it easy on yourself. That way, you might be able to delay it."

"Yeah," Jordan said, although he seemed not to be listening.

Later when the plane swooped down on the runway at Stapleton, he said, "Got your button-hook?"

Alex laughed. He pulled the little silver buttonhook out of his pocket and held it up. "Ready for anything."

When they came into the airport Jordan tensed. "I wish I knew who was meeting us."

"What's the difference?"

"I don't know. Different people . . . different treatment."

"Well, there's your answer. It's Mom."

She stood at the end of a line of people waiting to greet arrivals. For a moment she didn't see them and she strained forward, her face anxious and pale. Then she saw them. Her face changed at once. She smiled eagerly and tried to edge forward. She waved. She looked as she had always looked when they came home from anywhere — happy to see them, almost gay. She waved the car keys at them.

"Good old Ma," Alex said under his breath. He moved a little, unobtrusively, so that Jordan reached her first.

"Hi, Ma," Jordan said.

"Hi, dear." She reached up and kissed him lightly on the cheek. Her eyes swept his face for just an instant before she turned and kissed Alex. "We've missed you."

While they picked up the suitcase and when they were on the way out to the parking lot, she chatted easily, as if she had nothing on her mind. She said that Susan had called, Jenifer had been over to dinner, Tony had finished the first section of his dissertation, Skipper had a head cold and had played basketball on the first team in the game with Golden.

"What was the score?" Jordan opened the door of the car for her.

"I forget, but we won. Skip played very well although he felt terrible. I didn't want him to go."

Alex drove. Jordan sat half-turned so he could talk to his mother in the back seat.

"Did you have good food?" she asked.

"Most of the time. We had venison steaks one night. Really super."

By the time they got onto the Boulder Turnpike, a lull had occurred in the conversation. The things with which they could talk around the subject that was on their minds had begun to run out.

Finally Jordan said, "Did Terry call you?"

"Yes. She told me what Alex said."

"I'm sorry I didn't call you too, Ma," Alex said. "I was . . ."

"Oh, it was better the way you did it."

Jordan put his hand back and squeezed his

mother's gloved hand. "I'm going to be all right, Ma."

She caught her breath. "Do you mean . . ."

Quickly Alex said, "No, Ma, he means he's going to do as the doctor says, and he feels, you know, he can hold it off for a while."

"I know I can," Jordan said. "Ye gods, look at me! I'm healthy as an ox in every other way, and I'm young. Those things count for a lot."

"Of course they do," she said. "Of course they do."

"Terry told you I don't want people to know about it?"

"Yes. We didn't know whether you meant Susan . . . I suppose you'll want to tell her yourself."

"There's no need for her to know. Not now, anyway."

"That's not fair, Jordie," Alex said. "Susan ought to know."

Jordan set his mouth in a stubborn line. "Not now. I'll decide when she should know."

"Sure," Alex said. "It's your deal. I just meant . . ."

"Nobody outside the family. Except I suppose I can't prevent Terry from telling Pat."

"Pat *is* in the family now, Jordan," his mother said.

"Well, just don't let him start working me over. That bunch of unctuous clichés I do not need." Then he smiled at her brightly. "Alright, that takes care of all that. Now we can forget it. How's Em?"

"Oh, she's fine. She's such a comfort. She has

a present for you, by the way. A homecoming present."

"Yeah? What is it?"

"I'm sworn to secrecy." She hesitated. "We didn't tell her anything except that you have to take it a little easy for a while, but Jordan, I think she suspects there's more than that. She happened to come over right after Terry called, and she saw that I was . . . upset."

"Oh," Jordan said.

"If she suspects, she'll never mention it," Alex said. "Not until you tell her. I know Em."

"I know," Jordan said. "I just . . ." Then with sudden fierceness he said, "I cannot stand to have people pitying me."

"You'll never see pity in Em's face," Alex said. "All your lives she's felt the same pain you've felt, and the same joy. I used to think you two were like twins when you were little."

Jordan didn't answer. He was looking out the window.

When Alex turned into the street where they lived, his mother said, "One more thing — we haven't told Skipper. He heard what I told Em, and he accepted that. Somehow I couldn't bear to . . ." Her voice trailed away until it was almost inaudible. ". . . to tell him . . ."

"That's good," Jordan said. "No sense worrying the kid."

In the garage he went around to the trunk to get the suitcase.

"I'll get it, Jordan," Alex said.

"Don't be silly." He lifted it out and walked toward the back door. It was locked. He set down the suitcase and turned to get the key from his mother. She was still in the garage, and Alex had his arm around her. Jordan couldn't see her face, but he thought she was crying. "Hurry up, you guys," he said. His voice was sharper than he had intended. "Let's have the key."

"Oh, sorry, dear." His mother came quickly and handed him the key. She looked very pale, but there were no tears. She smiled up at him. "Didn't mean to keep you waiting."

Jordan wished he hadn't snapped at them. "That's okay. I'm just beginning to feel jet lag."

She looked at him quickly. "I've got a good lunch. I have a class at 1:40, but everything's all ready."

"Good. I missed your cooking." As he followed her into the kitchen, he thought, 'She'll always be looking at me like that now, with the anxiety not quite hidden.' For the first time he felt like crying.

Alex opened two cans of beer and brought one to Jordan while their mother got the lunch on the table. Jordan stretched out on the sofa. He felt very tired.

"I think you're trying to turn me into an alcoholic," he said to Alex. "Plying me with wine and beer . . ." He took a sip. "Mm. What a way to go."

"Wine and 3.2 beer won't lead you down the primrose path."

"I'm not fighting it."

At lunch Alex said to Jordan, "I'm working a two till midnight shift at the hospital. Will you be all right?"

72

Jordan put down his fork. "Alex, of course I'll be all right. And look, both of you — don't hover around waiting for me to collapse, okay?"

Alex looked hurt. "Sorry. I just thought you might be tired."

Jordan carefully buttered a hot roll. "I am tired," he said. "I didn't mean to sound like that. I appreciate your thinking about me. Only I don't want to be turned into . . . oh, you know, some damned invalid. At least not yet."

Alex said, "I know. We won't do that. It's just . . . a new situation. None of us are used to it."

"Let's say it never happened. Leave everything the way it was."

His mother said, "You do have to conserve your strength. But we understand how you feel, and we won't hover."

Jordan noticed lines around her mouth that he had never seen before. It made him feel angry that he had to put them all through this. It was bad enough to face it himself, without making everybody else suffer. He threw his napkin onto the table and got up. "Blast the whole rotten situation anyway." He stood in the bay window, staring at the big elm tree in the yard without seeing it.

Behind him Alex and his mother were silent for several minutes. Then Alex said in a normal voice, "If you don't want your crabmeat, can I have it?"

Jordan turned around, forcing a grin. "No, you cannot. I want it." He sat down and began to eat again.

"There's more," his mother said. She took Alex's

73

plate into the kitchen. When she came back, she said, "Alex, that's an awfully long stretch for you to work, right after getting off the plane."

"It's the price of getting those days off. I've got a chemistry exam on Monday, too. It's going to be a great weekend."

When Alex was leaving, Jordan followed him out to the yard. "Alex, thanks a lot for going to Rochester with me."

"I'm glad I could."

"I know it was pretty grim, and it's put you behind and everything . . ." He paused. "But I'm awfully glad you were there."

"Us middle brothers have to hang together." Alex got into the car. "See you later."

After his mother had left on her bicycle, Jordan wandered restlessly around the house. He found himself looking at it as if he were an outsider. 'The Phillipses need a new sofa,' he thought. He had had it vaguely in mind to buy one for his mother some day, until he'd found out how much a good sofa cost. He sat down at the piano and played a few chords. Tony was the one who had inherited their mother's talent for music. At one time all three of the older children had taken piano lessons, but only Tony was any good; and by the time Jordan was old enough, his mother had given up on all but Tony. Jordan could play a few songs by ear if he could transpose them to the key of C, but he was careful to play only when he was alone.

He walked around the piano, looking at the framed photographs of all the children at various ages. When a woman has five children, he thought, she has to buy a lot of picture frames. The only picture of his father that was to be seen in the house was an old snapshot that Skipper had framed. Skipper who had no recollection of him at all. It was a bad snapshot, slightly blurred, of their father stretching upward with a tennis racket in his hand, as if he were about to put a powerhouse serve over some unseen net. 'Showoff,' Jordan thought.

Upstairs he went into his mother's room and sat down on the bed. Everything looked different. He noticed things that he hadn't been conscious of for years: the framed Klee print that he had liked when he was little because of the free-floating balloons; the photograph of all of them when Skipper was about two; the pleasant scent that his mother used, which lingered in her room. He looked at the bedside phone and pictured her picking it up when Terry called with the news. It must have been a terrible shock. She was behaving very well.

He wanted to call Susan, but she hated having him call at the office. It was always frustrating, because she talked to him in a cold office voice that sounded as if she hardly knew him. He would call her at home later. It was going to be hard not telling her, but it would be worse if she knew. She wouldn't want to be bothered with a guy in the shape he was in, if she knew about it. No sensible girl would. He shivered.

He picked up the silver hand mirror with his grandmother's monogram on it, part of the set she had given his mother. He looked at himself in the slightly distorting glass. He had circles under his eyes and he looked pale. What would he look like in three months? six? a year? If he only knew what to expect, exactly what to expect, and when, it wouldn't be quite so bad. It was strange to think that a time would come, maybe soon, when no mirror would reflect his face. He put the mirror down, impatient with himself. You couldn't go around thinking that kind of morbid stuff.

He went back to his own room, and in a few minutes he fell asleep.

Eighth

Jordan was downstairs watching a football game on television when the family began to come home for dinner. His mother came first. She looked in at him and asked him if he'd like steak for dinner. She sat down on the arm of a chair opposite him.

"Sure. Fine."

"Did you get a rest?"

"Yeah." He didn't want her to fuss over him. He gave her a brief smile and looked back at the screen.

She got the message. "Good game?" She got up and started out of the room.

"Not too. More fumbles than anything else." He looked back at her. From the set of her shoulders she looked tired. 'Tired and worried,' he thought. But there wasn't anything he could say that would make her feel any better.

In a few minutes Tony came in, taking off his florist's jacket and throwing it down on a chair. "Hi."

"Hi." He was never as sure of what Tony would do or say as he was of Alex. Tony, they all liked to say, was "the deep one."

Tony sank into the big leather chair. "What a day!"

"Bad one?"

"Busy." He pulled a paper from his billfold. "Before I forget it, the VW now belongs to you." He tossed the registration into Jordan's lap. "You have to go down to the city hall and get it recorded."

Jordan stared at him in astonishment. "How come?"

Tony shrugged. "Ma and I got our heads together. We need a second car that isn't forever breaking down. I got a good deal on a '72 Opel, so we bought it together. It wasn't worth trading in the VW, so you're next in the line of succession."

Jordan swallowed. He was not fooled by Tony's explanation. They had arranged this so he could have a car. "That's great. Thanks."

"It's no great gift, really. It's going to need a valve job pretty soon, and God knows what else."

"Listen, let me help pay for the Opel."

"No, you'll need all you've got to keep the VW alive."

For a perilous moment Jordan thought he was going to cry. He gripped his hands together and stared at the TV. It was a surprise to find that kindness was so hard to bear. He felt Tony's hand on his shoulder for a second, and he heard Tony say, "I've got to get in that

78

shower before Skip and Alex get home."

Jordan called after him the thing they had been saying for years: "One of these days we'll buy a house with five bathrooms."

"You bet." Tony went up the stairs, but halfway up he turned and came back. Standing behind Jordan, he said, "And incidentally, if there's anything you need or want done or even if you just feel like shooting the breeze, give me the signal."

Jordan put his hand up and Tony gripped it for a second, and then went back upstairs. Jordan pressed the palms of his hands against his eyes until he was sure the treacherous tears were under control. He went into the kitchen and got a Coke.

"You'll spoil your appetite," his mother said.

"Not a chance. Hey, Tony told me about the car."

"Are you pleased?" She smiled at him.

"Of course. No more freezing to death on the old motorbike."

"I never liked the motorbike. I wish you'd sell it."

"Skip will want it."

"No, it's too dangerous. I'm going to get him a ten-speed bike for his birthday."

"Ma, have you come into a fortune or something?"

"No, I read an article on inflation. You save money and it just melts away in the bank. So I decided — carpe diem!"

"Carpe who?"

"Carpe diem. Seize the day!"

"Oh. Well, it's a good thing you read a lot, Mom." He picked up a raw carrot from a plate on the table. He waved it at her and went back to watch the rest of the game. Seize the day. It sounded like a good idea.

Skipper bounded into the house in his basketball practice clothes. "Hey, man! Welcome!"

Jordan flinched as Skipper hit him on the upper arm. "Watch it."

"I'm sorry, I don't know my own strength." He straddled the arm of a chair. "You developing a glass arm or something? How was Minnesota?"

"Chilly."

"Yeah? Did you go out with any Indian maidens?"

"Naturally." He watched Skipper closely for a few minutes to see if he suspected anything was wrong, but Skipper's clear gray eyes were as merry and disingenuous as ever. "I hear you played first string."

"Yeah, I was fabulous. Another Wilt Chamberlain, they're saying."

Jordan laughed. Skipper made him feel good, partly because there was nothing in reserve behind the jokes, no covered-up sadness. "You'd better start growing."

"No, it doesn't matter, because, see, I'm fast and sneaky. I stop and go like a quarter horse. That's what Em said. She's thinking of entering me in the rodeo."

"I can see it."

"What did those guys say is the matter with you?"

"Oh, some long Latin phrase."

"Meaning what?"

"Meaning take it easy for a while; pamper your muscles."

"Oh, I'm sorry I socked you. Did I hurt you?"

"It's all right."

"I'll have to remember that. Treat the old boy gently."

"Just for a while."

"Naturally. You don't think I could keep it up for long."

"Skipper, get ready for dinner," his mother called.

"Roger." He raced up the stairs.

Jordan closed his eyes. Already it seemed to him that he had never had that much energy. He got up and shut off the TV as the news came on.

After dinner Terry and Pat came over. Jordan was upstairs talking to Susan on the phone when he heard them come in. Susan had apparently been glad that he was back. She asked much the same questions that Skipper had asked, and he gave her the same answers.

"Did they mention tennis knee?" she said.

He laughed, but he felt a wrench of pain at the phrase. It seemed to him that he had moved into another world from Susan, somewhere a long way off, from which he could just barely hear her. "No, he didn't."

"You can have tennis knee in your elbow, too," she said, sounding grieved because he had laughed. "I mean it's a tennis elbow, or tennis shoulder, or whatever."

"Sure, I know. I just laughed because I feel a little hysterical. Haven't had enough sleep, and you know, jet lag and all."

"Will you be over tonight?"

He hesitated. He wanted very much to go, but he felt so tired he could hardly talk. "Honey, I can't tonight. Doctor's orders."

"Oh."

To cheer her up, he said, "Hey, guess what? Tony gave me the VW. I mean for good. It's mine."

Her voice lifted. "Oh, Jordie, that's wonderful!"

"Yeah. We won't be dependent on anybody for wheels."

"Listen, Ellie wants to use the phone, so I better hang up. Call me tomorrow?"

"Sure. Good night, Susie." He lay back on the bed after he had hung up. He wished he could skip seeing Terry and Pat. It would be all right to see Terry, she never made a fuss; but Pat . . . Maybe if he just stayed where he was, they'd leave. He turned off the light.

After a while he heard Terry's quiet voice in the upper hall. "Jordan?"

"I'm in Mom's room."

She came in and sat beside him in the dark. She put her hand on his head the way she used to do when he was little and had a fever. "Tired?"

"I really am."

"I went to see Dr. Parkhurst last night after Alex called. Alex wasn't too specific."

"He was upset."

"Yes, of course. Anyway, Dr. Parkhurst said when you feel tired, you should take it easy."

Jordan sighed. "I don't really see it like that."

"How do you mean?"

"A guy is dead a long time. While he's alive, he may as well live it up."

"It might shorten his life."

"What's the saying — a short life and a merry one?"

She was silent for a few minutes. "After I saw the doctor, I went for a long drive. I didn't pay any attention to where I was going, but I ended up in Longmont. Remember that little place where we used to go for hamburgers?"

"Yes."

"I went in and got some coffee. Some character came in and tried to pick me up, but then he got a good look and he saw a) that I was pregnant, and b) that I was crying. He took off in a hurry."

Jordan put up his hand and touched her cheek. "Don't cry, Sis."

"I love you, Jordie."

"I know. We're lucky that way; we've got a lot of love in this family. I always took it for granted before. Now . . . it's nice." After a moment he said, "Will Pat feel hurt if I don't come downstairs?"

"No, of course not."

"He won't preach at me, will he, Terry?"

"He'd like to, I guess, but I don't think he will."

"I don't think I could take that, and I don't want to be rude to him."

"I think he'll understand. To him, you see, the church is such a comfort. He wants everybody to enjoy it."

"Do you?"

She hesitated. "I'm not orthodox. I believe in God in my own way. My own simple-minded way, I guess."

"I guess it would be a comfort. I've never given it a whole lot of thought. I mean we went to Sunday School when we were kids, and later we went to church now and then, but less and less. When you haven't paid any attention to any god, you can't suddenly claim his help when you're in trouble."

"Why not?"

"Well, it doesn't seem fair."

"I doubt if God would worry about that."

"Anyway, I don't know if I believe in Him or not, so it would just be hedging my bets."

"I know what you mean. You feel you can't say 'I believe' just because it would be a help. But don't worry about it. It will either come or not come. You can't rationalize it." She smoothed back his hair, and they were silent for a few minutes.

"I don't want to die," he said. "I had a lot of plans. Damn it, I don't want to die!"

"All kinds of things could happen. They could find a cure, or the diagnosis could be wrong."

"It's a long chance."

"Jordie, every day of our lives is a long chance."

"Yeah. It's a funny feeling, though, Sis. Like with Tony I made that old joke about when we buy a house with five bathrooms, and I thought — 'I won't be here.'"

"Don't think that. Think 'I hope I'll be here.'"

"I don't like the idea of my muscles conking out." He gave a little laugh. "A guy spends all those years building up his muscles . . ."

"Jordan?" It was his mother's voice from the hall.

"We're in your room, Mom."

She appeared in the doorway. "Dr. Parkhurst dropped by to see you. All right if I turn on the light?"

"Sure." Jordan started to get up.

"Don't get up, Jordan." Dr. Parkhurst came in, making the room look smaller. "Hi, Terry. How are you feeling, Jordan?" He took Terry's place at the side of the bed.

"Tired, but otherwise okay."

The doctor took his pulse. "Knee all right? Shoulder?"

"Not bad."

"I talked to the Mayo fellow this afternoon. He's gone over it with you. My feeling, Jordie, is . . ." His voice broke and he looked away. He cleared his throat. "Play it cool. Give your muscles all the rest you can . . ."

Jordan felt betrayed. Somewhere in the back of his mind there had been a feeling that Dr. Parkhurst could stop this deadly thing. He'd always cured the other things — the flu, the measles, the skiing accidents. Wasn't he even going to try?

"Don't walk when you can ride," the doctor was saying. "Don't climb stairs when there's an elevator. You've got to pamper that muscular system."

"So I can last maybe eight months instead of five or six?" Jordan said coldly.

Dr. Parkhurst winced. "Jordan, people have

been known to live for years with this . . ."

"I know. Twenty years for one lucky character. Twenty marvelous years sitting around with muscles that wouldn't work. But he was unusual, Doc, wasn't he?"

"Jordan, I know you feel bitter . . . My God, if I could do anything . . ." His voice broke again. "I think the world of you Phillips kids . . ." He blew his nose and stood up. He spoke now in a more professional voice. "Rest up for a few days before you go back to classes. That was a tiring trip."

"What about my job?"

"Keep it if you feel up to it." He gave Jordan a long look, as if he were trying to find words for what he wanted to say, but then he turned away and left the room without saying good night.

Terry looked in. "I'll see you tomorrow."

Jordan forced a smile. "Right."

When they were gone, he went into his own room. He picked up a can of ski wax that Skipper had left on the bureau. No more skiing. No more tennis. No anything that mattered. He might as well be dead right now. For some reason he thought of the meteor that had zoomed over the Rocky Mountain states a few years ago, going 3,300 miles an hour just thirty-six miles up. If it had been thirty-six miles lower, an awful lot of people — maybe thousands, maybe the Phillips family — would have been wiped out without ever knowing what hit them. It was a crazy, random universe, and there ought to be a law against it.

Ninth

When Jordan came downstairs in the morning, everyone had gone. There was a note from his mother telling him there was freshly made coffee cake in the oven and bacon and eggs in the refrigerator. He drank the orange juice she had squeezed for him and poured out a cup of coffee. He fried some bacon and two eggs, and cut a piece of coffee cake. The doctor had said he might lose weight, but he had no intention of looking like some creepy skeleton.

He called his boss to tell him that it would be Monday before he could come back to work. The lawyer was his usual noncommittal self. He asked how the trip to Mayo had gone, but he didn't press for details. He brushed off Jordan's apology about not having been able to come in.

"Nothing too pressing. You can get caught up next week."

Jordan admired him. Not only because he was good at his profession but because of that reserved, logical approach to everything. If somebody told him he had a fatal disease, Jordan thought, he'd jot down the problems, think out the solutions, and proceed according to plan. No emotional ups and downs, no indecision, no wasting of time. That was the way to be.

He washed up his breakfast dishes and went out to the garage to look at his Volkswagen. He was poking around the hood when he heard Em's voice.

"Hi."

He looked up, glad to see her. He was always glad to see her.

"Hi yourself. Why aren't you on campus?"

"I cut my biology class to welcome you home."

"Ah, I shouldn't encourage you in such behavior, but I'm glad you did." He closed the hood of the VW. "How do you like my car?"

"Great. I heard you were inheriting it."

He wiped his hands on an old towel and followed her out of the garage. "Come on in. Mom left a pot of coffee. Of course she left a lot of other stuff, too, but I've eaten it. There might be a crumb of coffee cake, though."

They sat at the kitchen table and she chatted about various little things that had happened while he had been away: their friend Bill had broken up with his girl; Em's mother had gone to San Francisco to visit her sister; there was revolt brewing in the math class because the professor was using tapes instead of lectures; Em's horse had pitched her off and she had landed in the creek.

After a while he said, "You haven't asked me how things went at Mayo."

"No," she said, "I haven't, have I?"

"You've guessed they didn't go well."

"I know your mother was upset. But Jordie, you don't have to talk about it to me unless you want to."

"All right. It was bad news and I want you to know it, but I am sick to death of the details. Sick to death . . ." He gave an unhappy little laugh. "That's the right phrase, all right." He saw the pain in her face and he said, "I keep making great resolutions about putting it out of my mind, but before I know it I'm wallowing in self-pity again."

"And it's hard because you know it's making the others suffer."

"Yes." He was surprised that she knew that. "Not only because I don't like to hurt them, but because there's a . . . I don't know . . . a big load of emotion hanging over my head all the time. That sounds bratty, but I don't mean it like that. It's just that it's hard to be looked after and worried over and cried over. That's hard to take."

"Of course it is. Well, my friend, I won't cry over you." She smiled. "I came over to tell you I've got a present for you."

"I heard you had."

"You may not want it, and you absolutely must say so if you don't, because it would be a great mistake to take it if you didn't really want it."

"You've never given me anything I didn't want."

"This is kind of different, though." She got up.

"You have to come over to my house to get it."

He was grateful that she didn't say "If you feel like walking over there" or anything like that. "Okay, let's go."

They went through the gate in the wooden fence between their houses, and Em took him around to the kitchen door.

"Wait here." She went into the house.

He heard an odd scratching sound, but he couldn't tell what it was. Then she came out, carrying a Scottie dog. "Welcome home, happy birthday, Merry Christmas, or whatever." She put the dog down and handed Jordan the leash. "Do you want him?"

Jordan was delighted. "Of course I want him! I've wanted another dog ever since Flipper was killed."

"I thought you did."

"He's a very handsome dog. What's his name?"

"I got him from a classics major. I'm afraid his name is Cicero."

"An odd name for a Scot, but that's all right." He held his hand down for the dog to sniff. "Cicero, how are you?"

"He's eight months old, housebroken, a good watchdog, and reasonably obedient except when his Scottish obstinacy is working. He'll heel, unless he thinks of something more interesting to do. He'll come when you call him — usually. And he's loving."

Cicero having sniffed Jordan's shoes and trousers and hand, sat down and looked up at him with bright black eyes. Slowly he wagged his tail.

90

"He thinks you'll do," Em said.

"He's really great. Look at those bushy eyebrows."

"He's a good dog. I mean in AKC terms. I'll give you his papers."

"I seem to be making some marvelous acquisitions, with legal papers and all. First a car, now a Scottish dog who speaks Latin. Greek, too, I suppose."

"Of course."

Jordan sat down on the step and scratched Cicero's ears. The dog cocked his head toward him, wagging his tail harder.

"He likes that. You're good with dogs, Jordie; you should always have one."

For a moment the word "always" hung in the air between them. Em scooped up Cicero in her arms and put him in Jordan's arms. "Now he's yours." The little dog peered into her face. "Jordan is your master now."

Cicero gave Jordan a tentative lick on the ear.

"Will I do?" Jordan said. "Em, you were a doll to get him for me. I wouldn't have thought of getting a dog now. I'm really going to enjoy him."

"I hope so," she said. "If he's a bother or anything, you can give him back to me. One more animal around our place can always find a spot for himself." She patted Cicero's head. "I'd better get back to work. If you need anything, whistle."

"I'm going to be spoiled," Jordan said. "Everybody tells me 'if you need anything . . .' It's going to be a temptation to just sit back and whistle and watch you all run."

"That would be the day. I mean when you'd do it. So long, Cicero. Be good to Jordie."

Jordan carried the dog partway home and then put him down and led him. Cicero looked back several times to see what had happened to Em, but he came obediently. When Jordan lay down on the sofa, Cicero sat on the floor nearby. They studied each other.

"I'm glad you're here, Cicero. You'll be a good one to talk to. The nice thing is, you won't have any opinions about my future, or lack of. 'In today's poll on the question "Does Jordan Phillips have a future?"; seventy-two percent of those queried answered no. Twelve percent said yes. Fifteen percent had no opinion, and one gentleman in East Tincup said, "Who the hell cares?" Check your daily paper tomorrow for the results of the new poll.'"

Cicero got a running start toward the sofa, his short legs flailing like pistons. He just cleared the edge and landed with a thump on Jordan's stomach. He settled down to chewing the button on Jordan's shirt.

After a while Jordan sat up. "We have things to do, dog. First we drive our Volkswagen down to the store and get you some dog food, a bed, and something to chew on besides my shirt buttons. Then we come back here and start getting caught up on all the work we missed in class. All right?"

The puppy jumped to the floor, skidding on a small throw rug. When he had regained his balance and his dignity, he trotted to the door and waited for Jordan.

"Do you behave well in a car?" Jordan found the car keys, snapped the leash to Cicero's collar, and went out.

He had to discourage the puppy from sitting on his shoulder, but apart from that and the fact that Cicero barked furiously whenever he saw another dog, there was no problem. Cicero whimpered a little, but he sat obediently in the car while Jordan did his shopping.

It was an unseasonably warm Indian summer day. When he got home Jordan brought his books outside to the patio, where he could sit in the sun and study. He gave Cicero a marrow bone, which the puppy not only chewed enthusiastically but tossed and wrestled all over the grass. The patio, in the back of the house, was fenced in, so Cicero could explore without a leash.

Jordan had brought out a pad of blank paper that he borrowed from Tony's room. When he tore off a sheet, a folded piece of paper fell out of the pad. In Tony's scrawl there was a short quotation written on it.

And the words which carry most knives are the blind
  Phrases searching to be kind.

And Tony had written "Spender" under it.

Jordan thought about that for several minutes. It was probably true, he said to himself, and he wondered how it was that poets seemed to be able to say things sometimes that no one else had thought of. It was what made Tony seem mysterious, as if a poet had some kind of special

93

knowledge that the rest of them lacked. He decided he would borrow some of Tony's books of poetry and see what he could find. He might come across some absolutely amazing truth in just a few lines, a few words that would tell him some of the things he longed to know. There was a whole world of knowledge that he wanted to gobble up as fast as he could, while he had time. He would also borrow some of Alex's books in science. Anatomy, for instance. He had really only the haziest idea of what his body was like, what it did and couldn't do, and why. And now it seemed very important to find out. No more frittering away time watching TV or fooling around; he would spend all his time and energy learning and experiencing all he could while there was still a chance.

Tenth

Jordan found that he didn't need the doctor's reminder to "sit, don't stand," "ride, don't walk," and so on. His susceptibility to fatigue and aching muscles were enough. He avoided plans with his friends that would involve much activity, but they accepted his excuses without surprise, because ever since he had started working in the law office, he had had a shortage of time. Susan was not pleased when he ended dates sooner than he would have done, but she recognized that he was more tired than usual.

"When are you going to get over this?" she asked him. "What did those doctors say? You look so pale, Jordie."

"Oh, give it a little time," he said. "Don't worry about it." He dreaded the time when he would have to tell her.

He dropped a four-hour course to give himself an easier schedule. But in the law office he sometimes stayed overtime, after his work was done, reading.

"If I make it," he said at dinner one night, "I'm going to specialize in law that will help disabled people. They don't get a fair shake. Veterans, for instance. Those guys need a good lawyer."

"Right," Alex said. "I talked to some guy who had been in a Veterans' Administration hospital in Los Angeles. Guys from World War I, even, stashed away and forgotten."

"Disabled!" Skipper said. "I thought you were going to be a courtroom lawyer, star of the scene. What's the matter, don't you think you can hack it?"

"Shut up, Skipper," Tony said sharply.

"What'd I say? I only asked a simple question . . ."

"Knock it off. I get sick and tired of hearing you talk. Nobody can carry on a conversation in this house without you butting in with your smart cracks."

"I wasn't talking to you," Skipper said stiffly.

"Well, I'm talking to you."

"You're not my father."

"Thank God for that."

"Boys," their mother said, "that's enough. Be still, Skipper."

Skipper's voice trembled with indignation and hurt. "Why do I have to be quiet? Just because I'm the youngest . . ."

Tony slapped the palm of his hand on the table. "That's *enough!*"

Skipper shoved back his chair. "Oh, drop dead," he muttered. He picked up Cicero, who was sitting in the doorway, and went upstairs.

"Was that necessary?" Jordan said.

Tony flashed a look at him, but he didn't answer. He finished his coffee in one swallow and left the room.

"Oh, dear," their mother said softly.

"You'd better tell Skipper about Jordan, Mom," Alex said. "He doesn't understand why people get so edgy with him."

"I suppose so," she said.

"I ought to tell him myself," Jordan said.

"No," his mother said, "I'll do it."

"I'm upsetting the whole family," Jordan said.

"It's not just you with Tony," Alex said. "Bitsy is going to stay in Europe for another month."

"Oh?"

"She's dating some French skier."

"Oh, poor Tony," his mother said.

"You can't blame her," Jordan said, "with Tony's attitude toward marriage."

"Nobody blames her. But that doesn't make him any happier about it."

"I bet he'll never get married," Jordan said. "He's too complicated."

"I think it has to do with your father and me," his mother said.

"What do you mean?"

"I think he sees marriage as something likely to fail, and Tony hates to fail."

Cicero came back and sat in the doorway again, hungrily watching each bite of food that was eaten. Jordan was training him not to come any nearer the table during mealtime, but whenever Cicero thought no one was looking, he

97

inched his hindquarters a little nearer.

"Back, Cicero," Jordan said. "Back."

Cicero wriggled back to the doorway.

"Good boy."

"Have you fed him?" his mother asked.

"Yes. He eats like a horse."

"Growing boys are always hungry," Alex smiled at his mother. "Right, Mom?"

"Right." She got up. "I'll go talk to Skipper."

"I'll do the dishes," Alex said.

"I'm going out for a little while." Jordan felt suddenly that he could not stay in the house while his mother told Skipper.

Alex followed him to the back door. "You want company?"

"No, thanks, Alex. I'm all right." He went out quickly. He got the VW and drove out of the yard, but he stopped and went back to the house when he heard Cicero yipping. "Come on, Cicero." He got the leash and led the dog into the car. "Stay now. Don't climb all over me." Cicero sat up properly in the passenger's seat and pushed his black nose against the window. "You want some air?" Jordan opened the air vent a little, and the Scottie thrust his face into the opening. As Jordan drove down the hill, the night air blew Cicero's whiskers back. His eyes glazed with pleasure.

Jordan had a feeling of wanting to get away from the high, jagged mountains, which usually he loved. He drove east toward the plains. After a while he was out of the mountains, and the dark land stretched level as far as he could see. It soothed him. He tried not to think about

Skipper, hearing the depressing news from his mother. Poor old Skip. It's probably a good thing Tony is stern with him, he thought, because the rest of us spoil him. He's a good kid. People will like him better in the long run if he learns not to throw himself into the center of the stage all the time.

"It's tough to be the runt of the litter," he said to Cicero.

Cicero flicked an ear to show he had heard, but he didn't take his face away from the window.

"What's out there?" Jordan said. "What wonderful things do you smell?"

He began to think about Saturday night, the Thanksgiving ball. He looked forward to it with mixed feelings. If things went all right it could be a very good evening, but if his muscles balked, it would be disaster. His mother and he had argued about his going: she didn't think he should spend an evening dancing. Finally he had said, "Ma, you might as well give up. I'm going to that dance, come hell or high water." He could imagine Susan's reaction if he told her that he couldn't go. She'd been planning on it for weeks and she had bought a new dress. He'd just keep his fingers crossed, and Friday, when he got home from work, he'd take a long rest. The idea that he had to take a rest, like some old lady, made him sick.

He pressed down on the accelerator to pass a produce truck that was barreling along the narrow road in front of him. The Volkswagen shuddered and vibrated at the extra speed demanded of it. He would really have to see about a major overhaul on the engine. A valve job at the very least. He wondered how much it would cost.

For a few seconds the VW struggled along parallel with the truck, but then the driver obligingly slowed a little and let Jordan pass him. Jordan flicked his lights in a "thank you," and the truck returned the signal. It wouldn't be so bad to be a truckdriver, he thought, except that they put such pressure on you. But it would be a free kind of life, in a way, up there in that cab by yourself. He wondered what they thought about in all these long hours by themselves. Probably about whether their wives were being faithful while they were gone, and whether the union could get them a raise. But they must think about other things, too. He wondered what.

He slowed down a little as he passed through a tiny village, but then picked up speed again. He wished the VW was a convertible so he could put the top down and let the wind rush at him — but then Cicero would probably get blown right out of the car. He was glad Em had given him Cicero. The sturdy, independent little dog was comforting to have around.

He passed a sign pointing to Fort Collins. Em was talking about transferring to the Fort Collins campus to get a degree as a vet. Most kids outgrew their intention to be a vet, the way they stopped wanting to be firemen or astronauts, but Em was serious.

He passed a farmhouse whose lights glowed yellow in the night. He felt like driving all night, clear across Kansas, Missouri, Illinois, Kentucky, Virginia, right to the Atlantic Ocean, which he had never seen. All at once it seemed unbearable that he should die without having seen the Atlantic Ocean. He thought about his father up there in Maine. What was he doing in Maine? What kind of guy was he? How much of him had they all inherited? What if I went up there to see him, he thought? He wondered if his father would mind when his third son died.

The trouble was, it was hard to keep it in his mind as a fact that he had a fatal illness. Sometimes he could face right up to it for a few minutes, but most of the time it seemed unreal and he looked ahead into his life the way he always had. You couldn't believe a thing like that. To think of yourself as not existing was too much for the mind to grasp.

The VW suddenly went into a spasm. *Clank, clank, clank!* Jordan slowed down and pulled off the road onto a grassy shoulder.

"What now?" He found the flashlight and got out to look under the hood. He was not an expert with cars the way Alex was. He could not tell what was wrong. He checked the oil, but it was all right. While he was looking, the truck he passed sped by him, and he cursed himself for not having flagged it down. There were no other cars in sight. Leaving the hood up in case someone came along, he got back into the car to think.

At this hour he would never find a garage open, probably not even a gas station out here in the country. He would have to find a phone and call Tony or Alex. He ground his teeth in frustration and anger. He had gone on a pointless ride, and now they'd have to come all this way to get him. He felt helpless, like a baby.

"Well, come on," he said to Cicero. "We've got to find a stupid phone. God knows where." He took the dog out of the car and walked to the east for a few minutes, but there were no lights. "I guess we've got to go back to that farmhouse we saw. It must be at least two miles." He turned and started back. The night wind was sharp. He was wearing a lightweight jacket, having counted on the heater in the car. The fields on either side of the road stretched away in darkness, and overhead the sky was brilliant with stars. It was a beautiful night, he thought, for looking at, but not for walking two miles in. He tried not to think what would happen if his leg muscles rebelled.

He wanted to walk fast, from impatience and because of the cold, but he made himself settle into a steady stride. Cicero pattered along at his side, tugging at the leash every few minutes when there was a rabbit or something that only he could sense in the dark field. "Heel!" Jordan told him sharply, but Cicero had trouble keeping his mind on heeling. "I should have left you in the car." But he knew he couldn't have done that. Someone might have stolen him. Although that was hardly likely, considering that there seemed to be no one for miles around.

He was shivering and his muscles were beginning to ache and stiffen up with the cold wind. He tried to keep relaxed and to avoid the tension of worry, but the thought that his legs might give out, miles from nowhere, frightened him badly.

102

He began counting aloud, just for something to do. He counted to a hundred and then did it over again. Then he recited whatever came into his head that he could match his steps to. " 'This is the forest primeval, the murmuring pines and the hemlocks.' 'Mine eyes have seen the glory of the coming of the Lord, they have something-something-something where the grapes of wrath are stored . . . He has something-something-something with his terrible swift sword, and his truth goes marching on.'" The trouble was, there weren't many things he knew the words to. " 'Know ye all men by these presents . . . and the something hereinafter referred to . . .'"

He wanted to stop and rest but he was afraid to break his stride. The farmhouse seemed to be even farther than he had thought. He prayed the people in it would not have gone to bed. He prayed that they would have a phone.

Cicero was getting tired. His short legs had a hard time keeping up with Jordan. Without slowing down Jordan bent and picked him up and carried him for a while, but that really made his arms ache. He had to put him down again. "I'm sorry, Cicero. I'll slow down a little. Poor pup."

Then suddenly there was a light. The knowledge that he was almost there gave him new strength. He went to the back door, where the light seemed to be in the kitchen, and knocked. There was a wait before someone opened the door a crack and said, "Who is it?"

"I'm sorry to bother you, sir. My car broke down. Could I use your phone?"

The door opened a little wider and a man

peered out. "Yes, I guess so. Is that a dog?"

"Yes. He's all right. He won't bother."

"All right. Come in."

Jordan picked up Cicero, just to be sure he behaved, and went into the low-ceilinged kitchen after the man. A woman was sitting at the table — a thin-faced, middle-aged farm woman. She gave him an appraising look but she didn't say anything.

"Wants to use the phone," the man said to her. "Car trouble."

She pointed to a wall phone. "There it is."

"Thank you. I'm awfully sorry to bother you."

"No bother."

He put Cicero down, holding the leash under his arm, and dialed his number. Tony answered. Jordan told him what had happened.

"I'm sorry, Tony . . ."

"I'll come right out. Where exactly are you?"

"Wait a sec." He turned to the man. "How can I tell him to find your house?"

The man gave him some directions.

Jordan relayed them to Tony. "Got that? It's the only house on this stretch of road. You'll see the lights. I'm really sorry, Tony."

"See you shortly." Tony hung up.

Jordan said to the farmer and his wife, "I sure do thank you. How much do I owe you for the call? It was to Boulder."

"Nothing," the man said.

"That's very nice of you. I'd really have been stuck . . ." He stood there awkwardly, aching and cold still in spite of the warmth from the coal stove, and not knowing what to say. "I don't want to keep you up. I could wait outside . . ."

"Sit down, child," the woman said. "Harris, pour him a cup of coffee. He's shivering. He looks like he's coming down with something."

"That's very nice of you." He realized he'd said that before. "It does feel good to get out of the wind."

"You should dress warmer. Little old flimsy thing like that . . ." She frowned disapprovingly at his jacket.

"You a student at the university?" the man said. He put a mug of steaming coffee on the table and pushed a jug of cream and a glass bowl of sugar toward Jordan.

Jordan sat down stiffly. He had a feeling he couldn't have made it if the farm had been any farther away. "Yes, sir." Then he added, "But I live in Boulder with my family." In case the farmer had any prejudice against students.

After a considerable pause the man said, "What kind of dog is that?"

"It's a Scottie. Scotch terrier."

"Give the poor little thing some milk, Harris," the woman said.

"He'll spill it," Jordan said. "He's kind of a sloppy eater."

"No harm. Got to wash tomorrow anyway." She watched critically as her husband poured a saucerful of milk and put it down on the floor. Cicero thumped his tail. She laughed suddenly, startling Jordan. "Cute little fella," she said.

"He looks like them ads for Black and White Scotch whiskey," the man said.

"Always got whiskey on your mind," the

woman said, but she spoke amiably, as if she didn't really mean it. When Cicero had finished the milk in the saucer, he lapped up what he had spilled. "We're from Kansas," she said. "Only been here three months."

"Oh?" Jordan said politely. "Kansas is a nice state."

"Pull the armchair up to the stove, Harris," she said. "Child, you sit in the armchair. You're shivering."

"Thank you, I'm all right." Although he was cold, Jordan was so stiff he was afraid he wouldn't be able to get up from the hard wooden chair he was sitting on.

"Help him over there, Harris," she said. "The child don't feel good. Too far to walk in that wind, nothing but that little jacket on."

The man helped Jordan up. "Mother knows how it is not to feel too good," he explained. "She has the arthritis pretty bad."

"Oh, I'm sorry." He was eased into the more comfortable chair and felt the welcome heat of the coal fire. He felt dizzy. A refilled coffee mug was put in his hand. He wrapped his cold fingers around it and began to feel a little better.

"Are you an only child?" the woman asked.

"No. I have three brothers and a sister."

"That's good," she said. "That's the best way."

"Our boy was the only one," the man said. "We lost him."

Jordan looked at their worn faces. "I'm sorry." The conventional phrase was all he could think of to say, but he felt real pain for their lost son. He wanted to ask what had happened to him, had

he known he was going to die, had he been sick
or was it an accident, but he was afraid it would
be tactless. All he said was, "How old was he?"

"Twelve. Two years ago, that was."

"Twelve." Jordan shook his head. "I have a
brother fourteen."

"I hope the good Lord will give him a long
life," the man said.

"I hope so, too." He felt strange, as if he had
sat in this kitchen and talked to these people before. It's the dizziness, he thought. To reassure
himself he put his hand down and stroked
Cicero's ear.

"Would you like a dog, Mother?" the man
said.

"I wouldn't mind," she said. "Cute little fella
like that. Minds so good."

"I've only had him a little while," Jordan said.
"He was a present."

"We left Kansas to get away from the memories," the man said. "Too many memories."

"Mustn't talk sad, Father," the woman said.

The man gave a heavy sigh. "No. Nobody likes
sad talk."

"You're glad, though, aren't you," Jordan said,
"that you had him for twelve years? It's better
than if you hadn't had him?"

"Oh, my, yes," the woman said. And the man
nodded. "Yes, indeed. We are just a mite selfish,
you know, we wanted him longer. But we are
thankful for what we had." She moved stiffly as
if to ease her back. "Are you feeling a little
better?"

"Yes, I really am. That fire feels good. And the

coffee." He smiled and unexpectedly she smiled back, a luminous smile that lit up her long, somber face.

"Are you hungry? Father could make you a nice sandwich."

"No, thanks, really." Ordinarily he would have felt constrained with older people he didn't know, but now he asked them questions because he really wanted to know about them. He learned that the man was a wheat farmer and that so far he liked Colorado. They had been to Denver so the woman could go to the doctor and they could shop. They liked Denver.

The man said, "I rented a wheelchair for the day so I could take Mother all over without her being wore out and hurting."

"We had a nice day," she said. "We went to the May D & F to buy us some clothes, and Father got us a new TV." She pointed to a small color TV in the corner of the kitchen. "It works real good."

"We had our dinner at that Trader Vic's." The man grinned. "We had us a time, didn't we, Mother? Rum swizzles and all."

"It was lovely," she said. "Have you been there?"

"Yes. I like it," Jordan said, remembering the last time he had taken Susan there. He wondered what Susan would make of his new friends.

"We like those Polynesian spareribs," the man said. "Those are tasty."

By the time Jordan heard the sound of the Opel turning into the yard, he was almost sorry to leave the pleasant kitchen. He was warm, and his legs and arms didn't ache so much and he had stopped feeling dizzy.

Cicero, who had climbed into his lap, sat up and cocked his head.

"Look at that, Mother," the man said. "He hears their car."

Cicero jumped to the floor and ran to the door, whining softly.

"I forgot to ask your name," Jordan said.

"Ricker," the man said. "Harris Ricker."

"I'm Jordan Phillips." Jordan got stiffly to his feet, and the man held out his hand.

"Proud to know you, Jordan."

"If you ever come into Boulder, I wish you'd come by and see us. I'd like you to meet my family. We live at the top of Aspen Road."

"Mighty nice of you, Jordan. We thank you." The man went to the door and opened it as Tony came up on the steps. "Come in, come in."

Jordan went to the door. "This is my brother Tony. Tony, this is Mr. Ricker and Mrs. Ricker."

When the introductions were over, Mr. Ricker said, "You going to try and move your car tonight?"

"No, I'll have to wait till tomorrow," Jordan said. "It's really dead."

"What's wrong with it?" Tony asked.

"I don't know. A big *clunk-clunk* and it quit."

"I'll get out there in the morning and bring it over here with the tractor," Mr. Ricker said.

"Oh, I don't want to put you to that trouble."

"He don't mind," Mrs. Ricker said. "You don't want it setting out there. Somebody might steal it."

Jordan grinned. "Nobody'd want it."

"Just the same, they might strip it," Mr. Ricker said. "I'll get it come daylight."

"That's nice of you," Tony said. "And thank you for looking after my brother."

"Thank you very much," Jordan said. "I really appreciate how nice you were." He shook hands with them both.

"Come back," Mrs. Ricker said. "And wrap up warm, child."

When Mr. Ricker had guided them out of the yard and they were on the way back to Boulder, Tony said, "Quaint types."

"Don't laugh at them," Jordan said sharply. "They are good people. They were very, very kind to me."

Tony glanced at him. "Sorry. One gets the habit of being flip about people one doesn't know. It's a rotten habit."

"Their son died," Jordan said. "He was twelve."

"Oh. I see."

Jordan told Tony a little about them, about their coming from Kansas, about Mrs. Ricker's arthritis, and the fun they had in Denver.

"You really liked them, didn't you?" Tony said.

"Yes, I did."

"It's not like you. I mean, you've never paid much attention to people outside your own little circle."

"I know." He shifted his position so he could put his head back and look at the sky. "It's nice, isn't it, the way the sky out here comes right down around you like an umbrella."

"Yes. Kind of a nice change after the mountains."

"I wish I could paint it. Look at all the different shades of dark and light."

"You used to paint a lot when you were a kid."

"I know. But the teacher said I saw things all cockeyed. The kids always laughed. So I quit."

"Any artist worth his salt sees things cockeyed. Why don't you try it again?"

"I might," Jordan said vaguely. "Just for the fun of it." After a minute he said, "Hey, I just saw a star fall. Do they keep on falling till they burn up or hit something?"

"Beats me."

"I wish I knew something about astronomy. Alex told me a quotation, something about the universe being queerer than we know or can know."

" 'There are more things in heaven and earth, Horatio, than are dreamed of in your philosophy.' "

"It's kind of a nice thought."

When they got near Boulder, Tony said, "Mom told Skipper."

"How did he take it?"

"Hard."

Jordan sighed. "It's been on my mind all evening. He's too young to be hurt . . ."

"There's no age limit."

Jordan pressed his cheek against the window. "It doesn't make you feel too good to know that you're making everybody unhappy."

"When people love other people, they're bound to get hurt."

"I don't think much of that system."

Tony drove up the curve of Aspen Road and

into the Phillips' yard. "How do you like the Opel?"

"Neat."

At the back door Jordan stood still a minute, dreading to go in and face Skipper. "I'd better get to bed," he said.

Tony said, "I'll give you another quote, since you're collecting them, Byron this time. 'He did the best he could, with things not very subject to control.'"

Eleventh

There was no sound from the upper bunk when Jordan went to bed, and in the morning, although he was sure Skipper was awake, again it was silent. The others were halfway through breakfast when he finally came down. Jordan glanced up at him and was startled by how pale and ill he looked.

"Morning, sport," he said, trying to sound natural.

Skipper mumbled a good morning and sat down without looking at any of them. Alex and Tony exchanged glances, and their mother looked anxious. She looked as if she had been crying.

"Tony and I will go out and look at your car this afternoon," Alex said to Jordan.

"Oh, good. Do you want me to come?"

"No, no need for that."

"I'll be up a crick if I don't have a car for the dance Saturday," Jordan said. "I hate to take the Volvo."

"You can go with us in the Opel," Tony said.

"I didn't know you were going."

"Yeah. I'm taking Em."

"Em!" Jordan looked at him in astonishment. "Em?"

"Yeah, Em."

"You never took her out before."

"There's a first time for everything. Skip, pour me some coffee, will you?"

"You're too old for Em," Jordan said.

"I'm not marrying her, Jordie; I'm just taking her to a dance. I got the tickets when I thought Bitsy would be back."

"You could have sold them."

Half-exasperated, half-amused, Tony said, "I happen to want to go. Do you mind?"

"No, of course not. I'm just surprised."

"Em is a very attractive girl, and an excellent dancer."

"Sure. I know."

"Jordie still thinks of her in pigtails," Alex said, "riding bareback and all that. Like a movie. The girl next door."

"Oh, I don't," Jordan said. He felt vaguely disturbed at the idea of Tony taking Em to the dance.

"So anyway, you and Susan can go with us in the Opel if your car resists all blandishments."

"All right."

"Skipper, you didn't finish your breakfast," his mother said as Skipper got up from the table.

"I'm not hungry."

"You want a ride?" Alex called after him.

"I'll take the bike." The door slammed behind him.

Their mother shook her head. "He's so upset." Jordan sighed. "I'll talk to him later."

"What is there to say?" Tony said. "Let him come out of it in his own way."

"You should have let me talk to him last night, Ma," Alex said. "It was hard on you."

She suddenly began to cry. She pressed her napkin against her mouth, trying to stop. "I'm so sorry. I . . ." She tried to laugh. "Oh, I didn't mean to . . ." She got up and went into the kitchen. Tony followed her.

Jordan put down his fork and rested his head on his hands. He felt so heavy; it seemed as if he could never get up out of his chair.

Alex said, "Take it easy, chum. She's been too 'stiff-upper-lip' from the start. She had to cry sometime."

Jordan didn't answer. He couldn't think of anything to say. He was greatly tempted to go upstairs to bed and stay there a long time.

"Do you want me to call in and say you're not feeling well? You could go to class and come home."

"No," Jordan said wearily. "I'll rest late this afternoon. There'll be plenty of days when I really can't go in."

In a few minutes Tony and his mother came back. She was holding a damp handkerchief but she managed to smile. "I'm sorry. I didn't know I was going to do that."

"I don't think," Alex said, "that any of us ought to fight too hard against our feelings. I mean we can't go around wailing and rending our garments and all that, but if we try to behave as if nothing is wrong, the strain is going to get wicked for everybody."

"I'll talk to Skipper," Tony said. "In a way it's the hardest for him, I suppose. When you're that young and you feel the world is your oyster — which Skip did feel — you aren't prepared for the low blows."

"I'll talk to him," Jordan said. "I want to talk to him myself."

"All right." Tony looked at his watch. "I've got to shove. I'll drop you both off so Ma will have the Volvo."

When Jordan let himself into the office later, he found a note from the lawyer saying he'd been called away and was leaving a list of things for Jordan to do. Jordan was sorry; he didn't feel like being alone. But he settled down to typing briefs and composing the letters for which his boss had left only a sketchy indication of what he wanted to say. One of the letters was to a man in the country, a rancher, who had sent in a hand-written will. Following instructions, Jordan acknowledged receipt of the will and suggested it would be better if the man came in and let the attorney draw up a formal will.

I ought to make a will, Jordan thought. Not that he had much of material value to leave, but there was the VW, such as it was, that he would like to leave to Skipper. There was Cicero, whom he'd leave to Em . . . Then he thought: no, he would leave him to Mrs. Ricker. Cicero would have a ball on a farm, and the Rickers would love him. Em had her own menagerie. He'd leave his books to Alex, and his record collection to Tony, and there were his watch, and the gold nugget dug up at Leadville by his great-grandfather, and the money his grandmother had left him. With difficulty he brought his mind back to work. When he had time, he would definitely draw up a will. In an odd way it was a rather pleasant thought, leaving the things he loved to the people who would enjoy them.

Tony picked him up and took him home. Then he and Alex left to see about the Volkswagen. Jordan called Susan. She sounded happy and excited about the dance, and it cheered him to talk to her. He told her about the possible car problem and was relieved when she made no objection to going with Tony in the Opel. She described her dress to him in detail.

"You'll be the prettiest girl at the dance," he said.

"And you'll be the handsomest guy. 'Who is that gorgeous hunk of man with the dark red hair and the soulful brown eyes?' they'll say." She giggled. "Are you wearing your new suit?"

"Yep."

"I'll be the envy of the ball. See you Saturday."

He sat with his hand on the receiver for a minute, picturing her. She would look beautiful, all right. Everybody said she was a beautiful girl. He wondered whose girl she would eventually be. But that wasn't a line of thought he wanted to pursue. Seize the day! He got his English lit book and settled down on his bunk to get a little work done while he rested. They were reading Hemingway — *A Farewell to Arms*. He had been prepared not to like Hemingway because he had read references to the *machismo* and the showing off and all, but he found himself very much moved by the book. His instructor had said that Hemingway dealt with the "test," in a chivalric way; putting his heroes to the test like the old-time knights. After class a friend of Jordan's had said, "Prepare to hear about that 'test' bit till you're ready to throw up. Baker did his dissertation on the echoes of Arthurian legend in Hemingway."

Jordan had made the expected remark about instructors and their kooky ideas, but now that he was reading the book he saw what Baker meant. Maybe Gehrig's disease was his own test. If everybody had to go through some kind of hell to prove himself, this ought to qualify. It helped a little, even while he smiled at himself, to think of Jordan Phillips as the suffering hero.

He moved Cicero to a more comfortable position against his knees. "I see myself," he said to him, "standing lonely and courageous on a darkened plain, somewhere out by Fort Collins. You're the only one with me, the only one who understands." He scratched Cicero's attentive ear. You couldn't romanticize yourself too much, though, because that would be breaking one of the rules. He thought of something Tony had said once about an acquaintance of theirs who was showing extreme grief at the loss of her husband. How had Tony put it? "The sovereignty of sorrow doesn't release a person from human obligation." Something like that. At the time he had liked the sound of the phrase "sovereignty of sorrow" without paying too much attention to the meaning.

He flipped open the Hemingway book again. "Back to work, Cicero. Discipline is the watchword for Hemingway heroes."

Twelfth

Late in the afternoon Alex and Tony towed the VW into the yard.

"Piston rod broke," Alex said, when Jordan came downstairs to hear the news. Alex was well-smeared with grease. "I'm afraid she's out of the race for a while."

Jordan groaned. "Expensive."

"I'll pay for it," Tony said. "I should have had it overhauled before I gave it to you anyway. I knew it was in tough shape."

"Don't be silly. I'll pay for it."

Tony raised his hand. "Give me no argument, little brother. I am the eldest and I have spoken."

"You know, if I turn out to be okay, you guys are going to be sorry you squandered all this kindness."

"We'll take that chance."

"Mrs. Ricker plied us with homemade doughnuts while we worked," Alex said. "Man, were they good!"

"They're nice people."

"Mrs. R. has a crush on you."

"That reminds me, if anything . . . uh . . . happens to me, she's to get Cicero. She really liked him."

Alex finished washing his hands at the sink. "Why make it that kind of contingency? If you like her that much, get her a dog of her own."

"I never thought of that. That's a good idea."

"Then you can enjoy her enjoyment."

"I'll ask Em where I can get a good one."

Skipper came in while they were still talking in the kitchen. He looked more like himself than he had in the morning, but he was still very subdued and he avoided talking to Jordan.

"No wild adventures in the supermarket this afternoon, Skip?" Alex said.

"No. Except I dropped a jug of molasses."

"When our little brother drops something," Jordan said, "he knows what to drop."

Skipper glanced at him in a quick, self-conscious way, as if Jordan were a stranger. "It was a mess."

"Did they dock your pay?"

"Forty-two cents."

They tried to joke with him about it, but he went upstairs.

"I'll be glad when he gets the old bounce back," Tony said, "much as it sometimes bugs me."

"He'll be all right," Alex said. "It takes time."

But Jordan knew Skipper would never be quite his old carefree self again. All of them had changed some.

* * *

Saturday evening, when they left for the dance,

he noticed another change of a different kind: Em. He had never seen her dressed for an evening out, and it was a shock. She was wearing a long black skirt and a simple white square-necked blouse and earrings. Nothing spectacular in itself, he thought, and yet she looked quite sophisticated and a good deal older. He was impressed. People were so full of surprises. And he admired her manner with Tony. He'd have expected her to be a bit awed at going out with someone who must always have seemed to her like "an older man," but she was quite poised, casual, cool, even amused. It was a manner Jordan liked.

Susan, on the other hand, was keyed up, gay, full of chatter, and that charmed him, too. She looked very pretty in her new dress. He hoped Tony noticed how attractive she was. She loved parties and was in high spirits. She told Jordan he looked handsome and snuggled up to him in the back seat. He was pleased but also a little embarrassed when he noticed Tony's sardonic glance in the rear-view mirror. Double-dating with your brother wasn't the greatest idea in the world.

The men's gym was elaborately decorated for the dance and already crowded when they got there. Jordan had a moment of panic when they came in from the cool night to the hot and noisy gym. Lately he had begun to mind being hemmed in by a crowd of people. He supposed it was nerves, and the feeling that if he became ill, he wouldn't be able to get out quickly.

The four of them found a little table in a corner, and Tony went to get glasses and ginger ale. Like most of the others he had a pint of bourbon in his coat. It was against the rules, but the rule was, as Tony remarked when he poured out the drinks, "more honored in the breach than in the observance." He looked questioningly at Jordan before he poured his bourbon, and Jordan nodded. He would take it slowly, though. He wasn't sure what effect alcohol would have on him.

Susan was preoccupied in looking for Ellie, the girl who shared her apartment.

Teasing her, Jordan said, "Anybody would think you hadn't seen Ellie for months."

"Well, we arranged to find each other. She's coming with two guys! Her own date and his roommate. Business school guys."

Jordan didn't like Ellie, and he was chagrined when she turned up at their table with her dates and pulled up chairs to join them. He knew, from Susan, that Ellie thought Susan could do better than a struggling future law student. Ellie had an eye for the main chance, and he was not surprised when she confided — in a moment when Drake, the date, was gone from the table — that his parents were *the* Drakes of Colorado Springs and he drove a Mercedes. Tim Drake was good-looking, but self-assured to the point of arrogance. Jordan decided he couldn't stand him. His roommate, Peter, was quieter.

Tony and Em were already dancing when Susan decided at last that she could tear herself away from her friends to dance with Jordan.

While they were dancing, Susan said, "That Tim is cute."

122

"I like the other guy better," Jordan said.

"Oh, you just like to disagree."

He was dancing badly. Usually he and Susan danced smoothly together, but his legs seemed jerky and hard to control. It embarrassed him.

When they were all back at the table, Ellie said to Tim in the disparaging voice that she always used toward Jordan: "Jordan is prelaw, and one of his brothers is premed." She smiled sweetly at Tony. "What are you, Tony?"

"Prenatal," Tony said.

Peter and Tim laughed, and Ellie looked annoyed. Susan frowned. Jordan crossed his fingers and wished for time to pass. Susan liked to dance every dance but Jordan's legs were giving him increasing trouble. He had a horror of their giving out on the dance floor. He encouraged Susan to dance with Peter, although he knew she was puzzled and hurt. He would explain it to her somehow, later. It was very hot in the gym; he began to feel faint and his head ached.

Em said, "Jordan, aren't you going to ask me to dance?"

Tony took the cue at once and went off with Susan. When the others were gone, Em said, "Let's sit it out."

He was grateful, but he didn't like to admit it. "Afraid I'll walk on your feet?"

"No, I'm just tired. I'm not used to this wild night life." She smiled at him. "Would things go better if Tony and I got lost until it's time to go home?"

"What do you mean?" He knew what she

meant. Susan and Tony had never hit it off. Tony irritated Susan.

"Tony and Susan rub each other the wrong way. I think it's spoiling your evening."

He leaned his head on his hand. He felt giddy. "I'm just tired." But she was right; the evening was a disappointment. It was his own fault that Susan was dancing so much with Peter, but he felt jealous just the same. Peter was a goodlooking guy, and he could tell that Susan thought so. Well, it wasn't her fault. She loved to dance, and she had no way of knowing he didn't feel well.

Trying to get his mind off the way he felt, he said to Em, "You look very glamorous."

"Don't be misled by the disguise. It's just me."

"Well, that's a comforting thought." Anxiously he watched Susan and Tony dancing, hoping Tony wasn't bugging her. They didn't seem to be talking much.

Later, a little before midnight, Susan said, "Come on, Jordan, you've got to dance with me once in a while, you know." And as Tony and Em went off, she added, "Even if you'd rather stay here and talk to Em."

"Susie!" he said. "You've got it all wrong . . ." He stood up, but suddenly he was extremely dizzy. He grabbed the edge of the table.

"What's the matter?" Susan said. "Are you all right?"

"Yeah. Just a sec."

Tony was there at once. He pushed past Susan in his anxiety to reach his brother.

Not understanding, she said angrily, "Look out who you're shoving."

Em said something to her, but Susan was furious. "Who does he think he is?"

Ignoring her, Tony was helping Jordan back into his chair. "Just sit down, Jordie. Take it easy."

Susan said loudly, "Jordan, are you going to dance or not?"

Tony turned on her, his anger heightened by his worry. "Can't you see he's not well?"

"Shut up, Tony," Jordan said. He felt humiliated. "Susie, dance this one with Peter. I'll talk to you later. I'm sorry . . ."

"Are you really sick?" Susan said uncertainly.

"I'm all right, honey." As Peter came up behind them, he said, "Dance with my girl, will you?"

"With pleasure," Peter said.

"My tennis knee is acting up."

Susan looked at Jordan as if she didn't know what to think. "Oh, come on, Peter," she said finally.

"Let's get you home," Tony said to Jordan.

"I feel like I might faint."

"Keep your head down. It's so hot and stuffy in here it's enough to make a horse faint."

Jordan got up slowly, keeping his head down. When Tony took him by the arm, he said, "I don't want to make a spectacle of myself."

"People will just think you've had too much to drink, if they notice at all," Tony said. "Lean on Em and me."

Jordan's ears roared and the gym seemed to revolve at a tremendous speed. Fortunately they were not very far from one of the fire exits. They got him out and eased him down onto a cement step. Tony ran back in to get their coats and to tell Susan they were taking Jordan home.

By the time he came back, the cold fresh air had had its effect. Jordan could lift his head without fear of keeling over. "Susan . . ." he said. "How will she get home?"

"I told her I'd come back for her, but she said Tim and Ellie and Peter would take her home."

Jordan groaned. "She'll never forgive me. Did you say I was sick?"

"I took your cue. I said your knee hurt."

Tony drove the car as close as he could to where Jordan was, and Em helped him into the back seat. Jordan sat with his head back and his eyes closed. The world had stopped spinning, but he felt weak and sick. He put down the window and let the cold air wash over him.

"Well," he said after a while, "I guess that was my first and last ball."

Em turned around and smiled at him. "You never struck me as the social butterfly type anyway."

Jordan grinned weakly. "More the Marlboro man. The Hemingway hero. Lonely but undaunted."

"Yes," she said, "more like that."

Thirteenth

The doctor came soon after breakfast. When he had examined Jordan, he sat back and looked at him. "A dance," he said, "was a silly thing for you to take on."

"I'd made the plans a long time ago."

Dr. Parkhurst shook his head. "Sometimes plans have to be unmade."

"My girl would have flipped if I'd told her I wasn't going."

"Flipped!" the doctor said sharply. "Doesn't she care about your health?"

"She doesn't know about it."

"Oh. Well, that's your business, but I should think it complicates things unnecessarily not to tell her. You'll have to sooner or later."

"I don't want to lose her till I have to."

"Mmm. Think you'll lose her, do you?"

"Sure. She'd be a fool to hang around."

"Sometimes love makes fools of people."

Jordan shook his head. He wasn't ready to say that Susan didn't love him like that, but he knew she didn't, and in a way he was glad. It wouldn't be so hard on her. Some day years from now she'd come across a snapshot of him and she'd think, "Oh, that's that guy I used to go with, the one who died young . . ."

Dr. Parkhurst was still talking. ". . . and at your age it's hard to believe that life isn't going to be one glorious song, but believe me, death is not the only word that starts with that hard, remorseless D. There's disappointment, disillusion, defeat, dishonor, despair . . . Life is full of those D words."

"You're a poet, doctor."

"Yeah. Missed my calling." He snapped his bag shut. " 'Doctor' starts with a D too, for that matter." He stood up. "I think what happened to you last night might have been mostly psychosomatic. You were worried about not making it through the evening and you got sick. Perfectly natural." He put some tablets on the bureau. "Take one every six hours. And take it easy till you feel better."

"Placebos?"

The doctor laughed. "For a kid your age, you're very cynical. No, they are not placebos. They're something to quiet you down a bit."

"If I were a racehorse, that would be illegal."

As the doctor went out the door he said, "Skipper, the main trouble with your brother is, he's sassy."

Skipper came cautiously into the room. "How do you feel?"

"Better. The doc always makes me feel better. I don't know why." He wanted to keep Skipper in the room. It was the first time he had shown any wish to talk since he'd heard about Jordan's sickness. "How'd the game go last night?"

Skipper made a face. "Lost."

"How much?"

"108 to 78."

"Did you play?"

"If you could call it that. I practically lost the game all by myself."

"Oh, well, even Wilt Chamberlain has his bad days."

Skipper turned away. "I haven't been able to keep my mind on it lately."

"Because you're worried about me?"

Skipper shrugged. "I don't know." His voice cracked.

Jordan looked at his back for a moment. "I'm thinking about going up to Estes Park over next weekend. I'll probably leave after Thanksgiving dinner, with Cicero. That is, if the VW's fixed." He paused. "You want to come along?"

Skipper turned to look at him. His face lit up. "You mean it?"

"Sure."

"Just you and me?"

"And Cicero."

"Wow! You bet I want to come along. I'll go ask Ma." He ran out of the room and down the stairs two at a time.

Jordan shook his head. Why should that have made everything all right? Well, he was glad he'd thought of the right thing to do. He had intended to go up by himself. He wanted time away from the pressure of other people's emotions — but if he could jog Skipper out of his depression, it would be worth it.

When he thought Susan would be up, he went into his mother's room and called her. Ellie answered the phone.

"Susan's in the shower." She sounded unfriendly.

"Oh. I'll call her later."

"She won't be here."

"Oh? Then I'll call tonight."

"She won't be here then either. We're going to Colorado Springs."

Jordan tried to sound unconcerned. "I see. Thanks for telling me."

"To Tim's house. With Tim and Peter."

"Have a good time," Jordan said.

"Don't worry, we will." She hung up. He knew she wouldn't tell Susan he had called.

Jordan sat holding the receiver for a moment. After he put it back, he punched his mother's pillow with his fist. It wasn't going to work either way, telling her or not telling her.

He took one of Dr. Parkhurst's pills and got dressed. He felt shaky in his legs, and his hands shook so violently for a few minutes, he couldn't get his shoelaces tied. He heard Alex and Tony talking in the hall.

Alex said, "Do you have to work this afternoon?"

"No," Tony said.

"Want to run up to the mountains and get in a little skiing? Guy on the radio says they've had some powder snow."

130

"Sure. What time?"

"Oh, why don't we take off as soon as you're ready?"

"Right."

Jordan leaned his head on his hands. He felt sick with a sense of his own isolation. Of course they couldn't ask him, the way they always had. He could hardly walk up and down stairs properly, let alone ski. Thank God they hadn't asked him if he wanted to come along and watch. For the first time he really felt — not just thought about — what it was going to be like to watch other people's lives going on in a normal way and to be unable to move with them. He pulled hard on one of his shoestrings and it broke. He threw the shoe across the room and lay back on the bed, trembling.

A little later, when Alex looked in, Jordan pretended to be asleep. He heard them leave. He felt like lying where he was and never getting up. What was the point? Why make all that effort when in a few months or . . . all right, a few years . . . he'd be dead anyway? Why go around trying to look cheerful and making everybody else feel they had to look cheerful? He looked at his gun on the wall and for a few minutes he thought quite seriously about suicide. It would be painful for the family, but it would cut the agony short. They were going to have to go through it sooner or later, anyway. He could go up in the woods, leave a note or something so they'd know. . . . He got up and took the gun down and held it in his hands. The familiar smoothness of the stock felt good. It would only

131

take a minute. He knew how to rig a gun so he could pull the trigger with the gun aimed at his head. He stood for several minutes imagining it. Then he put the gun back.

For some reason that he couldn't quite define, he knew he could not do it. It wasn't fear; it seemed preferable to die a quick, self-chosen death than to wait around for his body to run down and give out. It would have more dignity, more an element of choice. One of the things he hated most about his disease was the helpless feeling that he was being kicked around by something entirely out of his control. And yet, he couldn't bear to cut life short before he had to. The doctors had said he might live several years. In several years he could see Terry's child get started as a person. He could see how Alex's marriage went. He could read a lot, and with any luck, ride around, see things, maybe even travel if he could get somebody to go with him. Grimly he saw himself in a wheelchair being pushed up a plane ramp, like a woman he had seen when they flew to Rochester. It would be lousy and he'd hate it, but he didn't hate the idea enough yet to kill himself. Once you pressed that trigger, you couldn't change your mind.

"Oh, hell," he said aloud. He rummaged through his bureau drawer looking for a new shoestring, gave it up, and put on his sneakers. He decided he had to get out of the house for a while.

No one was around downstairs but his mother, reading the paper and drinking coffee. She looked up with that quick anxiety she always had now. "Hello, dear."

"Hi." He got his sheepskin coat from the peg in the back hall and found his hard helmet. "I'm going out for a while."

"Jordan . . ." She hesitated. He knew she tried hard not to supervise him. "I wish you wouldn't take the motorbike. It's not safe."

"*It's* not safe or *I'm* not safe?"

She avoided an answer. "I've always been scared of that thing."

"I'm not going far. Just over to the dorm." He went out quickly, not wanting to talk about it anymore. He knew he was worrying her, but if she didn't worry about the motorbike she'd worry about something else. He was sick of being worried about.

The sky was the color of lead and there was a sharp chill in the wind. He wouldn't go far. Just cruise around. See how Nick's psych experiment was coming. Nick was doing a work-study project, something about monkeys.

He left the bike in the rack outside the dorm and went in. Halfway up the stairs his knees began to jerk. He remembered what Dr. Parkhurst had said about taking elevators, but it had never occurred to him to take an elevator in the dorm. He'd feel ridiculous, like some old lady. But when he got to the top of the stairs he had to cling to the iron railing for support. A couple of people passed him, glancing at him curiously, but he ignored them.

Nick wasn't in his room. Jordan wrote him a flippant note and sat down on the bed a minute. He had always wished he could live in a dorm, but now it was just as well he didn't. If you had to be sick, it was better to be sick at home. With sharp envy he looked around the cluttered room at Nick's things: tennis racket, a soccer ball, a microscope, a jumble of books and papers, and dirty laundry. The room was a mess, but it was the room of someone who was very much alive. Somebody with a future.

Impatiently he got on his feet and left, holding the handrail on the way downstairs. It would be nasty to take a plunge down those cement steps. Not to mention humiliating.

He rode around aimlessly for a few minutes and then turned down the street where Pat's church was. They ought to be out now, and maybe he could see Terry for a few minutes. For some reason she soothed him. She never scolded or criticized him, at least not since he was a little kid.

Church was out, but there were still a few people standing around talking to each other or heading for their cars. He saw Pat talking to two middle-aged women. He watched him a moment. I wonder why, he thought, clergymen clasp their hands behind their backs; don't they have any pockets? He himself kept his hands more and more in his pockets so people wouldn't notice the shaking. He was glad Jen had given him the leather wristband — it helped to hold that wrist steady. He wondered if it would look kooky if he wore one on the other wrist, too. Funny she should have chosen something like that. Maybe she had noticed that his hand trembled. He felt sensitive about it. He was like an old man with palsy or something.

He didn't see Terry anywhere. Pat was talking

now to a couple of young girls, and although he couldn't hear what he said, he knew the manner. Pat referred to young people as "youth," and he talked to them as if he were generations older. Actually he was only twenty-nine. For the first time it occurred to Jordan that Pat had kind of a hard role to fill, being all things to all people.

He wheeled the bike around and drove away toward the rectory. Maybe he'd get a few minutes alone with Terry.

She was still in her housecoat, looking very pregnant. She was glad to see him. "I goofed off on church. Come on in. I've got the fire going." She took his jacket and hung it up. "I don't think anybody who looks this pregnant ought to appear in public." She laughed. "It hurts my vanity. Besides, I can't kneel, and by the time I stand up for the responses, everybody else is sitting down again."

He sank into the low, comfortable chair by the fire, and she brought him a glass of sherry.

"Are you all right, Jordie?"

"Pretty good for a dying man."

"Oh." She poured some sherry for herself and brought a plate of buttered Melba toast from the kitchen. "It's one of those days, is it?"

He ignored the question. Terry had always had a way of not letting a person feel sorry for himself; but there were times, he thought, when he was entitled. He was not ready to be cheered up. "I saw your husband bidding good morning to the last of his flock."

She glanced at him. "Did you?"

"Does he really like going through all that?"

135

"Not always. But on the whole, yes."

"How could anybody?" Without waiting for an answer, he said, "Oh, I suppose it's not too bad a way to make a living. You make enough money to survive, and you're kind of outside the world's problems . . ."

She interrupted with a loud, "Ha!"

"What?"

"He's into more problems than you ever heard of, all the time. He's the center of the storm. There's one going on now that may wreck him, for all I know."

"Then why does he do it?"

She didn't answer for a minute. "I guess faith is the word. I mean he really has it. And he wants to share it. A lot of people see this in him, and they trust him because of it. And they're right to — it's very pure, Pat's faith."

"I don't really know what people mean by 'faith.' " He held up his glass to the firelight and studied it moodily. "I'd need a lifetime of study to find out."

"I don't think study has much to do with it. It's a . . . well, it's a leap in the dark."

"I'd want to know where I was leaping to."

She shook her head. "Nobody knows that, do they?"

"I'm a lawyer-type. I want proof."

"That's not the way it goes."

They sat in silence for a few minutes. Then she said, "Jordan, will you be the baby's godfather?"

He was startled. "Me? Why me? What does a godfather do?"

136

"Oh, stand up when the baby is christened and promise to see to his religious education, that sort of thing."

He sank a little deeper into the chair, leaning his head back. "You'd better get somebody who'll be around. Besides, I don't even see to my own religious education, as you well know."

"I'd like you to be the one though."

In spite of himself he felt obscurely pleased. It gave him a special kind of relationship with this baby. "All right, if you want. And if I'm still around."

"You're going to be around for a long time."

He shook his head, but he didn't say anything.

Pat came in with his usual bustle and hand-rubbing and broad smile. If he had a care in the world, Jordan thought, it didn't show. He chattered away to them about how the service had gone, who was there and who wasn't, how the choir had managed without their lead tenor, who was ill. The talk washed over Jordan, hardly reaching his conscious mind.

"Was Mrs. Benedict there?" Terry asked.

"No." After Pat said "no," there was a brief silence. Jordan looked at them, wondering what significance — if any — Mrs. Benedict's absence had.

"Who's Mrs. Benedict?" he asked, mainly because he had said almost nothing since Pat had come in.

Pat looked at Terry with an odd little smile. "She's one of our vestry, and the biggest contributor the church has. She's president of the Women's Guild and ..."

Terry finished. "And she's a cousin of the bishop's."

"Sounds formidable."

"Is formidable," Terry said. She got up. "Jordan, stay for dinner. It's roast lamb, which we can't afford but we have it sometimes anyway."

But Jordan felt too restless. "Ma would be disappointed. She has some prime rib and she's making Yorkshire pudding. The guys went skiing, so Skip and I had better do the honors."

"Well, stay as long as you can. I have to look at the lamb. I'll be back in a minute."

Pat prowled around the room restlessly. He made small talk with Jordan, but his mind seemed to be on something else. Jordan looked at him more attentively than he usually did, thinking of what Terry had said about problems. He wondered if Pat longed to have him ask for help, or if he was relieved that he didn't. What would he say if Jordan said, "Pat, I'm scared out of my mind"? Would he quote Scripture and let it go at that, or would he really try to understand? Jordan had no intention of finding out. He doubted anyway that anyone at all who was not in the process of dying would have any idea what it felt like. He would not have been able to describe it himself. Sometimes it seemed totally unreal, other times it was so real it made his teeth ache. It was too bad people didn't know, until they were about to lose it, how great just being alive really was. It made you want to touch everything, see everything, hold things in your hands, take deep breaths.

He stretched out his long legs and slumped

down further in the comfortable chair. Pat was talking about the last football game of the season. It distressed him that the Phillips boys weren't much for team sports, except for Skipper and the basketball team. They had always gone in for the individual sports: tennis, skiing, skating, golf, fishing, swimming. And Alex was an ardent horseman. Jordan had played some hockey in high school but had not planned to go out for it at the university.

In the midst of one of Pat's complicated descriptions of a play, the telephone rang. He jumped.

"Excuse me," he said, and went into his study and closed the door.

Jordan had no curiosity about Pat's affairs, but Pat's voice, trained to fill a church, was very audible, and the only way Jordan could not listen was to leave the room. He tried to think about something else, but that didn't work.

"I've been expecting your call, Mrs. Benedict," Pat was saying. "Yes, I . . ." He kept breaking off as if he were being constantly interrupted. At first he sounded agitated but as the conversation went on, his voice grew calm. "Yes, true, she did come to me. . . ."A long pause. "I couldn't tell you, Mrs. Benedict. The girl came to me as her priest. . . ."

Jordan heaved himself up from the low chair. He'd better join Terry in the kitchen. But at that moment Terry came into the room, wiping her hands on a paper towel. She gestured toward the study and said, "Benedict?"

"Sounds like it." Jordan sat down again.

Terry was frankly listening. She looked worried.

"I could not betray her confidence, Mrs. Benedict," Pat was saying. "I could only give her what I thought was the best advice . . . But she's not a child, Mrs. Benedict. She's twenty years old. She has a right to make her own mistakes. All one can do is. . . . Indeed I do understand and deeply sympathize with your feelings. No, you do me wrong. I would like to come and talk to you . . ." There was another long pause, and then Pat came slowly out of the study. He looked pale, but he smiled at Terry. "She hung up on me."

"Let her," Terry said. "She can't abuse you like that. After all the attention and help you've given that family. . . ." She pushed her hair back from her forehead. Her face was flushed.

"There, there." Pat put his arm around her. "She'll get over it." He turned to Jordan. "You must be wondering . . ."

"No, no," Jordan said. "It's none of my business. I was just going."

"Well, it's no secret now. The Benedict girl eloped with a young man her mother doesn't approve of."

"And that old witch blames Pat because he knew about it and didn't tell her," Terry said.

"I couldn't tell her even if I had wanted to. The girl came to me as her priest. It was a confidence."

"Is this the woman who's cousin of the bishop or something?" Jordan felt rather impressed with Pat. He wouldn't have expected him to defy the power in his church for the sake of a principle. He said something like that aloud, and Pat shook his head.

"The power in my church is not Mrs. Benedict," he said quietly. "It is not Mrs. Benedict I've given my life to serving."

"Can she get you fired?"

"Oh, yes. And very well may. But there are other churches." He squeezed Terry's shoulders. "We aren't afraid."

"No, of course not," Terry said. She had quieted down. "It just infuriates me when people are nasty to you."

"Ah, well. The bitter with the sweet. And Mrs. Benedict has been good to the church."

"She likes to run it. She's got a lady-of-the-manor complex. Everybody has to clear everything with Mrs. Benedict. Except Pat." She reached up and kissed his cheek.

Pat was composed and calm, but there was a faint flush in his cheeks and his eyes were unusually bright. "I think I shall take a short ride on the bike," he said to Terry. "I'll be back when dinner's ready."

He went out and in a minute they saw him wheeling his bicycle down the curve of the driveway.

"He always rides the bike when he has to let off steam," Terry said. "I hope he's careful. There's ice on the streets." She put out her hand as Jordan turned to go. "Stay a few minutes longer. Help me cool down. We won't talk about Mrs. Benedict. We'll talk about . . . what? How's Susan?"

Jordan made a face. "That's a touchy subject,

too. There's this new guy she's interested in." He told Terry what had happened at the dance.

"But she can't be angry with you for being sick!"

"Well, she doesn't know, you see, about . . . what's wrong with me. I think she thought I was being jealous of Peter. Which, I must say, I'm perfectly capable of being. In fact, am." He hoped she wouldn't say he ought to tell Susan about his illness.

She didn't say it. She only said, "When you talk to her, she'll get over it, whatever it is. She really likes you."

"I know. Susie's not one to languish and die for love, though. She has this protective shield. I think it has something to do with her family; they're a very quarrelsome bunch, apparently."

They sat in front of the fire for about half an hour, talking of different things. Then it was time for Terry to finish fixing the dinner, and Jordan left her.

When he came around the corner by the church, he stopped on an impulse and went in. It was cold inside and very still. He sat down in a back pew. The church was only ten years old, built in a modern style, with the upper half of the wall behind the altar made of glass, framing a view of the distant mountains. The church was dim on this cloudy day, except for two soft spotlights up in the beams that lit up the gold cross on the altar. There was one stained glass window near where Jordan sat, with a plaque saying it was given by Josephine Benedict.

Jordan hoped Mrs. Benedict wouldn't really

get Pat fired. He felt a new respect for his brother-in-law. He had done the right thing without concern for his own neck, and he hadn't made any fuss about it.

After a few minutes he realized he was not alone in the church. A figure that had been kneeling at the altar rail, at one side, stood up. It was Pat. Silently Jordan left. He felt as if he had come upon a private conversation.

Fourteenth

It was not until Wednesday, the night before
Thanksgiving, that Jordan was able to see Susan.
In the early part of the week she had always been
out or planning to go out. Ellie took pains to
tell him that at least once Susan had had a date
with Peter.

Jordan had thought long and hard about what
to do. It seemed to him that there was an in-
escapable choice between telling Susan about
his illness or ending the relationship on some
other grounds. Especially now that she had a
new friend, it seemed unfair to let her go on
thinking she owed anything to him.

He couldn't bring himself to tell her about his
disease. Not only would it be humiliating and
terrible to have to tell her, but her reaction would
be unbearable. He knew how she would be: she
would feel sorry for him, pity him, and at the
same time almost unconsciously start to break
away. He loved Susan very much but he understood her, and he knew she "looked out for number one," as she was fond of saying frankly. She
would feel guilty about leaving him but she

would do it, and in a way he admired her for it; it was more honest than hanging on because she felt sorry for him. But going through it would be awful. Telling her was simply an impossible idea; he couldn't do it.

So he was left with the alternative. When he dressed for the date, he looked at himself anxiously, as he did every day now, to see if he looked any different. As far as he could tell, he didn't. He checked the holes in his belt to make sure he wasn't any thinner. It seemed to him that unless he started to shake or jerk no one could tell that there was anything the matter with him. Once or twice his boss had asked him if he felt well, but he thought that was probably because he acted tired or looked tired. He had not told him that he was ill. He wanted to keep the job as long as he could, partly because he needed the money and partly because it was important to him to go on living a normal life as long as he could.

He knotted his tie carefully. He had dressed in his best suit because he was taking Susan into Denver for dinner. He couldn't really afford it, but if it was his last date . . . He shivered. It was going to be one of the hardest nights of his life.

The Volkswagen was back with a new engine that Tony and his mother had paid for. Jordan was going to pay them back part of the cost each week. He didn't like the idea of their paying it all. There was no need to baby him.

He drove down the Baseline Road with mixed feelings. He was eager to see Susan again but he dreaded it also. She was so pretty, it pleased him just to look at her, and she was very good company unless she was annoyed with him about something. I would not really have been the right person for her, he thought. They were so different in what they liked and the way they thought. She would have gotten more and more exasperated. In that kind of deal one or the other had to be dominated. He wouldn't have been, and she wouldn't have either unless marriage changed her a whole lot, and if it had, he supposed he wouldn't have liked that. Marriage had always seemed to him a terribly complicated business. If someone as even-tempered as Ma couldn't make it go, he thought, I'd never make it.

But when Susan opened the apartment door, all his rationalization failed him, and he felt intense pain at the thought of losing her. He put his arms around her and held her for a long moment.

She responded at first but then she pulled back, laughing. "Hey! You'll ruin my five-dollar hairdo."

"You don't need a hairdo," he said. "You're beautiful without it."

"You only think that because you've never seen me without it. Come on in while I get my coat. Is it cold out?"

"Kind of." He followed her into the apartment she shared with Ellie. Susan had a talent for making a place look nice. He stood looking out the picture window toward the east, and he suddenly remembered Mr. and Mrs. Ricker. He must ask Em about a dog.

"Where's Ellie?" he said, glad she wasn't there.

"Out with Tim."

"Oh?" He stiffened a little. "Did I keep you from going out with what's-his-name?"

"Peter? Don't be silly." She smiled at him. "Are you jealous?"

"Of course I'm jealous."

"Oh, Jordan. We've always agreed, haven't we, not to tie each other down?"

He tried to smile. "Agreeing is one thing; not being jealous is another."

She reached up and kissed him lightly on the chin. "Dopey. You know how I feel about you. I worried ever since the dance because I thought you were sick of me."

"Sick of you!"

"You never called."

"I did! Ellie said she'd tell you."

"Well, she never did. Where are we going tonight?"

"Laffite's."

"Wow! Can you afford it?"

"That's not a polite question." He held her coat for her. "No, of course I can't afford it, but I have to compete with those rich boys you're running around with." As she started to protest, he said, "No, no, I'm only kidding. I like Laffite's."

"Who doesn't?" She locked the door as they went out.

"And it's Thanksgiving and all that. We may as well live it up. Also, the VW has a new engine. And I could never get sick of you. What an idea!"

She snuggled up close to him. "What have

you been doing since I saw you? Is your arm feeling better?"

"Fine." It was true. He hadn't had any bad symptoms all week. Now and then he let himself think it might all have been a mistake.

He was glad he had reserved a table. The restaurant was full. They had oysters first, and then Jordan had a steak and Susan had lobster. Jordan ordered a bottle of wine, hoping they wouldn't ask for his ID. He couldn't legally buy anything but 3.2 beer. The waiter brought the wine without question. They lingered a long time over the coffee. Jordan kept watching Susan in the soft light of the candle, trying to imprint every moment of the evening on his consciousness. The thought of ending their relationship upset him so much, he wasn't sure he could do it.

"What's the matter, Jordie?" Susan put her hand over his.

"Nothing. Why?"

"You look . . . I don't know . . . sad."

He tried to laugh. "I'm regretting not having had the lobster. It was a great steak, but you can get a great steak other places. I should have had lobster."

"Next time you can."

"Right." Next time. He couldn't look at her. She was so pretty in the candlelight, it made him feel choked.

After dinner he drove around the city. The Christmas lights were already up on the business streets and even some of the homes were lighted. They drove slowly past the huge tree at the Civic Center.

"What are you going to give me for Christmas?" Susan said.

"I don't know, I don't know." His voice broke.

"Why do you sound so odd? Are you brooding about Peter?"

"No, no, no, I'm all right. Look at the huge blue spruce on that guy's lawn, all lit up."

"Pretty."

He thought, 'if we aren't tied to each other, the way she said, maybe it isn't necessary to do anything at all, just go on the way we are.' But he knew that was a forlorn hope. It wouldn't work.

When he finally pulled up in front of her apartment, he brought the subject up. "Listen, Susie . . ." He felt choked.

"I'm listening."

"I've been thinking, about you and Peter and all . . ."

"I knew you were."

"Not the way you mean. What I mean is . . ." He held the steering wheel tight in both hands and stared straight ahead. "I mean if I get to be a lawyer, it's going to take a long time — years — and then I have to set up a practice. It's not fair to expect you to think too seriously about me. I mean when you find another guy you like, don't feel there are any strings . . ." He couldn't go on. He felt her looking at him but he didn't turn his head. If he looked at her, he couldn't go through with it.

"Are you trying to ditch me or something?"

"Don't be silly. I'm trying to set you free."

"Jordan, you get so solemn about things. I *am*

free. We aren't engaged. Anything can happen. We both know that — we're realists."

He said, "Maybe we shouldn't see each other for a while."

"Okay, if that's the way you want it." Her voice was cold. "If you want to stay home and sulk about Peter . . ."

He banged his fist on the wheel. "Damn it, that's not it!"

Angrily she said, "Then what *is* it?"

He shook his head back and forth as if he were in pain. He couldn't speak.

She opened the car door. "Somebody ought to tell you that's not the best way to hang on to a girl." As he started to get out, she said, "Don't bother." She slammed the door and ran up the walk to the stairs.

Anguished, he watched her go, saw the blue door slam shut, watched the snow falling on the steps. He slammed the car into gear and drove out the Baseline, away from home. He drove fast, skidding on the curves and once almost hitting a parked car when snow clogged the windshield.

He came to a skidding stop beside a meadow outside Cherryvale, got out and scraped the thick wet snow off the windshield with his hands. He leaned across the hood of the car and put his head on his arms and wept.

Fifteenth

Thanksgiving dinner was at two o'clock so that Alex could leave for a second dinner at Jenifer's house and Jordan and Skipper could get up to Estes Park before dark. Jordan's mother wanted him to telephone ahead to reserve a cabin, but he preferred not to.

"There are always a few places that stay open all winter," he told her.

"But it's a holiday weekend. They might all close down and go away. Hardly anyone goes up there at this time of year."

"Don't worry, we'll be all right." He knew he was being stubborn about something unimportant, but to call ahead was a thing he never would have done, and she would not have urged him to do it under normal circumstances. And he was in a mood not to admit that circumstances were anything but normal.

He was half-regretting having broken off with Susan, and whenever the phone rang he tensed, hoping it would be for him. Several times he went upstairs and sat by the phone, wanting to call her. Once he dialed the first three numbers and then hung up. He would only have to go through it all over again another time if he smoothed things over now.

He was depressed, and it irked him to know that they all noticed it and tried to cheer him up. Even Pat was especially kind to him. He knew he was spoiling their day. Usually Thanksgiving was so pleasant. Their mother always cooked a big turkey with traditional vegetables, and Alex made the dressing. He experimented with different recipes in different years, and in his mother's cookbook on the blank pages at the back there were the recipes marked "Alex's chestnut dressing: 1971"; "Alex's cranberry dressing: 1972"; and so on. This year he had made it with cut-up dried apricots and a small apple. It was a success.

Tony usually brought out with a flourish the wine that he had made in the fall of the year before, which was sometimes good, sometimes not. This year he had omitted winemaking in favor of cherry bounce, made with pie cherries and sugar and bourbon. They had some after the mince pie.

"Only one for Jordan and Skipper, please," their mother said.

"Oh, Ma," Skipper said.

"You're too young, and Jordan has to drive."

"I don't think anybody is going to want much," Alex said. "With all due respect. It's very good, Tony, but it *is* sweet."

"It's a liqueur. It's supposed to be sweet."

Alex lifted his glass. "Then it's a success."

"I think it's lovely, Tony," his mother said.

"Thanks. It better be, after all the cherries I pitted."

Pat said, "Let's be flamboyant about this." He poured the cherry bounce over his second piece of pie and ignited it. The small blue flame flared for a moment and went out.

Skipper, entranced, had a second piece of pie and used the liqueur left in Alex's glass to make his own little flame. "How did you know how to do that, Pat?" he said.

Pat winked at him. "A man learns many things at the seminary."

"Did you know he could do that when you married him, Terry?"

"Of course. He has all kinds of hidden talents."

"Skip, are you packed?" Jordan said. "We ought to be taking off in a few minutes."

"Me, too." Alex got up and cleared away some of the dishes. "Tony, I'll wash if you'll wipe, and then I've got to go."

"You go now, Alex," Terry said. "Tony and I will do the dishes. Pat can put away."

"You're all so generous with my labor," Tony said. He clapped Alex on the back. "Go on, son. Jenifer is hanging out the front window looking for you."

"All right, thanks, Jordie, have a good time. You, too, Skip. Take it easy on that long hill." He kissed his mother. "Great dinner, Mom."

"He leaves with indecent haste," Pat said, looking owlish.

Alex laughed. "We're going out before dinner to look at a couple of apartments that were advertised in the paper. There's one on Grand-view that sounds good."

Terry followed him to the door. "The doctor says now that the baby might come the first week in January, like maybe the fourth."

"Gad!" Alex said. "Be sure he doesn't come before the wedding."

"I don't seem to have much to do with it."

"Well, think positive thoughts." He put his arm around her. "Every day, tell him 'Wait, baby. Wait till after Alex's wedding.'"

"I've told him — or her."

When Alex had gone, Jordan got the flight bag that he was taking to Estes Park and checked to make sure he had what he needed. He put in a couple of books and he took down his .22 and a box of shells. He and Skipper could do some target shooting. He was anxious to get out of the house. He felt an aching envy for his family and their futures: Alex and his marriage, his apartment, his medical career; Terry and her child; Tony and his writing. It had never occurred to him how much people, especially at his age, lived in their plans for the future. With any luck he would see Alex married and Terry's baby born, but beyond that, who could tell. He put his fur hat on the back of his head. "Seize the day," he said to his image in the mirror. "Don't waste time moping. Get on with it." He went down and packed the trunk with the box of food his mother had fixed, and with snowshoes, just in case.

He found that Tony had bought new chains for the VW. They were on the floor in the back.

He wanted to thank him but he knew Tony would just brush it off. He pointed out the chains to Skipper and said, "That's why we haven't really missed our old man. Tony looks after us like a father."

"I know." He settled Cicero in his lap.

As they drove north through the downtown area the sun came out from behind the clouds. It seemed like a good omen.

"It was a pretty good Thanksgiving," Skipper said.

"Very nice."

"Old Pat was really revved up, wasn't he?"

"Don't be too hard on Pat. There's more there than meets the eye."

"I guess so, or Terry wouldn't have married him. I'm not too crazy about ministers, though."

"That's narrow-minded, like saying you don't like the Chinese or something."

"Okay, okay." After a while he said, "Anyway, I guess it's really ministers' sons that bug me. There's this kid at school, Harry Wetherby. His old man is some kind of a parson, the kind who shouts a lot. Anyway, old Harry Wetherby bugs me. Last week he started in on what a lousy ball-player I am, and I was really teed off. I really swooped down on him and I said, 'Wetherby, if you don't buzz off, I'll kick you right in the bustard' . . . and . . ."

Jordan laughed. "Kick him in the what?"

"Bustard."

"I never heard that one."

"The great bustard is a bird, I mean a real bird. Ma gave me this twenty-dollar lecture on my language the other day. I'm not to talk vulgar or profane or obscene. So what I'm doing is, I'm making up my own bad language. Not even Ma could object to a bustard, right? But it *sounds* bad. It sure worked with Harry Wetherby. He took off like a big-bottomed frangipani."

"Skipper, you're unreal." But Jordan was laughing, and he felt as if he hadn't laughed for a long time.

"I've given this a lot of thought. I'm thinking of setting up a consultancy. You can see the ads: 'Has your life lost its flavor? Remember, it may be your language. If your business is doing badly and your wife runs away with the milkman, it may be because your expletives have lost their zest. A man *is* his language! Are you using the same tired four-letter words your grandfather used when his collar button rolled under the bureau? The same thing George Washington said when his dollar fell into the Rappahannock? The same things the first caveman said to the second caveman? Let the Phillips Brothers help you to new horizons. A new lease on language is a new lease on life!'"

"Oh, you're ringing us all in on this, are you?"

"Sure. I figure Alex can do the psychological testing, you know, tailor the language to the man. You can attend to the legal details, the contracts and all. And Tony will contribute words. Did you know Tony can cuss in Welch, Gaelic, and Chaucer?"

"He does quite well in modern English, when the occasion comes up."

"But that's all old-fashioned, you see? My aim

is to give the world a whole new vocabulary of pseudo-obscenities. Like if you say to some guy, 'You're a lousy rotten furred bird!' That's really effective. Try saying it. It sounds terrible."

"Furred bird. Yeah, it does sound pretty bad."

"All right. That's the story. When I'm world-famous, you'll be proud."

"My brother, the obscenity inventor."

"Well, it's not a crowded field."

Jordan negotiated the car out of a slewing half-spin. The road had become icy. There had been snow in the mountains. "Tony told me in England, when kids talk dirty, it's called 'talking rude.'"

"Talking rude. I like that."

"He said some paper had an article, and the headline was, 'Mum's Out — Dad's Out — Let's Talk Rude.'"

Skipper laughed. "That's cute."

"It was about how parents try to protect their kids from hearing and reading bad language, but if they got to hear how their kids talk to each other, they'd go into shock."

"Man, that's true. I mean, didn't you always feel it was the grown-ups you had to protect from the facts of life? I don't think they could take it."

They were in the deep canyon now, and the cold was bitter. Jordan turned up the heater, but it didn't keep out the bite of the cold. His arms ached. He hoped that place that sold coffee in the summer would be open, but probably not.

Unconsciously he speeded up, but the wheels spun.

"Oops! Watch it," Skipper said.

"Yeah. Sorry. I never did like this stretch of canyon road."

"It never gets any sun."

Jordan nodded toward a house set back from the road on the far side of a frozen stream. "Imagine building here. It'd be like living in a tomb. The valley of the shadow, or whatever."

They were both quiet for a while as the car climbed up the long, steep ascent. Spruce and pines and aspen were heavy with snow, and ice had frozen over the stream that rushed down the canyon in warmer weather.

"In one of the books Tony lent me, there's a quotation he wrote in, from Thoreau, something about, 'Winter is thrown at us like a bone to a famishing dog, and we're supposed to get the marrow out of it.' Tony crossed out 'winter' and wrote 'life.'"

"Tony gets depressed."

"I guess it's the occupational hazard of poets."

"What does that mean?"

"Oh, like a miner is likely to get black lung; a poet is likely to get black thoughts."

After a pause Skipper said, "I get black thoughts sometimes."

"Everybody does, chum. But we count on you to keep us cheered up."

"I know. The family clown."

"People need that, or they'd really go off the deep end."

Cicero woke up, sat up, and gave Skipper a lick across the face with his tongue.

"Cicero, cut it out. You're a clown. Lie down. Look out the window."

Cicero settled down on Skipper's knees and went back to sleep.

"A dog's life," Jordan said. "We should have it so good." He felt tired from the effort of holding the car against a skid, and the cold was beginning to bother him. But now the car was climbing up out of the canyon toward the high elevation of Estes Park and Rocky Mountain National Park. Long afternoon shadows slanted across the snow, and the white peaks of the mountains caught shades of blue and violet.

As Jordan slowed down, coming past the lake into the town, Cicero sat up and pressed his nose to the window. Jordan stopped the car. "How'd you like to run him up and down for a minute?"

"Sure. Come on, old Cicerone." He opened the door and the dog leaped out, barking and running in a wide circle in the snow. "Hey, the man said walk you up and down." He tried to pick up the leash, but Cicero managed to stay just out of reach.

Jordan laughed. "It's okay. Let him run a little. He's stiff." He stretched his own legs cautiously. The tension and the cold had made them stiffen up. I'm like an old man with rheumatism, he thought. I'm like poor Mrs. Ricker. He watched Cicero dash out onto the icy edge of the lake, skid, and sit down, looking surprised. Jordan had a stab of panic before Skipper coaxed Cicero back to the shore. The lake was not yet entirely frozen over, and in the middle the water looked black and sinister. Jordan had always liked winter; he loved to ski and to skate and play hockey and he had liked the invigorating sharp air of the Rocky Mountain cold. Now it occurred to him for the first time why people carried on so about spring. It wasn't just that it was pretty and mild; it was the new life of spring growing out of the old death of winter. But it took one to get the other. He remembered what Alex had said about things changing but not really getting lost. From some high school science course he remembered the laws of thermodynamics. How did it go? No new energy is created, no existing energy is lost; existing energy is simply transformed into something else. It was an awfully impersonal idea if you applied it to yourself, and yet he found it oddly comforting. I don't think I insist on being Jordan Phillips for all of eternity, he thought; in fact it might be horrible. Why not turn into . . . oh, a tree, or a cocky little meadowlark, or a Scottie dog?

He was still thinking about it when Skipper, cheeks glowing, got back into the car and pulled Cicero up onto his lap. Cicero's black nose was speckled with white frozen particles, half-ice, half-snow. His ears were cocked, and his black eyes under the bushy eyebrows shone with joy. It wouldn't be bad at all to become a Scottie. Jordan leaned over to rub Cicero's head, and he felt a warning spasm in his left leg muscles.

He sat up quickly, and in a voice that he forced to be casual, he said, "So now that you're all comfortably settled . . . how about changing places with me and driving up the road while I see what I can see in the way of a place to stay?"

Skipper looked at him quickly. "You're all right, aren't you?"

"Sure."

"Okay, good. I'd love to drive." He handed Cicero's leash to Jordan and got out.

Jordan pushed the gear up and carefully lifted his legs over into the passenger side. "Move, Cicero. I'm coming over." It was doing it the hard way for anyone as tall as he was, climbing over the gear box that way, but he was afraid just then to attempt walking around the car. His leg hadn't given out completely but he couldn't control the trembling. He eased himself into the seat and picked Cicero off the floor. "The trouble with a VW, it's too big."

Skipper still looked watchful. "I'll drive slow, right? You tell me in plenty of time when you want to stop or turn so I won't skid off the road . . . I haven't driven much on icy roads."

"You haven't driven *any* on icy roads. Okay, take it slow."

Skipper shifted smoothly and drove along the deserted and closed-up main street. Even the few places that had been open when Jordan was here with Susan were closed now. He felt a heavy sadness as they passed the café where he had taken Susan to lunch. Already it seemed like a long ago time, another life.

They went past rows of shops that in summer swarmed with tourists, but were now boarded up. There was no one at all to be seen.

"It's like being on the moon," Skipper said.

Jordan didn't answer.

"I hope you were right about a place being

open. It'd be a chilly night in the old sleeping bag."

Jordan hoped so, too. They could always drive back down to the valley, but the idea of the long drive was not a pleasant one.

Suddenly Skipper said, "Hey! There's life on this planet!"

Jordan leaned forward and peered through the faintly colored patterns that the intense cold was making on the windshield. Across the road there was a light in a filling station. "Good. Drive over there and we'll ask."

A man bundled up in a heavy hooded parka came trotting out to the car, his breath making little clouds of steam in the air like the balloons that cartoonists use for their characters' speech. As Skipper rolled down the window, the man peered in. "Evening."

"Would you fill 'er up, please?" Jordan said.

"Gotcha." The man pulled off one of his big woolen mittens and put the hose in the tank. While the gas was pumping into the tank, he came back to the window again. "Cool night."

"Right. Do you happen to know if there are any motels or cabins open?"

The man looked doubtful for a moment. Then he said, "There might be somebody up to Masons'. They're in California, but I think they left old Charlie up there."

"Where at?" Skipper asked.

"Up the road about a mile and a half, and then turn in a little, on your right. You'll see the sign." He attended to the gas and when he came back, he said, "You want to call up?"

"No, we'll go on up there and take a look," Jordan said. He held out the money for the gas. "Thanks a lot."

"If he ain't open, come on back and I'll see if I can find anybody at home wants to rent a room. Not too many folks up here right now."

Jordan thanked him. "I think I know where he means. Drive slow, and I'll keep looking," he told Skipper.

In a few minutes he saw the sign. "Turn right here, Skip. Take it easy. It's a narrow road, and there hasn't been much on it."

The snow was a good deal deeper up here than it had been back in the valley. It crunched under the wheels like breaking glass. Jordan hoped they wouldn't have to put on the chains. He wasn't sure he could make it. He was depressed. He wished he knew what to expect.

Skipper negotiated the steep, snowy hill expertly, and they came up into an area where there were eight or ten attractive little cabins and one larger one in the center. There were big pines all through the grounds, and in front of the main building a children's swing set and slide were coated with a thick frosting of snow.

"Thank God there's a light," Jordan said. "Skip, do you mind asking the man if we can rent a cabin?" He handed him his wallet. "He'll probably want to be paid ahead. Tell him three nights."

"Are you sure you're all right?" Skipper looked worried.

"I've been sitting too long in this bloody car. I'm stiff."

Skipper took the wallet and went up to the house and knocked on the door.

At first nothing happened. Jordan watched anxiously. He hoped it wasn't just a night light to keep burglars away. Then he saw the door open. A short, wiry little man with a beard stood in the doorway talking to Skipper. Then Skipper went inside.

In a few minutes he came running back to the car, grinning broadly, and the man went down the path to one of the cabins. Skipper opened the car door and got in. "All a-okay. I can drive a little closer. He's a nice guy. Going to start a fire for us."

Jordan leaned his head back and closed his eyes. "A fire! Right now I'd rather have a fire than a million bucks."

"He even likes dogs." Skipper maneuvered the car as close to the cabin as he could get it, and then jumped out and came around to Jordan's side.

Cicero took off at once to investigate the grounds. Skipper held the door for Jordan. "You want to lean on me?"

"Just till I get out, I think." He grabbed Skipper's shoulder and unwound himself from the cramped interior. "Guys built like the Phillipses ought to have Cadillacs." His leg jerked like a spastic.

"Or trucks," Skipper said. "Okay? Is your leg all right?"

"I'll use you for a crutch up to the porch, just to be sure."

By the time Jordan was inside the cabin the little man had a fire started. He was quite old, and his thick hair and his beard were gray like a grizzly bear's, shot through with black hairs. He had bright blue eyes.

"That fire will feel good," Jordan said.

"Man needs a fire in this kinda weather." He had an unexpectedly deep voice. "Brutal cold."

"We were afraid nobody'd be open," Jordan said. He eased himself into a chair near the fire. The sudden heat sent sharp little pains shooting up his legs, but he knew that feeling from staying out too long on the ice or out skiing and then coming in to a hot fire. That was normal.

"Nobody is but me," the man said. "The folks generally leave me here when they go off, in case somebody comes up to go snowshoeing or rabbit-hunting or somethin'. You fellas going snowshoeing? Lot of folks go in for that now, since the ski slopes got so crowded." While he talked, he was turning down the covers on the big double bed and the smaller one and checking the tiny stove and refrigerator. "You boys going snowshoeing?"

"I don't know. We brought 'em along. Mostly, though, we just wanted to get away from the city for a few days." Jordan shifted his leg. It was stiff, but it hadn't given out. It was his arms that really ached.

"I know what you mean. This is the only time I like it up here. I got more fondness for the jack rabbits and the deer and such like, than I have for folks." He grinned suddenly. His front teeth were crooked, giving him a boyish, impish look. "No offense intended."

Jordan laughed. "None taken."

"I'm an old mountain man." He stood with his arms akimbo, looking down at Jordan. "The way I spent the winter, year in, year out, I'd find me a clump of big trees in a holler, and I'd bed down there out of the wind. Keep a fire going most of the time. Hunt game for my food, buy a few vegetables in town when I needed to. Nobody give me any trouble." He looked wistful for a moment. "It was a fine life."

"Even in this kind of weather?" Jordan was thinking: what a wonderful way to live! "Even in the snow and all?"

"Oh, worse weather than this by a darned sight. Snow don't bother. You build like a lean-to of branches, out from the tree . . ." He stopped and rubbed his hands together briskly as Skipper stomped his boots on the porch. "Tell you all about it some time." He opened the door and Cicero shot into the room, a snow-covered fur ball, skidding, rolling over, and finally sliding to a halt at Jordan's feet. He cocked his head and looked at the little man.

The man laughed. "Cute little tyke."

Skipper staggered into the cabin carrying their two bags, the box of food, and an extra parka. Jordan started to get up to help him, and then sank back in self-disgust, knowing he couldn't.

The man said, "Here, let me give you a hand there."

The man must think I'm a jerk, Jordan thought, sitting here and making Skip do all the work. With all his heart he wished he were a tough mountain man.

Sixteenth

As the man left them, he said, "My name's Charlie Ellis. If you lads want anything, just yell. And if you hear any funny noises in the night, don't worry. There's a lot of deer prowling around here since the snow come." He looked at them shrewdly. "But you lads ain't tenderfeet, are you? Not from Philadelphia or any place like that?"

Jordan smiled. "No, we're from Boulder."

"That's all right, then. Had a couple, young married couple from Philadelphia, back here a few weeks, and the young lady had hysterics in the middle of the night 'cause she heard an owl. Made that poor husband get out in his nightshirt and search the grounds." He went out, shaking his head.

"He's all right," Skipper said. He arranged the parka over Jordan's lap with just enough room for Cicero's nose to stick out.

"What are you doing?"

"I'm getting you warmed up. Then I'm going to fix supper." He turned the dials on an old-fashioned dome-shaped radio. "You suppose this works? It must be fifty years old."

"Give it time to warm up." Jordan pulled the parka up a little further to cover his forearms. The heat was beginning to help, but when he tried to move his arms sideways, that strange little half-pain in his biceps caught him like a cramp.

Skipper chattered while he unpacked the food box, exclaiming over the things their mother had remembered to include. "How about turkey sandwiches and cranberry sauce? How does that grab you?"

"Very good."

"I'll make some instant coffee . . . Ah! Look what our admirable and splendid father-brother tucked in!" He held up a pint bottle not quite filled with cherry bounce. "How'd you like a shot right now, to stop your teeth from chattering?"

"I'd love it." He reached out to take the glass from Skipper when it came, but winced and put his hand down. "Bring it around front, will you? My arm's stiff."

"Okay. Can I have some?"

Jordan tried to joke because Skipper looked worried about his arm. "I guess so. I may get picked up for contributing to the delinquency of a minor." When Skipper didn't smile, he said, "What's the matter? You aren't going all gloomy on me, are you?"

"No. I just get sick of the baby jokes. I thought maybe this once we could just be two guys."

The radio suddenly blared into life, Johnny

Cash's voice filling the cabin. Skipper turned it down to a lower volume. " 'Ring of fi-yah,' " he sang with Cash.

"Skip . . ."

"Yeah?" Skipper was piling up sandwiches on a plate.

"I'm sorry about that feeble joke. You're right, we do treat you like a little kid sometimes. It's not that we think you are; it's just habit. Because you were once."

"Oh, I know. People get slotted. I went to one of Mom's lectures on campus one day, and I couldn't believe that it was our mother. She was somebody else altogether. People have different sides to 'em."

"Anyway, have some cherry bounce."

"Already had it." Skipper chuckled.

They ate in front of the fire, both of them very hungry.

"As we say every year," Skipper said when he had finished his pie and cheese, "I wouldn't have thought I could eat another meal for a week, after Mom's dinner, but look what I put away." He filled Cicero's dish with kibble and a little piece of turkey. "Cicero's a growing boy, all right. He eats like a Saint Bernard." He danced in front of the fire, singing "I Walk the Line." "Haven't those guys at that station got anything but Johnny Cash records?"

"Skip, do me a favor and bring in the .22, will you? I know there's nobody around, but I don't like to leave it in the car all night."

"No sooner commanded, sire, than done."

"Put your coat on . . ." But Skipper was already

out the door. He came back in a couple of minutes, bringing a cold blast of air as he came.

"Man, I mean it's *cold* out there! And the wind's come up. The sky is fantastic. The stars look like diamonds." As Jordan stood up, Skipper added, "I didn't mean you had to get up and look."

"I get stiff if I sit too long." He stepped carefully over to the wide window and peered out at the sky. "It really is clear, isn't it? What's that big one, right over the top of the tall fir?"

Skipper looked over his shoulder. "That's Venus. The one down lower might be Mercury. Gad, the visibility is good up here, isn't it?"

"Mercury looks kind of pale."

"Well, it's the smallest planet in the solar system, unless possibly Pluto. Until just a few years ago they thought it always had the same side toward the sun, but it doesn't. It makes a rotation every fifty-nine days."

"How'd they find that out?"

"Oh, they used a radio dish in the Caribbean somewhere, like Cuba or maybe Puerto Rico; I forget. They figured it from the Doppler effect . . . Well, it's kind of technical."

Jordan sat down again and stretched his legs toward the fire. "I didn't know you knew all that."

"Well, I like to read about it. I like the stars."

"Do you want to be an astronomer?"

"No, not really." Skipper put the dishes in the sink and put another kettle of water on the stove. "I used to want to be an astronaut, as you know. I know that's what all kids say, but I meant it. Only there's not much demand for 'em now. But

I want to work for NASA some way. Maybe a radio astronomer. My advisor at school has sent off for some dope on it." He came and sat on a chair arm, the dish towel in his hand.

"You never talk about this at home."

"Well, I'm afraid you guys would kid me."

"Skip, we'd be interested. We kid you, but you kid us, too."

"I know. Anyway, let me tell you about space. You ever hear of Bode's Law? This really fascinates me." When Jordan shook his head, he leaned toward him, his eyes shining. "Listen to this, Jordie. The distances between the planets fit a mathematical formula. What do you think of *that?*"

"What kind of formula?"

"Well, I don't remember the figures offhand, but this guy Bode worked out a formula that works, except that Neptune and Pluto are a little bit off, but not much. And one other thing: there was a gap between Mars and Jupiter where another planet ought to be to fit the formula. So a bunch of guys, around the end of the eighteenth century, began looking for it. They're called the 'Celestial Policemen.' "

"Did they find it?"

"Yes. It's a very small planet called Ceres. Right where it should be. But that mathematical formula — that really gives you pause, doesn't it? I mean, what can it mean?"

"I don't know. I find myself asking that question about an awful lot of things lately. I never realized there were so many questions to be asked."

"I saw this film the other day about the human brain. And speaking of what an intricate pattern the universe is — wow! dig that brain! What circuitry! It's got millions more connections than even the most complex computer. All in here." He tapped his head. "All we have to do now is learn how to really use it."

After a pause Jordan said, "I wonder if there's any chance of turning into a star when you die." He was looking out the window.

Skipper was quiet for a moment. Then he said softly, "You'd make a fine star, Jordie."

Jordan gave him a quick smile. "So would you, sport."

"Maybe we'll end up in the same cluster." Skipper stood up, changing his tone. "Hey, Cicero's gone to sleep on the big bed. Your bed, chum."

"He'll keep my feet warm."

Skipper washed the few dishes, built up the fire, and sat down in the other chair. Outside the wind had risen to a moan, but the cabin was snug. Jordan told Skipper about Charlie Ellis's sleeping all winter under a tree.

Skipper shivered. "He can have it."

For a long time they talked drowsily and listened to the radio and finally ate again. Then Skipper said, "Jordie, I don't know if I should mention this or not, and if I shouldn't, you say so." He paused, staring into the fire. "When I first found out about your being sick, I didn't think I could stand it. I thought I was going to . . . I don't know . . . crack up or something." He swallowed. "But when you asked me to come up here with you, I don't know why, but everything changed. I mean I want you to know that somehow it meant something terrific to me. Like we were brothers and we were a couple of men together and we could . . . you know . . . face up to things together. I don't know if I'm making any sense."

Jordan looked at his brother's face. The shadows and moving lights from the fire changed it. Skipper looked different, older, gentler than he had ever seen him. "You're making sense," he said. "I'm glad you feel that way. It's been a terrible shock for the whole family . . ."

"But worst for you."

"I thought so at first, but I don't know now. I think it's easier to take something that's happening to yourself than to someone you love."

"Does it scare you, Jordie?"

"At first I was scared blind. But you can't go on being that scared and that worried day in and day out. I mean, you begin to get used to it, and you even begin to think it may not be so bad." He gave a long shaky sigh. "Not that I'm looking forward to it. When I wake up every morning . . ." He shook his head. "There it is again."

"I think you're awful brave."

"No, I'm not." He watched a branch as the fire ran along it in a flicker like a snake's tongue. "Sometimes I think maybe life is really some kind of dream that we don't wake up from till we die." He got up and kicked a log that had slipped away from the flames. "But that's only sometimes that I think that. Well, what do you say, sport, time for bed?"

"All right. Will you be warm enough?"

"Sure, I've got a heated dog at my feet." He hugged Skipper as he went past him. "Sleep well."

"Right. I'll just sit up till the fire dies down."

"Don't drink up all the cherry bounce."

"Hey, I've heard of bourbon-flavored toothpaste. How do you think cherry bounce would do?"

"Yecch." Jordan undressed quickly and got into bed, maneuvering Cicero into the best position. The wind died down as suddenly as it had come up, and the night was absolutely still.

Seventeenth

Jordan woke up to find Skipper standing beside the bed with a cup of hot coffee. "Your morning beverage, sire," Skipper said.

"Hey, sport, you'll make a lovely mother." He sat up and took the cup. "I feel good. I slept like a log."

"So did I. And wait till you see the day." He pulled the curtains aside at the window. It had snowed another half-inch or so during the night, but now the sun was out and the world sparkled. "No wind, either."

After breakfast Jordan said, "What do you want to do?"

"How about a little target shooting?"

"All right. Let's drive up the road a way and find some place where there's nobody around."

"That should be easy."

They found a little road into the woods about a mile beyond the village limits. Skipper set up the empty can that had held their breakfast fruit juice. Jordan couldn't get his arms up to hold the rifle in the usual position, but he shot almost as well holding it against his hip.

175

"You look like a Western movie," Skipper said. "I wish I could shoot as well as you do." He held the squirming Cicero in his arms.

"You don't take enough time." Jordan gave him the gun and watched him, making suggestions. Skipper's score improved.

"Much better. Anything you do that involves a target, like placing a tennis ball or golf ball or shooting, hold on to your position a beat longer than you think you need to. Otherwise you're apt to jerk away too soon."

They spent about an hour, with Skipper doing most of the shooting. The sun was dazzling on the snow when they came out of the woods.

"Let's drive up into the park," Jordan said. "You drive."

Skipper drove slowly up to the entrance to Rocky Mountain National Park. There were no rangers around, but the barriers were down so he drove in.

All around them the towering mountains glittered in the sun.

"It's like sitting on top of the world," Jordan said. He thought of Susan's saying she hated Colorado. How could she? It was so beautiful.

"Want to drive up to Bear Lake?"

"Sure, if the road's open."

Skipper drove in second gear most of the way. The road had been cleared, but it was slippery. On both sides the evergreens stretched away, their branches now and then snapping up suddenly and discharging the load of snow.

They left the car and walked in to Bear Lake. It was no more than a snowy depression in the ground now, except in a few places where the ice showed. Cicero took off into the woods.

"It doesn't look like the same place we had a picnic last spring," Skipper said.

There were rabbit tracks around the lake, and as they walked toward the other end, they saw signs of deer. In the woods a partridge whirred up and flew off. As they stood to watch it, a doe stepped out of the woods a little farther along. They stood very still, watching her. At first she didn't notice them. She was having some trouble as her sharp hooves sank deeply into the snow. Then she caught their scent and swung her head toward them. For a long moment she looked at them, her nose twitching, her large dark eyes showing no alarm. When she did move, she turned back toward the woods, floundering a little and almost losing her balance. Then she was gone.

"The snow is hard on them," Jordan said.

"Well, they've got the rangers to look after them. She wasn't scared of us, was she?"

"No. They're safe from hunters here."

"I don't like hunting, especially for deer."

"I used to like to hunt. I don't think I would do it now."

Across the lake two magpies dove at something on the ground. When Jordan and Skipper approached, the birds flapped up into the air. The torn carcass of a rabbit stained the snow.

"Somebody got him," Jordan said.

The magpies circled, the sun making their black and white feathers vivid.

"Lucky for you guys," Skipper said to them.

"Mother Nature is a cruel old hag."

"To quote one of your favorite ditties, she never promised you a rose garden." As Cicero came racing toward them on his short legs, Jordan said, "Grab him before he gets at the rabbit."

Skipper scooped up the dog, and they walked back to the car.

They had lunch at the cabin. Jordan settled down in front of the fire to read, but Skipper got his snowshoes from the car and went for a hike with Cicero.

After a while Jordan found himself listening for their return, and even getting up every little while to look out the window. The wind had started in again, but gently, bending the tops of the trees and frosting the ground with blown snow. Jordan looked at the children's slide and tried to imagine Terry's child sliding down it.

He had always liked to be left alone when he didn't feel well, but lately he found he hated it. Maybe, he thought, I'm afraid I may die alone, but what of it? Animals are supposed to prefer to die alone; why not man? It was bound to be a lonely business, any way you did it.

He put on his sheepskin coat and went over to the main cabin. Charlie Ellis answered his knock.

"Come in, lad, come in. Saw your brother and the pup go off. I was coming over to see if you'd like some popcorn. Come in and sit down. Nothing like hot popcorn when you ain't feeling too chipper."

Jordan sat down, wondering why Charlie

thought he wasn't feeling chipper. Was the man a mind reader? He watched Charlie vigorously shaking an old-fashioned wire cornpopper over the open fire.

When it was done, Charlie dumped it into a bowl and poured on melted butter and sprinkled salt. He shook the bowl to mix it up. "You dive into that now while I fetch the coffeepot." He disappeared into the kitchen and came back with an old enamel coffeepot and two mugs.

"This is great," Jordan said. He helped himself to another handful of popcorn. He had never tasted such good popcorn. "Why did you think I wasn't feeling good?"

Charlie shrugged. "When you live like I do, you get to noticin' everything. Probably notice things that ain't even there. Didn't mean to rub you the wrong way."

"No, you didn't. I just wondered. This is wonderful coffee."

"They got lots of new ways to make it, but I stick by the old dump-it-in-and-boil-it system. Just boil 'er a minute and then let 'er set till the grounds settle out. About all you can do when you got nothin' but a campfire."

He sat in a big armchair with his legs propped up on a straight chair. "Had a pretty good life, I have, by and large, but now the old bones creak, and I got to take it easy. So here I am." He looked at Jordan with his bright, searching eyes, like a bird's eyes.

"You must have done a lot of interesting things."

Charlie began to talk about his life. He told

tales of driving a mule train loaded with dynamite along the Snake River in Wyoming, "trail just wide enough for the wagon, and a thousand-foot drop-off near enough I could wave my hand over it." He talked about acting as a guide in Yellowstone Park in its early days as a park, and about manning a fire lookout in Montana's primitive area, "I mind the time I had to wade down the river with the animals and keep duckin' my head under water to keep from being burnt to a cinder." He told about hair-raising encounters with angry grizzlies, and being trapped in a canyon with a charging moose. He talked about wolves and wolverines and an eagle that knocked him off a ledge. Jordan listened, fascinated.

When Charlie stopped for a minute, Jordan said, "Were you born in Colorado?" Charlie shot a look at him and Jordan thought, what an odd face he has; sometimes he looks very old, other times, like now, he looks like a young man. And the expressions kept changing, now brooding and somber, now eager, now sardonic, now gentle.

"I was born in Vladivostok," Charlie Ellis said.

Jordan gasped. "Vladivostok in Russia?"

Charlie's crooked-toothed grin was impish and young. "Only Vladivostok I know of."

Jordan felt silly. "Yes, that's right. I was just surprised. You seem so . . ."

"So American? Well, that was eighty-six years ago. Pa brought us to America when I was two. He got sick of pogroms. We spent a couple years in Brooklyn, New York, and then we come out to Colorado in a wagon. That makes me almost a Colorado boy, wouldn't you say?"

"Sure." Jordan felt dazed. He couldn't believe the man was eighty-six, to begin with. And a Russian Jew. And . . . were his stories true? In the firelight the man almost looked like . . . what? some kind of fancy, not real. If I was a poet like Tony, he thought, I'd say maybe this is the face of death — this changing, quizzical, sad, mischievous face with the eyes that look right into you. But, thank God, I'm not a poet. Things as they are, are puzzling enough. But what if things aren't as they are, or as they seem? He felt a little dizzy. He reached for his coffee cup but his arm jerked. He moved around in his chair so he could reach it more easily.

Charlie Ellis moved the cup toward him. "Here, you can get at it better from here, not work your arm so hard."

Jordan stared at him. What did he know about Jordan's arm? The guy was eerie.

Charlie didn't wait for the question. "Nothing remarkable about that. I noticed from the start you got trouble with those arm muscles. Like I say, a man alone has to notice everything or he may not live out his eighty-six years." He chuckled. "And wouldn't that be a pity." He watched Jordan. "You worry too much, lad. Take 'er as she comes." He took off his shoes and wiggled his toes.

At least, Jordan thought, there's no cloven hoof. He was trying to jolt himself out of these fancies. He had never been a fanciful person; he was the legal mind, the facts man. Did this crazy disease change your mind as well? In order to stop his train of thought, he said, "Tell me some more."

"Ever hear of HAW Tabor?"

"The Silver King?"

"The same. When I was a boy, I was HAW Tabor's stablehand for a while. Saw him make all those millions in silver up to Leadville and saw him die broke. Knew Baby Doe Tabor, pretty as a picture, she was, and hard as nails. Took him away from the first Mrs. Tabor and set Denver society on its ear. They had a daughter named Silver Dollar. She died a dope addict in some Chicago honkytonk. When he was dyin', HAW said to Baby Doe, 'Baby, hang on to the Matchless.' He always believed the Matchless mine would make another fortune. Baby Doe moved up there, dead broke, lived in an old shack by the mine portal all alone for years and years." He paused and shook his head. "I seen her in the village one day, goin' through trash cans. A hag, she was, with rags on her back and gunnysacks for shoes. Her that had been such a beauty. If I was a moral man, I could find you a moral there. They found her dead, finally, frozen stiff in that shack of hers, the place stacked to the ceiling with newspaper clippings about the great Tabors."

Jordan knew the Tabor story — probably everyone in Colorado had heard of it, and there had been shows and books about Baby Doe. He tried to remember what the dates had been; could Charlie really have been old enough to work for the Tabors? He must ask Tony.

182

He glanced at his watch and was startled to see how late it was. Outside the shadows were deepening. "My brother ought to have been back before this." He got up. "I'd better go look."

Charlie stood up. "I was thinkin' the same. May have run into a mite of trouble. I tell you what, lad, you build up a good fire over to your place and heat up some soup or tea or whatever the boy likes. I'll go out and get him."

"I can look for him." It annoyed him to think that this old man would be more competent in finding Skipper than he would be. And he was frightened. What if something had happened?

"I know the lay of the land. I'll pick up his tracks." Charlie had already taken down a pair of snowshoes that hung on the wall and was putting on his parka and mittens. "Nothin' to worry about. Easy to find in this snow. He might have lost his bearings back there in the woods." With remarkable ease and speed for an old man who had said his bones creaked, Charlie went out on the porch, hung a rope over his shoulder, checked the shells in his gun, put on his snowshoes, and started off in the direction Skipper had taken.

Trying to fight down panic, Jordan went back to his cabin and relaid the fire, laboriously handling the logs without being able to lift them far. He put a kettle of water on the stove to heat, and then he began to pace. He never should have let Skip go off alone. He thought of him as knowing his way around in the woods, but actually Skipper had almost always been with one or another of his brothers. He had never had to take the responsibility himself for noticing where he was going and all that. The deep snow could be treacherous, too, hiding crevasses, deceiving entirely. If anything happened to Skipper . . . He made himself sit down.

He wished he had insisted on at least going along with Charlie. Charlie was an old, old man. He might collapse himself. And that eerie something about him, the way he seemed to know things that no one had told him, the way he looked at you, his strange background . . . In spite of trying to be rational, Jordan was frightened. That line about 'There are more things in heaven and earth, Horatio . . .' could be comforting under some circumstances, but it could also scare the hell out of you. Hamlet had never specified that the 'things' were good things.

"Oh, what is the matter with me?" he said impatiently aloud. "I'm carrying on like some wild-eyed Gypsy." He got up and made some sandwiches with a can of tuna fish and some mayonnaise. Skipper would be hungry. He dumped some kibble into Cicero's dish. Cicero would be hungry, too.

At last he heard a faint bark. He threw open the door, not even noticing the cold blast of early evening air. A squirrel scampered off the step and disappeared. As Jordan strained his eyes to see, a small black spot appeared at the top of the slope.

"Cicero!" he shouted.

And Cicero ran toward him as fast as he could, his legs flailing the snow. He kept falling down and getting up and coming on. Jordan caught him up in his arms, feeling him shiver. "Where's Skipper?"

And there was Skipper, trudging over the rise carrying his snowshoes, and right behind him, brisk as ever, came Charlie Ellis. Jordan felt thankfulness rise in him like a tide. But he made himself stand still and act casual. At Skip's age, kids hated a fuss.

"Hi," Skipper said. He was grinning, but he looked tired and dirty, and there was a nasty red scratch across his face.

"Where you been?" Jordan said.

"Oh, I fell into the black hole of the universe trying to rescue your dog, who needs some lessons in woodsmanship, I might add." He came in and collapsed into a chair. "What have you got to eat?"

In the open door Charlie Ellis nodded to Jordan, smiling, and turned away.

Jordan went out onto the porch. "I want to thank you."

Charlie gave his expressive shrug. "What for? For makin' an old man feel useful for a few minutes?" He waved his hand. "Warm him up and he'll be fine."

For a second Jordan watched him go, and at that moment it seemed to him that Charlie Ellis looked more like a small, gnarled angel than anything else.

Eighteenth

Skipper was getting out of his coat. His face was red from the cold, and he was stamping his boots to get his feet warm.

"Take off your boots," Jordan said. "Get up to the fire. I've got some coffee." When he tried to pour it, his hands shook so badly he spilled the first cup and had to pour another, measuring out the instant coffee powder with a trembling hand and using both hands to steady the tea-kettle. He felt weak with relief, almost sick. He had never been a great worrier, as Tony was, but his new physical weakness, which kept him from feeling he could cope with emergencies, was frightening. "Skipper, get your boots off," he said again, more sharply than he intended.

Skipper glanced around at him. "Just a minute, Jordie. I'm trying to get the ice out of Cicero's paws. It hurts him."

Jordan bit his lip to keep from saying, "Do as I tell you!" And it struck him that when parents snapped at their children that way, it might be

186

because they were anxious or frightened. "You'd better get your own cup," he said, making his voice mild. "I keep spilling it."

"Sure." Skipper came at once and took his cup and Jordan's to the table near the fire. He began to unlace his storm boots. He looked serious. "I guess I scared you, and I'm sorry. It was an accident."

"You've got to be careful in the woods," Jordan said. "You've got to learn to think ahead, Skipper. Don't just sail along as if you're at home. The woods are very dangerous if you don't pay attention to what you're doing." He sat down and reached for his cup, but his hands were still shaking. He put the cup down again with a clatter.

Skipper drank some of his coffee. "That tastes great, Jordie." He stood his boots a little distance from the fire. To Cicero, who was stretched out close to the blaze, he said, "You all right now, old-timer?" Cicero rolled his eyes up at him and thumped his tail without taking his head from his paws.

"What actually happened?" Jordan said.

"Well . . ." Skipper took another long drink of coffee and stretched his toes toward the fire. "Cicero took off after a rabbit. The rabbit zigged and Cicero zagged, and he skidded on a ledge . . . I mean it looked like a ledge to Cicero and me, but actually the snow had frozen out beyond the ground in a kind of lip, you know? And it didn't hold, and poor old Cicero shot down into this kind of tiny canyon. It was too steep for him to climb back up again and there he was, barking like a maniac. At first I didn't see how I

187

could get him and get back up myself, because the sides all the way around were very steep and covered with ice. There was a pine tree growing down there but it was no help because it was just a dwarf, Alpine-type, you know. Well, I was going to come back for you, but I hated to do that . . ."

"You should have."

"But I had this neat idea. I took off my snow-shoes and tied the laces of one of them to a tree that was real near the edge. Then I hitched the second snowshoe to the first, and my belt to the second snowshoe . . . you follow?" Jordan nod-ded. "All right. I lowered this ladder over the side of the little canyon, see? It didn't reach the ground, but by jumping up I figured I could catch hold of the belt and pull myself up to Snowshoe Number Two, and then to Snowshoe Number One, and . . . well, it seemed like a brilliant idea at the time."

"But it didn't work."

"No. I went down like a dream, half using the ladder, half just skidding down, the way Cicero had. Poor little bustard, he was so glad to see me. He'd been really shook up by that fall, but he wasn't hurt. So I tucked him in my parka, and I made a leap for the belt. Caught it on the third try, and I began to climb. I won't say it was easy, with this squirming pup inside my jacket . . ."

Jordan was beginning to relax. His hands were steadier. "It sounds like that hideous story in the *Book of Knowledge* about the boy who hid a fox inside his coat — I forget why — and the fox ate his stomach."

"Yaa!" Skipper made a face. "Cicero wouldn't

do a dirty thing like that, but he did want to get his head out to see what was going on. Even so, things were going pretty well. I got my hands onto Snowshoe Number Two and gave a big heave and . . ." He spread his arms out dramatically. "The lacing of Snowshoe Number One broke."

"God! You could have broken your back."

"We landed on soft snow. We sat up, Cicero and I did, and we sang a short chorus of 'Right Back Where I Started From,' and then we decided to scale it like the Matterhorn. Only we didn't have ice picks. As fast as we found a toehold, we lost a handhold. Got a handhold, lost a toehold. By actual count we fell back into that little hole in the ground seven times." He held up his hands. They were badly cut and scratched.

"Why didn't you say so?" Jordan went into the bedroom and got the first-aid kit. "Wash them off first. Hurry up, Skip. You don't want to get infected."

Wearily Skipper got up and washed his hands. "Jordie, you're acting like a den mother."

"I want to get you home alive."

"I think you'll make it. We both feel fine. Only a little achey and scratchy and hungry."

"I made sandwiches." Jordan got the sandwiches, but before he let Skipper eat, he helped him put Band-Aids on the worst of the cuts. "Is that about when Charlie showed up?"

"Yeah. Cicero heard him coming and he barked him in. Charlie had a rope. No problem from there on in."

"Thank God for Charlie."

"I don't suppose we were in any real danger. I was trying to figure out how Charlie made that canopy of boughs when he used to sleep under his tree all winter. I could have done that . . . I had my knife. And we were sheltered from the wind down there. I didn't have any matches, though, for a fire."

Jordan pulled a pack of matches from his pocket and tossed them to him. "Always have matches with you in the woods. Better still, I'll get you a metal match when we get home. Regular matches can get wet."

"You sound like I'm going to be the new Dan'l Boone."

"No, but you've always been with one of us when you went camping. You might as well learn to do it right by yourself." He grinned suddenly. "You did say you weren't a baby anymore."

Skipper bowed. "*Touché*, sire."

They ate up everything that was left in their mother's picnic hamper, and then they settled down to play Patience and listen to the radio. Both of them were tired enough to go to bed early.

In the morning the temperature had climbed and there was a light rain falling. They drove into town and found a little grocery store open.

"Let's ask Charlie Ellis to dinner," Skipper said. "Get some steaks, okay?"

Jordan got three steaks, some instant mashed potatoes, a big can of baked beans, a six-pack of beer, and a frozen pie.

"I'll cook," Skipper said.

The man who waited on them looked amused. "Pretty good cook, are you, young fella? Pretty good at defrosting?"

"I win prizes for defrosting at the county fair," Skipper said, "and I have two blue ribbons in instant mashed potatoes."

The man laughed. "Then you won't never need to get married."

Skipper added two huge chocolate bars to the grocery basket at the last minute. "To go with the snails and the wine," he said to the grocery man.

Charlie Ellis seemed pleased at their invitation. He came over promptly at 6:30, wearing a clean shirt and freshly shaved. It was a pleasant evening, with Skipper listening wide-eyed to Charlie's inexhaustible store of reminiscences.

A satyr? Jordan thought. Is that what it is he reminds me of? It was the eyes, mostly, with their penetrating gaze and their odd look of secret amusement, alternating abruptly with ancient wisdom. But maybe that wasn't what a satyr was. Jordan found that words meant more to him than they had; he wanted to know the exact meaning of a word before he used it, as if it would help to get closer to the truth — although the truth of what, he did not know.

When Charlie finished a story about the time he worked for the Cable Mine in Montana, where the biggest gold nugget in the world was found, Jordan said, "Charlie, you ought to be a millionaire, all these things you've been in on." He caught Skipper's quick look of disapproval. Had he sounded skeptical?

Charlie seemed unperturbed. "Easy come, easy go."

When he left at the end of the evening, he said, "Before you go, I got a little present for you." He was looking at Jordan. "Don't take off till I see you."

"If it's going to rain all day, maybe we ought to go tomorrow instead of waiting till Sunday," Jordan said.

But Skipper said, "Oh, let's not, Jordie. Let's wait till Sunday."

By morning, the rain had cleared. The ground was slushy, but in the afternoon it had already frozen into ruts and irregular patterns. Cicero slipped and slid as he tried to run across the places that had been smooth with snow.

They drove up into the park as far as they could, until they came to roads where the winter barriers were up. The woods had changed dramatically since the day before. Snow that had partly melted and then frozen again into ice turned the trees into shining crystal.

"Some of those trees look like a bunch of darned chandeliers," Skipper said.

They stopped, and Jordan got out and put his hand on the transparent ice that turned a birch trunk to glass. "Look!" He pointed to a spider's web that glittered like an intricate diamond net. "Wow!" He patted the tree gently. "Maybe I'm a pantheist. Is that the word?"

"A which?" Skipper was examining the entrance to some small animal's den.

"Pantheist. Maybe that's not the word. I could

worship trees and spider webs and ice crystals and mountains . . . what's the word for that?"

"Cicero, cut it out!" Cicero also had discovered the den and was digging at it furiously. "Cicero! That's breaking and entering." Skipper hauled him off.

The ice on the tree trunk began to melt under Jordan's hand, and his fingers started to ache with the cold. He took his hand away and put it in his pocket. "I don't know why," he said, "but I kind of respect nature because it doesn't know I exist; it isn't going to make anything easy for me. Why should I like that? I don't know."

"Your dog," Skipper said, shooing Cicero away from the hole again, "is a second-story man at heart. He's got no morals." He ran away from the hole, trying to lure Cicero. "Come on, Cicero, come on, boy. Let's play fox and geese. No, no, that's not the way it goes. *I'm* the fox . . ."

Cicero chased Skipper, jumping up on his legs and finally tripping him up.

Skipper rolled over in the snow with Cicero climbing all over him. He sat up, covered with snow, holding Cicero in his arms. Cicero yipped delightedly.

"Cicero, cut it out. That's my ear you're chewing."

"Let's go," Jordan said. "Where shall we have lunch?" They had brought sandwiches with them.

"Oh, I don't know. We'll come to a good place."

Skipper drove back down the icy road very slowly, skidding every few minutes. "I'll be an experienced winter driver by the time we get home." After one long skid, he said, "It'd be fun to go down this road real fast and then jam on the brakes."

"Don't be stupid." Jordan worried about Skipper. He could remember all too well the idiotic things a fourteen- or fifteen-year-old boy could think of to do, sometimes the dangerous things. At that age you thought nothing could hurt you; you were in command. "It's a good way to kill yourself."

"Don't worry, Jordie. I'm not as stupid as I sound."

"Good."

Skipper laughed. "One thing about being the youngest — you don't build up much conceit. According to my brothers, I haven't done anything right since I was two."

Jordan grinned. "What did you do that was so great when you were two?"

"I was *cute*. I was an adorable child."

"As a matter of fact, you were a demon."

"Nah. I know better. I got the pictures to prove it."

"You used to bite people."

"That was you. *You* bit people. Em's mother's got a scar to this day."

"Well, it's hereditary. Ma says our old man bit people when he was a kid."

"Probably still does. Did you know Alex invited him to the wedding?"

"No, I didn't. What if he comes?"

"He won't come. He's not interested in us."

Jordan thought about it for a minute. "I sort of wish he would. Not for the wedding, because that would spoil it for Mom, but sometime. I'd like to get a look at him before I . . . you know, I'd like to see what he's like."

"I'd just as soon not. He sounds like a furred bird to me."

"He can't be all bad or Ma wouldn't have married him."

"We all keep saying that about Terry. I don't see that it's necessarily so. A woman can make a mistake."

Jordan pointed to a sunny place by the side of the road. "How about there for lunch?"

"Right on." Skipper accelerated a little and then put on the brakes. The car skidded.

"Skipper!"

"Sorry. My foot slipped."

Cicero leaped out to hunt for new game. Skipper got the sleeping bag from the car, and they sat down on it in the sun and opened the sandwiches. Skipper had made enormous three-tiered sandwiches with peanut butter, salami, mayonnaise, and tomatoes.

"Good Lord!" Jordan said. "What a sandwich!"

"My own creation."

"I'm sure." He opened his mouth wide and bit into it. He chewed it thoughtfully.

"Better than you expected, eh?"

"Not bad. But it *is* unconventional."

"Anything worth doing is worth doing well, old boy. Just remember that as you go through life and . . ." His voice trailed off, and he busied himself with opening a Coke.

After a minute Jordan said, "I'm having a good time. I'd like to live in a place like Estes."

"All the time?"

"Yeah."

"In the summer it's full of tourists."

"Well, then I'd go somewhere else for the summer."

Skipper handed him another sandwich. "You'd never get to be a big shot lawyer up here."

"My ideas about that are changing. I'm not even sure law is what I'd want."

"How come?"

"Well, since I've worked at the office, I've begun to realize that lawyers aren't all Oliver Wendell Holmes, and they don't all the time deal with big issues. It's more like Joe Smith is suing Bill Jones because he borrowed his lawn mower and didn't return it, or Mrs. La-de-da is contesting her Uncle Billy's will, or Mr. So-and-So didn't pay his alimony. You know, trivia. That's a lawyer's bread and butter."

"What about those handicapped people you were going to represent?"

"It was a nice idea, but first I'd have to find handicapped people who wanted to be represented."

"Then what do you want to be?"

"I think I might want to be a . . ." He stopped. "It sounds crazy, but I think I'd like to go to art school."

"Art school. That's a switch."

"Not entirely. It's always been in the back of my head. I don't think I have much, if any, talent, but the desire might make up for it. Like if I could paint that tree back there, the birch . . . not necessarily the way it looks, but the way it *means* to me. I don't know if I could ever do it."

He shrugged. "Anyway, it's a moot point."

"I do vaguely remember Ma used to plaster the bulletin board with stuff you'd painted at school."

"My art teachers thought I was lousy, but that might be because we didn't see things the same way. I didn't realize that at the time, so I just quit."

"Well, do it again."

"I'd have to learn so much. It would take too much time."

With sudden passion Skipper said, "Jordan, stop talking about yourself in the past tense. You could have years yet. Don't quit now."

Jordan was surprised and a little offended. "I'm not quitting. I'm just trying to be realistic."

"How can you be 'realistic' when you don't know what the reality is and neither do the doctors? I hate it when you sound like everything's all over."

"All right, all right. We'd better get back to the cabin. It's getting chilly." Jordan was quiet on the way back to the cabin, but just before he got out of the car he said, "I was right to bring you along. It's been a very good weekend."

Skipper smiled. He opened the car door, and as Cicero scrambled over him and jumped out, he said, "First one to the cabin gets the second chocolate bar."

Nineteenth

When they were ready to leave at noon on Sunday, they went over to say goodbye to Charlie, and to return the platter on which he had brought them a stack of buttermilk pancakes for breakfast.

He came out to the car with them, and when they were about to go, he gave them each a present. To Skipper he gave a horseshoe. "That's off the best mule I ever drove, name of Sampson, died forty years ago. It'll bring you luck."

"Gosh, thanks, Charlie," Skipper said. "Don't you want to keep it, though?"

"Had my share of luck already. It's time to give away a little." To Jordan he handed an old, soiled piece of heavy paper that was folded in four, the creases worn and greasy with age. "This is for you."

Jordan unfolded it carefully. It was a stock

certificate for two shares in the Matchless Mine. It was made out to Charles Jack Ellis, and it was signed "Horace A. W. Tabor."

" 'Course it won't do you any good, but it's kind of an interestin' souvenir of the old days," Charlie said.

"Thank you very much," Jordan said. "I really like it. I like things like that."

Charlie nodded. "Thought you did." He stood back so Jordan could start off. "Come back some time. Enjoyed your visit." His eyes were kind as he nodded his goodbye.

As Jordan drove the car along the main street of the town, he said, "I wonder if he gave me that paper because he thought I didn't believe him."

"I thought you didn't myself."

"I wasn't sure whether I did or not. I guess I was wrong."

"You didn't like him too much, did you?"

"Sure I liked him. I hardly knew him. I don't get strong feelings about people I've just met." But to himself he thought: 'I might have been jealous because he's had such a long life and so much adventure.' He felt as if he owed Charlie an apology.

It was a cloudy day with a smell of new snow in the air, not as cold as it had been coming up. After a while Jordan's wrists ached, but he didn't want Skipper to drive on the main road. The snow crews had removed most of the snow from the road, but there were still patches of ice, especially in the canyon where the sun couldn't reach it. Jordan was impatient now to get home.

Once he spun sideways on a strip of black ice that looked like the hardtop.

They got home in the middle of the afternoon. Alex was in the kitchen watching Jenifer make a *quiche Lorraine*. Their mother was upstairs reading freshman themes, and Tony was in his room working on his dissertation. They all gathered at the dining room table to join Skipper and Jordan in a cup of coffee and to hear about the weekend. Jordan thought his mother seemed relieved that they were home. He knew she must be carrying a big load of worry.

"Bitsy's back," Tony told them.

"Did she have a good time in Europe?" Jordan said, and then realized that was the wrong thing to say.

"Great," Tony said, with the downturn of the mouth that meant he was unhappy. "She got engaged to the French skier."

No one spoke for a moment. Then Jordan said, "The fortunes of war."

"You did keep harping on how you weren't going to get married," Alex said. "You can't blame her."

"Who blames her? I was just supplying the news." Tony refilled his coffee cup and went upstairs.

When he was gone, his mother said, "He minds."

"Alex is the only Phillips who's lucky in love," Jordan said.

"And me," Skipper said. "I got 'em swooning everywhere."

Jenifer linked her arm with Alex's. "We're so lucky it scares me."

"Don't let it scare you," Jordan said. "Enjoy."
He smiled at his mother. "Seize the day." He
made himself a sandwich and went in to lie down
on the comfortable old sofa. He was very tired
and his arms and wrists ached, but he felt like
staying close to the family.

Jenifer went back to her *quiche*, and Alex
joined Jordan in the living room. Cicero curled
up in a happy circle at Jordan's feet. Skipper
brought Jordan some aspirin and then retired to
a corner of the room to do his algebra. After a
while Alex and Jenifer went for a walk and
Jordan slept.

When he woke, the room was filled with late
afternoon shadow, and through the window he
could see the intensely blue air that sometimes
came for a few minutes before darkness fell. 'I'd
like to paint that color,' he thought, 'with the bare
black branches of the oak tree spread across it
like a Japanese print.'

The fire in the fireplace was burning low. Skipper was half-asleep in his big chair, and at the
other end of the room Tony was playing the piano
softly. Was it Debussy? Jordan could hear his
mother in the kitchen, and the house smelled
deliciously of roast lamb. He felt not exactly
contented, but more at peace than he had been
for some time, perhaps because he was too weary
to feel emotion. He was sorry about Tony and
he wished he could help, but nobody could help
with the real problems, it seemed, except to just
be there in case someone was needed. He had
never thought Bitsy was the right girl for Tony,
but he knew he could be wrong. Nobody knew
who was right for whom. He wondered what

Susan had done over the weekend. Maybe she had gone home to Pueblo, although she didn't go there much. He thought of dialing her number and just hanging up if anyone answered, but that was a sick thing to do. Forget it. He turned over, and Cicero fell off the sofa with a thump.

Jenifer came in from the kitchen, carrying a plate with wedges of *quiche* arranged on it. Alex followed with paper napkins and a pitcher of cider. Skipper woke up with enthusiasm and helped himself to two pieces.

"Skipper!" Alex said. "Don't be a pig."

"No kidding, I thought it was one piece. I mean, they're so thin."

A few minutes later Alex looked at the empty plate and at Jenifer's bemused face and laughed. "You're in for a lot of shocks, angel. In your house you work and slave and make a *quiche*, and the three of you take a nice leisurely hour to eat it. Here it's all gone before you get to sit down."

"That's fine," Jenifer said. "It's flattering to the cook when it all disappears fast."

"In that case," Tony said, "you'll find the flattery in this family absolutely overwhelming."

Later, when they were having dinner, Tony said, "I didn't tell you, did I — I've got a new job."

His mother looked up quickly. "What job?"

"As of a week from tomorrow, I'll be tending bar at the Harvest House."

They all looked at him in surprise.

"You mean give up the flower shop?"

"Yep."

"Why, Tony? You liked it so much."

He was carving the lamb with his usual skill. "I did like it, but it doesn't pay enough. I'll get three times as much, with tips, at the Harvest House."

Jordan was upset. "You'll work three times as hard and at least twice as long . . . what's your shift?"

"Six to midnight."

"You'll hate it. You don't like mobs of people. You hate drunks."

"People in bars are not necessarily drunks."

Jordan put down his fork. "Why is it so necessary to make all this money? You'll be through graduate school next summer."

"I like money."

"You're doing it because of me. You think it's going to cost a lot. Well, it isn't, because I don't intend to let it . . ." He broke off. He was upsetting them all except Jenifer, who looked puzzled. "We'll talk about it later."

"No, we won't, Jordan, because it's all settled, and for my own reasons. I don't have to account to the family for my actions, do I?"

"Of course not," Jordan muttered, but he was distressed. Tony had been happy at the florist's shop; he would hate bartending. He wasn't the gregarious type. Alex could do it perhaps, and he himself could, but not Tony. And he knew it was for him. But one thing he was determined not to allow was for the family to be dragged into debt on his account. No hospitals, none of that stuff. If it came to that, he'd rather take his .22 and go off in the woods and get it over with. The feeling of peace he had awakened with was gone.

He went up to his room after dinner, too depressed to stay downstairs with the others. But after about an hour he heard Terry and Pat come in. He made himself get up and go down.

He sat on the couch beside Terry. Pat and Tony were engaged in one of their theological arguments. Skipper came and sat in the wing chair near Jordan and Terry.

"Feel better?" he asked Jordan quietly.

Jordan nodded. He hadn't realized when he was well what a luxury it was to be able to have a mood without everyone checking up on it and worrying about him.

Tony and Pat were arguing about Easter and the resurrection.

"Everything that dies shall live again, and everything that lives shall die," Pat said sententiously.

"Consider the amoeba," Tony said.

"The amoeba?" Pat said blankly.

Skipper said, "It toils not, neither does it spin."

Terry giggled. "Why don't you guys knock it off for once?"

'She's nervous,' Jordan thought; 'life and death are not safe subjects in this family any more.'

"What about the amoeba?" Pat said.

"It doesn't die. Unless somebody eats it. It doesn't die a natural death. All these bland generalities we have for everything, they usually aren't true."

"If you cut a starfish into five parts, you'll get five live starfish," Skipper said.

Alex raised his eyebrows. "What I value about Skipper is his flare for the relevant. Why don't we talk about something pleasant? Like my wedding. Let's all discuss what you're going to give us for presents."

While the chatter went on, Jordan leaned his head back and closed his eyes for a few minutes. Terry touched his hand.

"Why don't you go to bed, love? You look beat."

"I am beat. But we had a very good weekend. Any static from your friend Mrs. Benedict?"

"Plenty of static but so far no serious interference."

"Are you feeling okay?"

"Oh, yes. Pat has morning sickness, but I feel fine. Did I tell you I'm naming the baby Jordan?"

Jordan felt tears sting his eyes. He looked away. "What if it's a girl?"

"Jordan would be a nice girl's name."

In a minute he got up stiffly, turning sideways so he could push himself up with his right arm. He saw Jenifer looking at him in a puzzled way. As he passed Alex, he said, "Tell Jen. She's in the family now."

"Tell me what?" Jenifer said.

He winked at her. "Secret stuff." He walked slowly out of the room, easing himself along from one piece of furniture to the next. The family conversations went on, he thought, as they would always go on, with or without him.

Out of the strands of conversation behind him, he heard Pat say, "I'm not an old fogey, you know. I've read Darwin. I know all species change and adapt . . ."

And Tony's voice saying, "Consider the sow-bug."

"Sowbug?"

And as Jordan went up the stairs, Skipper's voice above the others saying: "He toils not, neither does he spin."

Jordan laughed. Poor Pat. He always walked into the traps. But he didn't seem to mind. Maybe it made him feel like a part of the family. He had been an only child and an orphan, reared by a grandmother. He must have had a lonely life before he met Terry.

He walked upstairs slowly, leaning on the banister. Downstairs anxious faces would be turned toward him to see that he made it all right, anxious ears would listen for a fall. And now Jen would be added to the list of the watchful worriers. There was a strange ambivalence in the attitudes of the living and the dying toward each other, a drawing closer and at the same time an alienation. He was moving into a realm that they couldn't imagine, that he would not have been able to imagine himself, and it made a gulf between him and them.

In his room he closed the door and leaned against it for a moment. Walking up the stairs was getting to be an effort. He could feel the disease speeding up. He sat down at the old desk that he and Skipper shared and began to clean his gun. He oiled it carefully. Then he took down his hunting knife and wiped the carved wooden handle with a little oil. Tony had had that knife custom-made for Jordan, by a friend who was in the business of making special gunstocks. Jordan was very proud of it. He wished he could be buried like the Indians or the Egyptians, with his favorite things around him. Buried! What a nasty idea. What if he just said, "I *won't* die. I will not!"

He stood up suddenly and hurled the knife with all his strength at the doorframe. The point of the blade sank into the wood, and the knife vibrated for a moment. He was surprised that he had that much strength left in his wrist. He went over and pulled the knife from the door. It left a thin line of splintered wood. He felt exhilarated, although he knew it had been a stupid, dangerous thing to do. Someone might have opened the door at that moment . . . But they hadn't. He put the knife back in its sheath, undressed, and went to bed. He was going to have to buy some regular shirts, maybe a new flannel shirt. Anything that pulled over his head was too hard to manage now. Better get some wood putty tomorrow and fill up that crack the knife had made, before his mother saw it.

He was almost asleep when Alex came quietly into the room and looked down at him.

"Awake, Jordie? Jen wants to say good night."

Jordan tensed. He was too tired for any emotion. But he said, "Send her in."

Alex went out and in a moment Jenifer came in. She sat down on the edge of the bed. "I've got a secret to tell you."

"Shoot."

"All my life I longed for a brother, and I used to wonder what kind I wanted, because he had to be just right. All of a sudden I find I've got one, and he's better than anything I ever thought up." She ducked her head under the overhead bunk and kissed him on the cheek. "See you later, chum."

She was almost out the door before he could say, "Good night, Jen."

Twentieth

"All right," Dr. Parkhurst said, "you can put your shirt on." He leaned back against the wall of the examining room. "You're doing too much, Jordan. You've got to slow down." He frowned. "I don't understand the rapid weakening in your hand muscles. Have you been doing anything unusual?"

"I work them with a handball every night."

"You what?"

"I work with a handball, grasping it, you know, to strengthen the muscles."

Dr. Parkhurst was exasperated. "Jordan, will you for God's sake let *me* do the prescribing? That's just the kind of thing you should not do."

Jordan was angry. After all that painful, tedious exercising, why should he have to be bawled out as well? "I want to strengthen them."

"But you're doing just the opposite. Jordan, it isn't a weakness in the muscles, per se; it's a disease, a wasting disease. What you need is to rest them, not overwork them. Please, Jordan, I do know what I'm doing."

Jordan struggled with his shirt, not answering. He felt sore not only in his body but in his mind. Dr. Parkhurst reached over and helped him with the sleeve.

More gently the doctor said, "I don't want you to cut down your time unnecessarily."

"There's not a whole lot of it, is there?" Jordan sounded almost accusing. "I'm not going to be one of those rare twenty-year men. More like a few months, isn't it?"

Dr. Parkhurst sighed. He looked tired. "I don't know. No, it won't be any twenty years, but that could be just as well. What about school? Do you have to take a full load?"

"I might drop out after Christmas. What's the point, after all?"

"Well, it isn't that. It's just that you're doing too much."

"The other day in sociology I nearly blew my top. Two guys and the instructor argued for twenty minutes . . . *twenty minutes* . . . about where you draw the line between the lower middle class and the upper lower class. I haven't got time for all that crap."

Dr. Parkhurst smiled. "I remember sociology. If you're going to drop out after Christmas, why not make it now?"

Jordan shrugged. "All right. Do you think Mom will be upset?"

"I think she'll be relieved. She worries about your seeming so tired, forcing yourself to keep going and all." He put his hand on Jordan's arm. "And Jordie, I didn't mean to bark at you about those exercises."

"That's all right."

"We're all kind of tense over this thing."

"Yeah." Jordan struggled with the buttons on his shirt. "So I'll go the route with the administration and get myself dropped." He looked up. "If you've got a minute, there are a couple of other things . . ."

"All the time you want, Jordie."

"Number one, I want it understood that I'm not ever going into any hospital or anything like that. That would eat up all my family's money. No matter what, Doc, no hospital."

Dr. Parkhurst looked thoughtful. "I don't anticipate your having to, but what if you needed hospital attention? I hate to bind myself."

"How could I need it? They don't know how to treat my disease. Maybe I might . . ." He shuddered. "I might get helpless altogether and need a nurse or something, but a nurse at home would be a lot cheaper than a hospital."
I really want you to understand . . . I refuse to go to a hospital."

Dr. Parkhurst hesitated and then nodded. "All right, Jordie. Understood."

"And the other thing . . ." This was hard to say, but he had been giving it a lot of thought. "Would there be a research place or a medical school or something that would like to do a post-mortem or whatever you call it? I mean, if it's such a rare disease and all, they might be curious . . ." He felt like throwing up. The only way he could talk about this was to think of it as having to do with something entirely outside himself.

Dr. Parkhurst looked as if it were hard for him, too. "Yes, indeed, there are such places. Washington Medical School, for one. And I know they'd be very interested." He made his voice as impersonal and cool as Jordan's. "It might help them solve the problems of the disease. It might help to save lives."

Jordan swung down off the examining table. "You get the papers or whatever, would you? I imagine there's stuff to sign."

"I'll have Miss Whiting write for the papers today. Or maybe call. The mails are so bloody slow."

Jordan grinned. "You don't have to be all that eager, Doctor. I'll be around a little longer."

Dr. Parkhurst laughed too heartily. "You bet you will, boy. I'll drink to that."

Jordan said, "It will save the family a lot of fuss and money, too. No hoopla at the funeral parlor and all." He tried to laugh again, but it didn't quite come off. "Of course it will do Pat out of a fee."

Dr. Parkhurst opened the door for him and rested his hand on the back of Jordan's neck for a second. "Remember, old boy, slow down. I can't guarantee anything if you go galloping off in all directions at once."

"You can't guarantee anything anyway." He grinned at the doctor and went on out through the crowded waiting room. People with head colds waited, people with rheumatism, people with acid indigestion. They'd make it. But at the door he met a young woman and a little girl, the woman a former student of his mother's, and he remembered hearing that the little girl had leukemia. She wouldn't make it. He looked at her with a feeling of comradeship. Dr. Parkhurst's failures. She was a pretty little kid. A burst of rage made him kick open the door that led outside. What a lousy business, picking on little kids!

He drove over to the campus and annoyed somebody in a Mercedes by beating him to a parking space. He was not in the mood to be generous.

Getting himself removed from the university student body was even more complicated and time-consuming than getting enrolled had been. Some day, he thought, the world will hang itself in red tape. Tired and exasperated, he went into his mother's office, but the woman she shared it with said she had already left to go shopping.

In the parking lot someone had parked just behind him, leaving the car locked. He had to wait twenty minutes in the cold afternoon wind before the owner finally showed up. Jordan recognized him, an upper-classman and a Sigma Nu, who was in his sociology class. By campus rules of hierarchy Jordan was the "inferior," but he was so angry at having to wait that he told the older man off in the strongest language he could think of. The Sigma Nu started to argue but then, perhaps impressed by the fierceness of Jordan's attack, he shrugged, got into his car, and drove off.

At home Jordan had time for a long, hot bath before anyone else came in. It calmed him down. Getting emotional upset him too much, made him feel sick. He washed his hair and shaved, two things that were getting harder to do because of the trouble in raising his arms. Pretty soon he'd have to start going to the barber shop.

He dressed, getting out a clean shirt, and then he lay down. He felt better. Rage, like despair, was a hard emotion to sustain for any length of time. After a while it didn't seem worth the bother.

It felt good to be out of the university, much as he had liked it. It had become more and more difficult to do all the little things you had to do — just to get from one place to another, for instance, or to make himself heard in class because, although he didn't like to admit it, his voice was not as strong as it had been. And keeping up appearances with his friends was a strain. The jokes, the horsing around, the casual push and shove tired him. And yet it was the end of something he had cared about, one more thing to go. His life was being sliced away, like a whittled stick. He turned on his side to steady his leg, and Cicero snuggled up to him. He would have to check with Em to see if she'd heard of another Scottie for the people out in the prairie. She had promised to ask.

He looked at the thick sociology book on his desk and was glad he didn't have to finish the reading assignment. Sociology annoyed him, or at least the instructor he had had annoyed him. All that jargon.

"Tomorrow," he said to Cicero, "we go to the library and check out books on astronomy, poetry, anatomy . . . no, we can borrow Alex's anatomy book . . . but a book on crystals, and some history books, early stuff, like the Bronze Age people, the early Indians, that kind of stuff. We may as well end up knowing a little something, old dog."

Cicero burrowed his cold, wet nose into the palm of Jordan's hand.

"All right, and a book about dogs. Who knows, they may inherit the earth."

Twenty-First

He parked in front of Susan's apartment house with the sense that this was something he had done in the distant past. He had hardly been able to believe it when he heard her voice on the phone. She had sounded odd, and she'd said, "Jordan, I just want to ask one question: were you serious when you said you weren't going to see me anymore?"

He had not been able to answer for a moment; his voice had failed him entirely. Then he had said he would like to see her that evening. He had decided, after he'd hung up, that he must tell her what was going on. She had swallowed her pride to call him; he would swallow his.

He sat in the car for a moment, to pull himself together. His hands were shaking, and his heart pounded. If she wanted to keep on seeing him, after he told her about his sickness, he would be very happy. He had missed her painfully. She was always in his mind, even when he was talking or thinking about other things.

He knocked on the bright blue door. It opened almost at once. He had almost forgotten how pretty she was. Although he hadn't planned to, he learned forward and kissed her. "Hi, Susie," he said.

"Hi, Jordan. Come in."

She had made the room inviting. Fire in the little fireplace. Candles burning on the mantel. Soft lights. Stereo playing quietly.

He sank down in a chair by the fire after she had taken his coat. "How are you?"

"Fine."

"I missed you — and that's the understatement of the year."

She came and sat on the divan. "I missed you, too. I kept thinking you'd call."

"I had a reason."

"I know. But I don't see him anymore."

"Not that reason. I'll tell you before I leave." He got up and sat beside her, holding her hand. "Have a good Thanksgiving? How was Pueblo?" He felt terribly nervous.

"I didn't go to Pueblo. I went to Colorado Springs. It was a disaster."

"Oh?" He didn't want to hear about Colorado Springs. He had this moment, this short time, and he knew already that it wouldn't last.

But she told him anyway, a long story about a house party at Tim's, with Peter on hand, Tim's family away, lots of drinking . . . Jordan watched her face, not really hearing all she was saying.

"I don't think I'm a prude," she ended, "but I don't go in for orgies. Do you think I'm a prude?"

"Of course not." He put his right arm around

her. He could just make it. If she had been on his other side, he wouldn't have been able to. What a situation, when you can't get your arm around a girl! "It doesn't mean you're a prude just because you're not decadent."

"Do you think I'm frigid or anything?"

"Don't worry about such things. You're fine." But he knew there was an element of coldness. He had always told himself that he would teach her to overcome it, but could he have?

As if to prove to him or to herself that she was, as she kept saying, "perfectly normal," she was more loving with him than she had ever been. She moved away from him after a while and said, "I'll get some beer."

"Who needs it?" He could hardly bear to see her disappear into the little kitchen. She might vanish. Everything he loved seemed to tremble on the brink of vanishing. He started to get up and follow her, but he gave up trying to move.

She gave him the tall, foaming glass of beer. "You've lost weight," she said. "You should eat more."

"Why don't you marry me and see that I do?" He said it lightly; it was the kind of thing they had often said to each other, knowing that it would have to wait. But now she glanced at him sharply.

"I would if you would. I mean now, not a hundred years from now."

He felt the pulse in his throat beating. Why not? Why shouldn't they get married and have what time was left? He knew she was reaching out to him because Peter had let her down, but he also knew she was fond of him — and she wouldn't have to put up with him very long.

"Well, it takes a few days to get the license . . ."

"Jordie! Do you mean it?" Her face lit up. "Listen, I could keep on working till the end of your school year, and then you could get a job . . . If I talk to Mr. Jacob at the plant, I know he'd find you something . . ."

He took her hand in both of his. He felt so happy, he was almost light-headed. "Wait a sec. First I have to tell you something . . ."

Her face fell, and she pulled her hand loose. "Oh, sure. That's how the story always goes, isn't it? Everything's great, except for the part that starts 'First I have to tell you.' That's the killer. I knew you were just putting me on."

"But I wasn't putting you on. My God, Susan, I'd give my right arm to marry you . . ." The phrase stopped him. More quietly he said, "I'd give my life. But that's the point."

"What's the point?" Her face was turned away from him, but he thought she was crying.

There was no gentle way to do it. "I'm dying."

She gave him a startled look. "Why do you say stupid things like that?"

"Because it's true."

"True?" She stared at him. "Dying? What do you mean?"

"You remember when I went to Mayo . . ."

"Sure, but you said you were all right."

"Not exactly. I have something incurable called amyotrophic lateral sclerosis."

She kept on looking at him, horrified. "Jordie!"

She put her arms around him and began to cry.

He held her close, like a child, while he answered all her questions. Was he sure? How long did he have? Would it hurt? He felt calm now, with the calmness of hope laid low.

In one moment of whistling in the dark, he said, "We still could get married, though. We'd have a little while together. I've quit school, but I'm keeping my job. It doesn't pay much, but if we both . . ." He saw her face and stopped.

"Jordie, it wouldn't be practical."

"No, I guess not."

"I couldn't work and take care of you, both . . ."

"I was asking you to be my wife, not my nurse."

"I didn't mean it that way. Oh, don't be hurt. Jordie, I feel so terrible. I can't bear to think . . . But I was just trying to be practical, too."

He smiled at her. "Sure, I know. It wouldn't work."

"I'm glad you see. You don't feel hurt, do you? I didn't mean to hurt you."

"Of course not. Hey, you didn't drink your beer." He picked up his own glass and held it out to her for a sip. He saw her draw back quickly, and although he meant to make it a joke, his voice was bitter as he said, "It's Gehrig's disease, angel, not leprosy."

She gasped. "Don't say things like that."

"I mean it's not catching." He looked at his watch. "I'd better split; it's getting late. You have to go to work tomorrow." He was careful not to touch her again. Until then he hadn't thought about other people's revulsion toward disease. You couldn't blame her. She was a healthy girl. She didn't want to be made love to by a dying man, a diseased man. He shuddered. Death had more faces than he had stopped to consider.

He left her in tears, but there were no ways that he could think of to comfort her.

"Call me, Jordie. Soon."

"Sure. Don't worry."

She followed him outside. "Take care of yourself, Jordie."

"Right."

So that was that.

Twenty-Second

The next day, when he went to the office, he
told the lawyer about his illness. Mr. Parson's
long, narrow face looked sad, but he didn't say
very much. He would be glad to have Jordan
stay on as long as he felt like it. He praised
Jordan's work and his intelligence.

"If there's anything I can do at any time,
please let me know." He laid out the afternoon's
work and left for the courthouse.

Jordan felt relieved.

When he got home that evening, he found a set
of watercolors and some brushes on the desk. A
note said: "Paint me a masterpiece, Pablo. Love,
Skipper." He was touched that Skipper had
remembered their conversation and had taken
the trouble to get him paints. It might be fun
to try, but he wished he knew something about
technique. There might be a book in the library.
He opened the tin lid and looked at the colors.
He didn't even know if he wanted to paint in
watercolors or oil or pastels or what. It was sad

to be so ignorant. He wrote a note and tacked it to Skipper's bunk.

TO MY PATRON:
My heart is grateful for Your Grace's generosity. All my labors will be dedicated to Your Grace.

Your humble servant,
PP.

He went downstairs and let Cicero out the back door, following him out for a breath of fresh air. Tony had driven the Opel into the garage, and he stood at the fence talking to Em. They looked excited. Em called to Jordan.

"Come hear the news!"

Tony turned toward him, his face aglow. "Guess what?"

Jordan smiled. "I've never had a good answer for that one."

"He's won a grant!" Em said. She looked very happy.

"What grant?"

Tony grinned broadly. "The Eugene O'Neill Foundation. They give a few writing fellowships every year. The winners go to their place on Long Island, and their play gets produced, and critics come from New York."

"You won that?"

"Yeah. With that play I wrote last summer, the one about the old silver miner who comes back to Central City in the tourist season."

"Tony, that's wonderful! A production and everything!"

"They'll probably tear it to shreds, but I'll learn a lot."

"And you'll be where you belong. Can Em and I come and see it?"

"Front row center, opening night. I've got to go tell Ma." He waved to Em and ran into the house.

"Isn't that wonderful!" Em said.

"Terrific. He deserves it. He works hard."

"And he's talented."

"Oh, yes. I'm really happy he got that." As Cicero raced toward him, Jordan said, "Did you find me a pup for the Rickers?"

"I haven't found a Scottie, but I know where you can get a very cute little Westie bitch. They look like Scotties, you know, only they're white and a little smaller."

"The other dog in the Black and White ad."

"Yes. She's too small for a show dog so you can get her cheap. She's seven months old and very sweet."

"How much?"

"He said thirty, but I think you can get it for twenty."

"Will you get it for me? I'll bring the money over."

"Sure. I can go out there day after tomorrow."

She agreed to go out to the Rickers' with him to deliver the dog. He was pleased that she had found a dog for them. They had been on his mind. Of course they might not actually want the dog, but he thought he could tell if they didn't, and he'd figure out a way to withdraw it without embarrassing them. But he was pretty sure they'd like it. He remembered how they had lit up over Cicero.

When Alex came home, he, too, had news. He and Jenifer had found a place to live. "It's on Grandview, one block from campus. It's half of a rackety old Victorian house, in lousy repair, but the rooms are big and it's got character. Oh, and a view."

"Yeah, I know that street," Skipper said. "You've got a wonderful view of my school. Especially the football field."

"We'll raise our sights," Alex said. "We'll look to the mountains." He went to call Jenifer to tell her the news about Tony's fellowship.

Jordan said to his mother, "It's nice to see everybody getting the breaks."

"Yes, isn't it?" She smiled and turned away, but not so quickly that he didn't see the tears spring to her eyes. Skipper saw it too, and he tried to cover the moment.

"Have you painted your masterpiece yet?" he asked Jordan.

"Give me time, man. Give me time."

"All right, but I expect diligence. Hey, Ma, can I eat and run? I've got basketball practice."

"Come out here," his mother said. "I'll fix your plate."

After dinner Alex drove his mother and Jordan downtown to see his apartment. The tall, rather ugly nineteenth century house had been divided vertically. It was set close to the hill that plunged steeply down to the high school playing fields. Cicero set forth at once to explore the hillside, but Jordan called him back.

"Too many cars down there." He snapped on the leash.

"I rented it from someone who claims to be a real estate agent," Alex said, unlocking the front door, "but she is obviously a working witch. It's possible the house is haunted. Jen found an 1897 newspaper in the cellar with blood on it."

"Old blood, I hope," his mother said.

Jordan wandered around studying the big empty rooms, following a habit he had lately developed of trying to fix every detail in his mind and even to project how the future would look. He could see Alex standing with his elbow on the marble mantel over the fireplace that didn't work. He could imagine rows of books on the two-feet-wide window sills. He could see Jen standing at the chipped kitchen sink, looking out the window toward the mountains in the north as she washed the dishes.

"Jen is going to have problems with this stove," his mother said. "It's ancient."

"She'll cope," Alex said.

"Don't be that way, Alex," his mother said, a little sharply. "In this day and age a woman shouldn't have to 'cope' with primitive stuff like this."

"Ma, it's the only place we've seen we could afford."

"All right, but you help her."

"You know I'll help her."

She went into the big back hall. "She can do the laundry at our house. I doubt if you could connect a machine here . . ."

"Even if we could afford one. Mother, I'm your son Alex, remember? I'm not Paul Getty. For the next few years we are going to be poor as church mice."

"Is Jenifer going to keep on teaching at the kindergarten?"

"For now."

"Then you could afford a washing machine. But I don't think you could connect it. This is a really old house." She pointed to an overhead kitchen light with one naked bulb. "Be careful about the wiring. It's probably defective."

Jordan laughed. "Ma, stop being the consumer's advocate. This is Alex's first home. I think it will be swinging. I can see it now, when Jen gets through with it . . ."

Alex looked grateful. "We'll have to ransack our attic and Jen's family's, too, for furniture. And then we thought some of that unpainted pine stuff they have down on Pearl Street. We can paint it some jazzy color."

"Yes, that's good," his mother said. "Be careful about the secondhand stores. Don't buy beds secondhand. They might have bugs."

"We can have some beds from Jen's folks that they don't use."

His mother pointed up at the living room ceiling. "I like that chandelier."

"Wow!" Alex said. "She likes something!"

"Oh, honey, I didn't mean to downgrade it. It must have been a gracious home at one time. I just want to make sure you're practical. Don't forget, I had to spend years worrying about things like this."

"I know. I'm only kidding. I know you'll like it when it's fixed."

"Of course I will." She opened a corner cupboard. "That's a nice glass door. You know, Alex, I'm probably carping because I can't stand to see the first bird leave the nest."

"I'm not flying very far."

"You will." She took a deep breath. "But that's what it's all about, I guess, rearing you up so you can."

When they got home, Jordan went into his mother's room. "I know what I want to get them for a wedding present."

"What, dear?" She was lying on the bed. She looked tired.

Jordan sat down beside her. "One of those electric oven deals. You know what I mean? You can roast a turkey or whatever."

"A Westinghouse roaster. That would be nice, Jordan. That stove is a horror."

"All right. I'll look at them tomorrow morning."

"Do you want me to do it for you? The stores are a madhouse with Christmas shoppers."

"No, I want to do it."

Later he went downstairs and joined Tony, who had come in from work and was watching television. The show was a rerun of an old movie, Laurence Olivier in *Wuthering Heights*. Tony chuckled from time to time at the flagrant passions of the film, but Jordan liked it. He was moved by the wild solitude of the Yorkshire moor and the intensity of the emotion. He could believe Heathcliff and Cathy, although he found the David Niven part a little hard to take.

"Wait till you see the death scene," Tony said. "It beats *La Bohème*."

But Jordan was impressed by the scene in

which Wanda Landowska played the harpsichord. He had never known a harpsichord could
sound so abandoned.

Tony pointed. "Look at the spider going
across the tube."

A small house spider raced partway out onto
the glass of the TV screen, stopped, and went
on again.

"He doesn't know he's walking on Olivier's ear,"
Tony said. "He's got his own network."

Jordan watched the spider's erratic progress.
"Which is the real show, his or Olivier's?"

Tony smiled. "And how many other networks
are there that we don't even know about?
World's within worlds, the word within the
word." He stretched. "I'm going to hit the sack."

Jordan stayed until the end of the movie, and
by that time the spider had scurried out of sight.

Twenty-Third

During the holidays Jordan was usually home alone in the mornings with his mother. Alex was working full-time at the hospital. Tony slept late after his job at the hotel and then went to the campus library to work on his dissertation. Skipper was at the supermarket in the afternoons and in the mornings he scouted out odd jobs shoveling snow and running errands for people.

Jordan was glad his mother was home. He dreaded being alone. He was feeling noticeably weaker, although he tried to conceal it. His mother never mentioned it, but she made excuses to save him from going up the stairs and she usually drove him to work. He knew she was worried about his ability to drive, and she was right. His reactions had slowed down. He would soon have to give it up. One more thing.

230

What would he be left with in the end?

He and his mother had not had much leisure together for a long time. Often they sat at the kitchen table late into the morning, talking about all sorts of things, except what was happening to Jordan. He asked her questions about the family background, which he had never paid any attention to before. She liked to talk about her mother, whom they had all loved and who had died the previous winter.

When he asked about his father, she was not as informative. "I really don't know much. He left home when he was seventeen. His parents had a small department store in Massachusetts. They died long ago, I believe."

One morning she came downstairs and found him making a list. "Christmas list?"

"No, I'm making a rough draft of my will so I can take it to the office and get it properly drawn up." He looked up and saw her wince. "Ma," he said gently, "facts are facts."

She turned away without answering.

"I was thinking about the money. I've the thousand Grandmother Jordan left each of us, and some more I've saved. I think it should go to you."

"I don't want it," she said in a low, tight voice.

"But you ought to have it."

"I don't want it," she repeated sharply. She rattled some dishes in the sink and started the hot water. "Leave it to Skipper for college."

"All right. That's a good idea." He wrote it down. "One other thing . . ."

She said, "Do we have to talk about this?"

"Ma, I'm not trying to upset you, but I do need your advice."

She poured washing powder into the hot water and let it foam up higher than was necessary. "All right, what is it?"

"About the VW. I'd like to leave it to Skip, but it will be almost two years before he can get a license . . ."

"Leave it to Terry."

"Terry? I hadn't thought of that. They have a car . . ."

"Pat has a car. Terry is stuck in that house all the time. A woman needs to escape."

"All right, fine. The VW for Terry." He wrote it down. Looking at her tense back, he folded the paper and put it in his pocket. "I didn't mean to upset you. Things have to be faced."

"I can't face them as well as you do. I'm sorry."

"I'm not too good at it myself. But you get used to an idea, even that one."

"I don't." Her voice was fierce, and she had her head bent over the dishes. "I am not resigned. I shall never be resigned."

After a moment he got up and put his hands gently on her shoulders. "How about if I take you to the Hungarian restaurant for lunch? I don't have to go to work today, you know."

She tossed her hair back so she could look at him. Her eyes were full of tears. "Lovely." She forced a smile.

Jordan went upstairs feeling depressed. He sat down by the window to have another go at the picture he was trying to paint. So far his painting had been a dismal failure. He had tried to do a view of the Flatirons from his window — just the peaks soaring up above a nearer hill — but all he got was a blob.

"I want a certain color," he told Skipper, "and I put it down, and then I see, like for instance, the snow has blue in it. So I add a touch of blue and it looks awful. So I try some brown to kill the marshmallow look, and I get mud. Every time I end up with mud."

"So paint mud," Skipper had said. "You could be the Mud Painter of the Rocky Mountain West."

Jordan had picked up some oils, and he was trying those now. Also he had gradually diminished his subject until now his goal was to get at least a recognizable likeness of the upper half of an oak tree in Em's yard, it's black branches spread out against the sky.

Tony had told him about a method he'd read about that an early twentieth century artist named Maxfield Parrish had used to get a vivid color of sky. "He was a pop artist, mostly an illustrator, actually," Tony said, "but he was a good technician. I read about this method just the other day. It seems to me he started with blue cobalt with a little linseed oil in it and let that dry. Then add umber glaze and let that dry. No, I'm wrong . . . before the umber, you varnish the blue and let it dry. The varnish is the key to the whole thing. After the umber, a little white and I think a little pink. I may have it wrong but you might fool around with it."

Late last night Jordan had applied the varnish

to the cobalt. Now while he was waiting for that to dry thoroughly, he practiced sketching the branches of the tree. It was astonishing how hard it was to get it right. He held up a little plastic ruler to his eye and tried to measure the proportion of the lower branches. He'd have to fill in the top of Em's father's garage, just the top of it, below the branches, because it was important that part of the tree be hidden. He tried and erased and tried again. It was frustrating and fascinating. What he wanted seemed to be always just beyond him, like something glimpsed from the corner of the eye. And his hand was so unsteady.

He was both glad and sorry when it was time to get dressed to take his mother to lunch.

They had a pleasant meal of good Hungarian food. Jordan thought his mother seemed much more cheerful. After lunch they did a little shopping. Jordan picked out the electric oven for Alex and Jenifer, "one with all the gadgets," he told the salesgirl. And he did a little Christmas shopping. He had never been so interested before in choosing just the right Christmas present for everyone, but he had to shop in small doses because he got so tired. Today he bought the Gelb biography of Eugene O'Neill for Tony and a stuffed animal for his unborn nephew or niece. It was a soft, fluffy rabbit, caramel-brown with amber eyes.

"Young Jordan will go ape over that," he said to his mother.

They went home then, and as his mother drove the Opel into the yard Em came over, carrying a small white puppy.

234

"Em's got the Westie for the Rickers," Jordan said. He got out awkwardly, trying to hurry the slow, jerky legs. "Let's see him, Em."

"It's a her." Em put the dog down, and the puppy sat demurely, looking at Jordan with serious dark eyes.

"I like her. She's a serious dog."

"She can be playful. She's awfully little, way below standard but otherwise okay. I got her last night and she's behaved like a perfect lady."

Jordan's mother bent down to pat the puppy. "She's a love, Em."

"When do you want to go out to the Rickers'?" Jordan asked Em. "I've got the afternoon off. Are you free?"

"Yes. I can go now if you like."

"Take the Opel," Jordan's mother said. "Let Em drive it, Jordie. She's never driven it."

He winced a little at his mother's transparent effort to keep him from driving. It was humiliating, but she was right. "You want to drive?"

"Love to. Wait till I run home and tell my mother where I'm going."

"I'd better go in," Jordan's mother said. "I hear Cicero complaining."

"I'd better leave him home this trip. They might not hit it off."

"Thank you for the lunch, darling. I had a lovely time. Keep wrapped up warm, won't you? You wear that fur hat on the back of your head like a skullcap. Pull it down to keep your ears and neck warm."

"Yes, Mama," he said, laughing at her. "Will do, Mama."

When Em backed the Opel out of the yard,

Jordan stretched his long legs out as far as he could and put his head back. He was tired, but not unpleasantly. He felt more languid than anything. The little dog sat on his lap, alert and watchful. "What's her name?"

"Snowflake."

At the sound of her name, the puppy cocked her head at Em.

"Cicero is probably having a temper tantrum. He's not used to my going off for very long without him. If he ever knew I was out with a strange dog . . ."

"You spoil him."

"Sure I do. But so does Skip, and he'll be Skip's dog . . . someday." He hadn't meant to get into that. He and Em never talked about his health. She never even asked him how he felt, and he was grateful for it.

As if she hadn't noticed what he had said, she began to tell him about her plans for transferring to the campus at Fort Collins. She was going to do it in the fall instead of spending another year in Boulder as she had planned. "My mind is made up, so I might as well get with it." She told him she wanted to have a complete clinic, treating farm animals and horses as well as pets.

"I can see the reaction of those farmers when this pretty little girl shows up to deliver a calf or something."

"If I do a good job, they'll accept me fast enough."

"You're a good, gutsy girl, Em."

She looked pleased but she said, "That's probably not the most gallant thing you can say to a girl."

As they got closer to the Rickers' house, Jordan began to get nervous. "Maybe they won't remember me. Or anyway they may think I'm crazy, giving them a dog when I hardly know them."

"It's not like giving them the Hope diamond. They're farm people. They'll understand the gift of an animal. I think they'll be pleased."

When Em turned into the yard, Jordan said, "Snowflake, you be good now. If you want to do anything disgraceful, wait till after we've gone."

"She wouldn't dream of doing anything disgraceful." Em stopped the car at the back door. "Shall I come with you or not?"

"Oh, God, yes. I need moral support." He handed the dog to Em so he could get out of the car, holding onto the door.

When he knocked, it was a long minute before anyone answered. He was beginning to feel acutely disappointed. But then the door opened in Mr. Ricker's slow, cautious way.

"Mr. Ricker, do you remember me? I'm Jordan Phillips . . ." He felt panicky at the blank look on the man's face. But then slow recognition and pleasure lit up Mr. Ricker's face.

" 'Course I remember you. You and your little dog. Come right in. Mother will be glad to see you. Speaks of you often."

Jordan introduced Em, and they were ushered into the big kitchen. Mrs. Ricker sat in her same place, as if she had not moved since he was there before. Her eyes shone with delight.

"The child has come back to see us, Father,"

she said. Stiffly she held out her hand to Jordan, and stiffly he took it.

"How've you been, Mrs. Ricker?"

"Can't complain, child. You're looking thinner. Is this your young lady?"

Em blushed, and Jordan said, "This is Emily Faulkner, my next door neighbor and one of my oldest friends." That was a stupid way to define Em, he thought, but what could he say?

"Where's your dog? You got another one there. Look, Father, isn't he a cute one?"

"Other half of the Black and White label," Mr. Ricker said, chuckling.

"It's a she," Jordan said. "Her name is Snowflake."

Em put Snowflake down. The puppy sniffed around the room for a minute and then sat down in front of Mrs. Ricker, studying her.

"Oh, she's nice. Here, you folks, sit down. Where's my manners? Father, make some tea."

"We can't stay . . ." Jordan began, but she cut him short.

"You can stay for a cup of tea."

"I love your Christmas tree," Em said.

Jordan hadn't noticed it. It was a tall spruce, decorated with red and silver ornaments and lights. "It's a beauty."

"She's a live one," Mr. Ricker said. "I'll plant 'er out back after Christmas."

"We do that, too," Jordan said.

"We went into Denver and got them ornaments," Mrs. Ricker said.

"Did you go to Trader Vic's?" Jordan asked, smiling at her.

"You bet we did," Mr. Ricker answered. "Had rum swizzles."

"The child will think we're a couple of old soaks," Mrs. Ricker said.

Jordan laughed. "I wouldn't say that."

While the tea was being made, they talked about the weather, about crop prospects, about how much the Rickers had liked Jordan's brothers. They asked about the VW: was it all right now?

When Mr. Ricker poured the tea, he also poured some warm milk in a saucer for Snowflake, who lapped it up delicately as a cat.

"Good manners," Mrs. Ricker said.

Jordan swallowed. For some reason it was hard to get to the point. "I brought her for you."

They both looked at him in surprise. Then, with no protests or exclamations of astonishment, they accepted it.

"Well, that's about the nicest Christmas present we'll get, Mother," Mr. Ricker said.

And Mrs. Ricker, looking at Jordan with her luminous smile, said, "One of the nicest we ever got in our lives."

Jordan was immensely relieved. No fuss, no long explanations, nothing but understanding and acceptance. He had been right: they were great people. He tried to stoop to pick up the puppy and put her in Mrs. Ricker's lap, but he had to put out his hand quickly to brace himself on the table. Mrs. Ricker said nothing, but he knew she saw. Em quickly picked up the dog and gave her to Mrs. Ricker.

"She's seven months old and she's had all her

shots and all. I've got a list here of what's she had and when she'll need a booster." Em got it out of her pocket.

"Em is studying to be a veterinarian," Jordan said.

"Well, then, we'll know where to go if we ever have any questions," Mr. Ricker said. "Will you write down your telephone, young lady?"

"Yes, of course." Em wrote her name and number on the paper.

"We not only got us a nice little dog," Mr. Ricker said, "we got a vet to go with it."

Mrs. Ricker was giving all her attention to Snowflake, who leaned against her confidingly.

"She's your dog already, Mother," Mr. Ricker said.

"Snowflake," Mrs. Ricker said softly. "Good doggie."

When they left, amid good wishes and Merry Christmases, Mrs. Ricker clung to Jordan's hand for a moment.

"Eat more, child," she said softly. "You're too thin. Take care of yourself."

To his own surprise he leaned over and kissed her cheek. He had never done that sort of thing in his life. Her eyes filled with tears, but she smiled at him.

"Merry Christmas," he said quietly, "and a happy, happy New Year."

She nodded and smiled, but she couldn't speak. Snowflake stared at Jordan with her grave scrutiny.

"Snowflake, you behave like a lady." Moved by a depth of feeling that he didn't really understand, he left quickly.

Em slammed her door and called a last good-bye as the Opel engine roared. In a minute the Ricker house was out of sight in the broad snowy landscape. "What sweet people," she said. "That woman really loves you."

Jordan didn't answer. He was afraid his voice would break.

When at last he could trust himself to talk, he said lightly, "Poor old Em. You're always being tagged as my future wife."

She smiled. "Tony thinks I'm madly in love with you."

"Are you?" He knew she wasn't, but for a second it struck him that it might be quite pleasant if she were. A man should be entitled to one broken heart left behind when he went.

"We've always been so close it would seem like incest, wouldn't it?"

"I guess it would. You're like my twin."

She was silent for a while. "I'll tell you a secret if you swear never to tell."

"Sworn."

"I'm in love with Tony."

He stared at her in amazement. "You're kidding!"

"No, I've been in love with him for years."

"Does he know it?"

"Of course not. I'm the little kid next door who always bugged him." She paused and then added softly, "But he did take me to the ball."

"Well, I'll be damned — and I thought I knew you."

"You're too close to me to see."

"Listen, Em, it's a wonderful idea, you and Tony. You'd be just what he needs."

241

"Unfortunately, it's his decision."

"Em, hang in there. Don't give up."

"Oh, I won't give up," she said. "Don't worry about that."

It was a very comforting idea. He began to whistle softly under his breath. A good day all around, a good day.

Twenty-Fourth

It was Christmas Eve. A little before five o'clock Jordan came out of the office building where he worked. His boss was going to the Bahamas, and he had given Jordan two weeks' vacation with pay. When they had said goodbye and exchanged holiday greetings, the question hung in the air, whether Jordan would be able to come back, but neither of them spoke of it. Earlier Jordan had asked him if he would like to start breaking in someone else. He was worried because he was not able to get as much work done as he always had. But the lawyer had said no, "We won't worry about that until we have to."

Jordan usually waited in the lobby for one of the family to pick him up, but tonight he stepped outside. It was unseasonably warm, and the western sky was pale gold. Up and down the street Christmas lights glowed, and last-minute shoppers hurried in and out of the stores. Across the way a Santa Claus leaned against a telephone pole and wearily swung his bell. In the music store next to the office building the p.a. system was playing "Hark, the Herald Angels Sing."

Jordan leaned against the stone wall of the building. He was a few minutes early. In his pocket he had his mother's Christmas present, a small unset emerald on a delicate gold chain. It had cost him ninety-five dollars and tax. He kept touching his pocket to make sure it was still there. He usually spent fifteen or twenty dollars for her present, but this was special.

He looked up the street for either the Opel, the Volvo, or the VW, but none of them was in sight. A group of people swung out of the office building, arms around each other, drowning out the carol with a bawdy song, moving unsteadily toward the parking lot. Office party, Jordan thought; hope they get home without a crash. Merry Christmas, everybody.

Some children, about seven or eight years old, swirled out of the alley like blown leaves. They were playing a game, and they regrouped near Jordan. A little girl in a red snowsuit stood in the middle of the circle that the others made. They chanted to her: "Crocodile, crocodile, may I cross your golden river in your little golden boat?" And she sang out loud and clear: "Not unless you're wearing PURPLE. Those who aren't get chased."

The children looked themselves over hastily. One child pulled out the top of a lavender sweatshirt. "Purple, purple!"

The others found no purple, and they were chased by the child in the red snowsuit. She was a very pretty little girl, blond and brown-eyed. Jordan watched them with amusement. He called a warning as one little boy dashed off the curb. The child reversed his path and was caught by the little blond. The boy looked at Jordan reproachfully, as if it were his fault.

"You're it, you're it," the little girl cried out. "I caught you, Herbie Plummer."

"Crocodile, crocodile," began Herbie Plummer, and got a chorus of protests because he wasn't playing it right. Above the shouts his voice rose ". . . unless you're wearing ORANGE. Those who aren't get chased." And he started the chase at once.

Two of the children, the little blond girl and a boy, skittered backward against Jordan's legs. He caught at the coping on the building behind him and saved himself.

The little girl looked up at him. "Are you drunk, Mister?"

"No, just unsteady on my pins."

As they ran away he heard their voices, the little boy saying, "What'd he say?"

"Steady on his pin." They both looked back at him.

"Merry Christmas," Jordan said.

They giggled and ran.

Tony pulled up to the curb in the Opel and opened the passenger door.

"Sorry, am I late?"

"No," Jordan said, getting in carefully. "I was early."

"What are you looking amused about?"

"Kids." Carefully he stretched out his legs.

"You know, young Jordan might not be a boy at all. He might turn out to be a little girl in a red snowsuit."

"Coming in snowsuits now, are they?" Jordan laughed. "Merry Christmas."

"Merry Christmas, kid."

He took Jordan home and then he went to the Harvest House to work. When he came home shortly after midnight, Jordan and Alex were playing checkers in front of the fire. Behind them in the corner the big Christmas tree glowed with lights.

"Big night?" Jordan asked, as Tony came in and threw himself into a chair.

"Yes. If I have to wish any more drunks a Merry Christmas, I'll cut my throat."

Alex got up and got Tony a beer. "Busman's holiday."

Tony pulled off the metal tab and threw it into the wastepaper basket. "Ma gone to bed?"

"No, she took Skipper to the midnight service at Pat's church."

"Oh, yeah, I forgot. Poor Skip."

"It won't hurt him," Alex said.

Tony made a face, but Jordan said, "I agree. If you live in a Christian culture, you ought to know what it's all about."

"Just in your own field," Alex said, "how do you read Yeats or Eliot or . . . well, the bulk of Western literature, I suppose . . . if you don't know what Christianity is about?"

"Anyway," Jordan said, "religion preaches the qualities that man needs to survive, like love, compassion, brotherhood . . ."

"What is this I've stumbled into?" Tony said. "The Old Philosophers Club?"

"We were just talking about religion before you came in."

"Did you convert each other?"

"No," Alex said. "We just agreed that people need something to hang onto, if they can, and brotherhood and love are a step up from human sacrifice and hanging dissenters."

Jordan turned his beer can upside down, and Alex got up to get him another. "I wish I had a very exact, literal belief in some religious system. It would be such a relief." He held out his hand for the beer. "Thanks. All I can say is, I believe in the on-going-ness of life. The going-on-ness."

"Too much beer," Tony said.

"No, I think the same, cold sober, although I might not get into that word. I do not believe in nothing. How's that for a positive statement?"

"What are you giving me for Christmas?" Tony said.

"None of your business."

"Tony was always the one who sneaked down before anybody else was awake," Alex said.

"The oldest brother has some rights," Tony said. "The rights of primogeniture." He looked at his beer. "Where did we get all this elegant Tuborg?"

"Jordan's friend Nick brought it over for Christmas. His old man owns a package store."

"I wonder what our old man owns," Tony said. "Two shirts and collars, five dollars."

"He hasn't sent me a wedding present yet," Alex said.

"You are the most gift-grabbing bridegroom I ever heard of," Jordan said. "All you think of is gifts, gifts, gifts."

"If a man goes through a church wedding, he's entitled to some reward."

"You get my present tomorrow," Jordan said. "I may put it in your stocking."

They stayed there, talking, until Skipper and their mother returned from the midnight service.

Jordan thought Skipper looked quite handsome and grown up in his new suit. He was proud of him, and yet it was a little sad when the baby of the family grew up.

After they had gone to bed, he said to Skipper, "Let's make it a good Christmas." No one had given any indication that it would be his last, but he knew that they knew. He had lost a lot of ground in the last month.

"That church thing was really nice, Jordie." Skipper seemed unusually serious. "I wish you'd been there. All the candlelight and the carols and all. And Pat didn't seem like Pat at all."

"I know."

After a long pause, Skipper said, "Good night, Jordie."

"Good night, sport." He turned over carefully, trying to find a comfortable position. Good night for all the Christmases to come.

Twenty-Fifth

Christmas had gone reasonably well, with everyone working to make it a success. Working, in fact, almost too hard. Jordan felt the general strain. His legs bothered him so much that Skipper and Alex had to help him downstairs. He hated that, and he was worried about the wedding. What if he couldn't get through it? Not that that would be the end of the world, but for him it would be a major disappointment.

"You ought to let us fix you a bed downstairs," Alex said.

"The hell with that," Jordan said sharply. "We aren't going to turn this house into a nursing home. When I get to the point where I can't make it up and down stairs, I'll stay in my room."

"It was just a thought," Alex said mildly.

"We can always help you up and down," Skipper said.

"The languishing invalid," Jordan said bitterly. But then he saw that he was making them all feel bad, and with an effort he changed his tone.

"It'd ruin your throwing arm, sport."

He stretched out on the sofa during the exchange of presents, and after dinner he stayed only a short time before he went up to his room. He could feel what was almost a sense of relief when he left the room. He was an obstacle now in the smooth running of everyone's lives. They had to stop everything and think about him: did he feel all right? was he comfortable? was he much worse? The undertow of grief pulled at them all and wore on their nerves. His mother was sharp with the other boys but never now with him. The boys snapped at each other but never at him. That kind of considerateness was horrible. It made him feel more like an outsider than anything else could have.

There was a wedding rehearsal the next day, but Jordan begged off. He spent the day in bed. Pat and Alex could tell him what he was to do as best man, and it was understood that if Jordan didn't feel up to it, Tony would step in. But Jordan was determined to do it himself. He had practiced it over and over in his mind. If he held himself very stiff and rigid, and took small, careful steps, he ought to be all right. He didn't have to walk far, after all. And Alex said if he felt faint or anything, he could just quietly step out the side door into Pat's office or he could sit down in the front pew with his mother. But Jordan wanted very much to bring it off properly, the way it was supposed to go. There would be about a hundred fifty people there, lots of them friends of Jenifer and her family. He wanted Alex's family to come off well. Tony was going to get him to the church a little early so he could see exactly where he was to stand and so on.

At a little before six he heard someone come in downstairs, and then Skipper's running leaps up the stairs.

"Hi."

"Hi," Jordan said. "What are you doing home? Why aren't you at the rehearsal dinner?" Skipper was wearing his good suit.

"Oh, I chickened out. All those people; I don't even know half of them."

Jordan was not fooled. Skipper had come home because he knew Jordan hated being alone. "You don't have to miss the dinner, sport. Why don't you go back? I'm all right."

"Nah, I don't want to go. Honest, Jordie. Jen's mother keeps telling people I'm Alex's cute little brother." He made a face. "I've had that."

Jordan was too glad to have him there to argue. He had been working on his sketches of the tree, trying to get it right and not being satisfied.

Skipper made turkey sandwiches and brought them upstairs, and after they had eaten, he went to the window with the telescope that Jordan had given him. "This is the neatest thing I ever had, Jordie. I can see all kinds of stuff."

"Let's have a look." Jordan fixed it to his eye and stared at the heavens, now brought so startlingly close. "You really can see quite a lot. Look at that moon!"

Skipper took it back. "I wonder if it was a comet or what, that the wise men saw."

The telephone rang. He handed the telescope

to Jordan and went into their mother's room to answer it. Jordan looked at the stars again. He was thinking about the distance, and the fact that some of the stars he was looking at now had actually ceased to exist, possibly millions of years ago. Wasn't that what they said? It boggled the mind. A person's sense of fact got all jostled up.

Skipper came into the room and said in an odd voice, "Jordan, your father is on the phone. What shall I say?"

Jordan stared at him in astonishment, and in spite of his surprise, he laughed. "*My* father?"

"Well, our father. You know who I mean."

"Who does he want?"

"He asked for Alex and then for Mom. I don't know what to say to him. He said, 'Which one are you?'"

"I'll talk to him." Jordan swung himself around and went slowly into the bedroom across the hall. He felt very peculiar. He had never spoken to his father, or at least not that he could remember. He sat down on the bed and picked up the phone. "Hello?"

"Hello, who is this? Alex?" The voice sounded like Tony's and for a second Jordan wondered if it were a practical joke. But the voice wasn't quite like Tony's, and Tony hated practical jokes. Anyway, Tony was at the rehearsal dinner.

"This is Jordan." He tried to make his voice strong so his father could hear him. It had gotten weaker lately.

"Jordan? This is your dad."

"Oh. How are you?" He felt like Skipper — he didn't know what to say. "Alex isn't here.

They're having a rehearsal dinner."

"I see. Why aren't you there?"

He couldn't think of an answer so he pretended not to have heard. "Mom is there, too. Can I give them a message?"

"Yes. I was going to come to the wedding; Alex sent me an invitation . . ." He said it apologetically, as if he had to explain. "I drove down to Boston last night to get a plane to Denver, but there's not a seat available." He sounded aggrieved.

"It's Christmas." Jordan thought of Tony's saying 'the old man never did anything right in his life.'

"Yes, I'm well aware of that now. I'm very disappointed."

"Alex will be, too. I'll tell him." Then suddenly he was afraid his father would hang up. He would never have a chance to talk to him again. He couldn't let it go, in this stiff little dialogue between strangers. "I'm sorry you can't come. I'd like to have talked to you."

His father's voice sounded warmer, almost eager. "I'd like to talk to you, too, all of you. I wish you'd come see me some summer."

"I've thought of it, but I've always worked."

"We'll have to plan it. You'd like Maine. You've never been here, have you?"

"No, I haven't been much of anywhere."

The operator broke in to say the time was up. Jordan was glad when he heard the clank of more coins and then his father's voice again. "Hello?"

"Are you still in Bangor?" Jordan asked.

"Yes. I'm teaching French and Spanish in the high school."

"Do you like Bangor?" At transcontinental rates, tell me all about Bangor. But his father seemed as anxious to talk as he was.

"Yes, it's very nice. A biggish city for Maine, and it's inland, you know. '. . . out of the swing of the sea.' That's a line from Yeats that I always liked. Do you read poetry?"

"I've been reading it lately." And that line, he didn't say, is from Hopkins, not Yeats.

"What are you majoring in? What are you going in for?"

"Well, I was going to go into law . . ."

"Do it then, Jordan, do it. Don't say 'was.' Make the most of your opportunities."

"Yes, I'll try to do that."

"Well . . ."

"Do you have any family back there? Relatives?"

"Relatives?" He sounded puzzled.

"I mean, have I got cousins or uncles or whatever?"

He hesitated and then said vaguely, "Yes, there are some. I've never kept in touch." He paused. "How's your mother?"

"She's fine."

"Tell her I asked."

"Sure, yes, I will." He tried to think of something else. There was so much to ask. But he couldn't say, "What are you like? Are you happy? Am I anything like you?"

"Tell Alex there's a wedding present on the way and I'm really sorry to miss the festive occasion. Maybe I'll make it for *your* wedding." When Jordan didn't answer, he said, "I enjoyed talking to you, Jordan. Call me sometime."

"All right." Jordan's voice was choked, and he wasn't sure his father heard him.

"So long, then."

"Dad?" It was hard to say, a rusty unused word.

But his father had already gone. He heard the click of the receiver in Boston. Slowly he put the phone back. Skipper was in the doorway.

"What did he want?"

"He was going to come to the wedding, but he couldn't get a plane."

"Wow! What a narrow escape!"

"It wouldn't have killed anybody if he'd come," Jordan said. "He's our father, after all."

"I know," Skipper said hastily. "I just meant . . . I mean Tony would have had a fit. And Mom."

"It wouldn't have killed them. It wasn't much for him to ask." He got up. He felt like crying. "When you get married, you invite him, you hear?"

"Sure, okay, Jordie." He followed Jordan back to their room. "It gives you an eerie feeling, doesn't it?"

"Yes." Jordan lay down and closed his eyes.

Twenty-Sixth

All four boys crowded into their mother's room to get their ties tied and the ruffles of the rented shirts properly in place.

"We look like the cast of a restoration comedy," Tony said, squinting down at the buttons of his waistcoat.

Jordan sat on the bed waiting his turn. He felt shaky, but he was concentrating with all his strength on holding himself together.

"My vest won't button," Skipper wailed.

"Oh, my God, it won't!" Alex said. "Ma, look! Skipper, how could that be? You tried it on at the rental place . . ."

"I was thinner then." Skipper strained to close the gap.

"Don't! You'll burst the buttons," his mother said.

"Well, what do I do? Saunter down the aisle with my vest unbuttoned? 'This is a real informal wedding, folks . . . Come as you are . . .'"

Tony was laughing. "Just stoop your shoulders. Don't stand up straight."

"I could quit breathing till the ceremony's over."

"This isn't funny," Alex wailed.

His mother pushed him away. "Alex, do stop dithering." She fussed with Skipper's clothes. "You'll just have to keep your jacket buttoned. It's supposed to be buttoned anyway. I'll pin the vest . . ."

"Ma!" Alex said. "Please. I'm responsible for those clothes . . ."

"Alex, darling, do go away somewhere."

Tony maneuvered Alex to the door. "There is nobody so unpopular as the bridegroom on a wedding day. Go hide somewhere."

Muttering, Alex went out of the room.

"Alex the unflappable," Jordan said. He had his legs up on the bed, and he was leaning against the headboard. He was glad his family was such a bunch of nuts. He'd know them anywhere. If they were a constellation, the astronomers would say, "What's that odd group of stars? I never saw so much light."

When his mother had finished with Skipper and Tony, she tied Jordan's tie and arranged his shirt. "There. You look beautiful."

"You got me mixed up with the bride. Nobody notices the best man."

"I notice him." She kissed his cheek.

"You look pretty good yourself. And you smell like Paris in the spring, however that is." He smiled down at her. She did look very young and pretty in her soft pink dress.

Tony and Jordan went to the church early, and Tony showed Jordan where to stand, what to do on which cue. "You've got the ring, I trust."

"Yeah." He felt it every few minutes to make sure it was there. "Tony, I'm quite sure I'm going to make it all right, but if I don't, the big thing is for you to get into my place fast and let me get out of there so it's not a disruption or anything."

"Sure. Don't worry. They won't be looking at you, anyway. Everybody will be swooning over the bride and crying; that's what they do at weddings."

"Show me where you'll be standing."

Tony took his place. "Pat says we're an intrusion. There aren't supposed to be a couple of extra brothers standing up here. Skipper told him we were groom's-maids." He laughed. "Why don't we wait in Pat's study? You can lie down if you want." He led the way into the little study. "This is where Pat naps when everybody thinks he's mulling over his next sermon."

Jordan lay back on the leather couch, and by the time the rest of the wedding party arrived, he was almost asleep. He sat up and combed his hair, smoothed down his clothes, and checked for the ring. He felt nervous, but he was fighting against it. 'You'll be all right,' he kept saying to himself, 'you'll be all right.'

People came and went. He could hear the hum of voices. Alex, looking quite composed now and very good-looking, said, "Here we go, chum."

As he took his place beside Alex in the church, he stood stiff, fixing his gaze on the lectern. After one glance at his mother and sister, who sat in the front row not far from him, he tried to forget that there were all those people out there. He listened to the wedding march. He saw Jenifer, looking amazingly pretty, coming to the front of the church on her father's arm. He saw Pat facing them, looking benign, and he saw Tony and Skipper, Tony interested and ever so slightly amused, Skipper self-conscious and a little scared. He thought, 'my mother's raised some nice-looking kids.'

Alex stepped to Jenifer's side. The service was going on. He didn't try to hear the words. It wouldn't do to scatter his attention. His job was to stand there and hand over that ring at the right moment. He reached inside his pocket for it, bracing his elbow against his side to steady the shaking in his hands. He drew it carefully from his pocket — and dropped it. He heard the tiny gasp that his mother made, and he saw Tony look at him quickly to see what had happened. No one else had noticed. He would have to pick it up. Stooping was something he avoided, lest he fall. But he had to pick up the ring. Now.

He heard a slight movement behind him, and he turned his head and frowned sternly at Terry. She was leaning forward as if to get up. But if she came and picked up the ring, she would have to cross a distance of several yards. It would be very noticeable. He was the only one who could do it inconspicuously. If he didn't fall.

Slowly and very carefully he leaned down, bending his knees as much as they would bend and then putting his hand down. If he began to fall, perhaps he could brace himself with his hand. But he must not fall, must not fall. His fingers touched the cool metal of the ring. He got hold of it. Holding his other hand away from his body a little to balance himself, he straightened slowly. He could feel the letting go of the tension in his mother and sister, who had virtually stopped breathing while he stooped. He glanced at Tony and winked.

It was the moment to hand the ring to Alex. He gave it to him. He felt immensely pleased with himself. He could even hear the words now. "With this ring I thee wed." He wasn't worried anymore. Things would be all right now. Hey, Mr. Hemingway, I just passed my test. Well, one of them, anyway. He exchanged quick grins with Skipper.

Alex kissing Jenifer. The triumphant recessional music. His mother going out on an usher's arm. Terry. Bride's mother. Everybody. Alex is married!

He let himself be taken to the reception at the Harvest House for a few minutes. Then he'd have to split. Awfully tired. Champagne. Tony disappearing for a few minutes because he wanted his colleagues in the bar to see what a dandy he was. Jenifer's mother saying, "You boys looked so lovely. Such a lovely family." Dr. Parkhurst saying, "Good work, Jordie! Man, when you dropped that ring, I thought I'd faint! Never expected you to make it. Very good work. But go home now and rest." Jenifer giving him a loving kiss. Em smiling. Alex's fraternity brothers passing glasses of champagne. Skipper grinning from ear to ear, forgetting and unbuttoning his jacket, hastily buttoning it up again. Finally Terry taking his arm and saying, "Hey, brother, let's you and me sit down before we fall down," and guiding him to a comfortable chair. "Weddings are not for pregnant women. I'm such a reminder — it seems indelicate." She got him a plateful of very good food.

"Well, that was young Jordan's first wedding," Jordan said.

She laughed. "Thank God she had the sense not to insist on firsthand participation."

"It seems pretty firsthand to me. How you feeling?"

"Resting uncomfortably. But things could pop . . . if you'll pardon the expression . . . at any minute."

"Good. The sooner the better."

A little later she drove him home and came in with him. He lay down on the sofa. His head ached. "Listen, go back and enjoy yourself. I'm all right."

"No, I'd rather be with you. If you don't mind."

"Mind!" He smiled at her. "It was a nice wedding, wasn't it?"

"Very nice. Jen is a good kid."

"And so is Alex."

"And so is Alex."

After they had talked about the wedding for a while, he said, "I worry about that christening business."

"Afraid you won't feel up to it?"

"I don't mean that, although I guess that's possible. I worry about making all those promises that I can't keep."

261

"Everyone understands."

"But the kid's left high and dry. Do you think Skip could act as my delegate?"

"Sure. Don't worry about it."

"I mean afterward. I want to be there if I can make it, but later he could see that Jordan does what he's supposed to do, like go to church."

"I don't think he'll have much chance of not going. He or she."

"Okay. I won't worry about it." He was silent for a few minutes. "Life seems to have turned into a series of ceremonies. Thank God you won't have to go through a funeral service; that would spoil all the nice ones. I'll be long gone to the medical center . . ."

She put her hand over his mouth. "Don't."

"All right. Only — can I say one thing?"

"If it's not sad."

"No, I don't think it is. Skipper said Ma wanted to have a memorial service, but I want to leave some directions for that. Will you take charge of seeing they're followed?"

She smiled and nodded. "Bossy old Jordan."

"Right. Well, I want it to be a happy occasion. First of all, I want Tony to play the organ, I want him to play something happy. Then I don't want Pat to say anything personal. No eulogy. Understood?"

She nodded.

"You'd better make notes."

"I'll remember."

"I suppose Pat has to say something, so have him read one of the cheerful psalms. There are cheerful psalms, aren't there? And then, like the old New Orleans deals, very happy on the way out. I want Tony to play 'When the Saints Go Marchin' In,' real loud and gay. Got that? And then . . . and then . . . listen now, Terry . . . everybody come back here for a party."

"Jordie!" She was half-protesting, half-laughing. "You're making me laugh at something I don't want to laugh at . . ."

"That's the point. I want no solemn goings-on. A good party back here with lots of food and Tony to tend bar. Skip can crack all his best jokes. Ask the Rickers to come, and a guy up in Estes Park named Charlie Ellis . . . Skipper knows. Play Louis Armstrong records. Just like an old-time New Orleans funeral. Or a good Irish wake. Everybody enjoy themselves."

She leaned back and looked at him. "And shall we sell the screen rights?"

"By all means. But about the service — will you do it?"

"I'll do my best."

"That's usually good enough." He closed his eyes for a minute. Talking so much tired him. But you couldn't let the chances go by. 'The days dwindle down . . .' He'd always thought that was a song for old men. More quietly, his eyes still closed, he said, "It's a funny thing, isn't it, how young Jordan and I will be passing each other in that little zone between worlds . . ."

Softly she said, "I hope young Jordan is just like you."

"No," he said, "young Jordan will be young Jordan. Not just like anybody."

Twenty-Seventh

Young Jordan was born a day ahead of schedule, eight-and-a-half pounds, a boy. Jordan was impatient to see him, but Dr. Parkhurst had forbidden him to go to the hospital. "Can't have you picking up a staph germ or something. There's no place as unhealthy as a hospital."

Jordan began to worry about the baby. "What if he picks up something?"

"He's in a glassed-in enclosure, all very sanitary. He's fine."

Jordan had to content himself with cross-examining his mother about the baby.

"He's very good-looking," she told him. "Big blue eyes with dark lashes and a little cap of soft dark hair."

"I thought babies were bald and red and wrinkled."

"And hideous," Skipper added.

"Not Phillips babies. You were all very nice-looking."

"Does he look bright?" Jordan asked.

"Darling, he was four hours old when I saw him."

"But couldn't you tell?"

"I'd say he looked as bright as a four-hour-old baby can look."

When Terry and the baby went home, Jordan and Skipper went to see them. Tony had already been to the hospital, and Alex was still at Vail on his honeymoon. Jordan had telephoned him when the baby arrived.

Jordan was nervous. "I feel as if I'm meeting some great personage, and I'm worried about whether he'll like me."

Terry was just changing him when they got there. "Well, here he is." She sat the baby up to face them.

Jordan was awed. "He *is* beautiful!"

"Aren't you afraid you'll drop him?" Skipper asked.

"Don't worry. As soon as I get a diaper on him, you can hold him."

Skipper backed away. "Oh, not, not me. Jordie can hold him."

"No, my arms aren't strong enough."

With a speed and expertise that surprised her brothers, Terry got the baby diapered and in plastic pants and a little terrycloth pullover. Holding him with one arm, she turned the little rocking chair in the bedroom so Jordan could sit comfortably. "Just sit there. I'll support him." When Jordan sat down she put the baby in his lap and knelt beside them, her hand against the back of his head and neck, and the other hand on his side. "Jordan, this is Jordan."

The baby stared unblinkingly at Jordan.

"Hello," Jordan said. He patted the baby's fat little knee. "You look very bright to me." He touched the baby's curled fist, and the small hand grabbed his finger. "Look at that reflex!"

"Of course he's bright," Terry said. "What'd you expect?"

"Well, you never know." Jordan stared back into those deep blue eyes. He was even more moved than he had expected to be. This was a real person.

Suddenly the baby opened his mouth in a wide grin. Jordan could hardly believe it. "Look, he's smiling at me!"

"Or laughing," Skipper said. "He looks like a first-class joker to me."

"Are you going to be a comic like your Uncle Skip?" Jordan said to the baby. "Terry, is he warm enough?"

"Sure. He's fine." She picked him up. "I have to feed him now."

They watched, fascinated, as she fed the baby from a bottle.

"He takes to the bottle like an old toper," she said, lifting him up on her shoulder and rubbing his back.

"What's that for?" Jordan said.

She laughed. "That's called burping. I can see you haven't had much experience with babies."

"How do girls know all this stuff?"

"They learn it. Anyway, I had four younger brothers."

"Gad!" Skipper said. "Did you burp me?"

"Often."

"What an indignity."

The baby fell asleep before he finished his bottle. They watched as Terry tucked him into his crib, and Jordan lingered a moment more, looking down at that round face. "Jordan Phillips Patterson," he said softly. "God bless."

Skipper made coffee for them while they waited for their mother to come back from the market to pick them up.

"It must be a fantastic experience to have a baby," Jordan said.

"It is."

"It's the kind of thing people take for granted, being born or dying or whatever, and yet when you think about it, it blows your mind."

"All that DNA working away," Skipper said.

Terry said, "Don't turn him into a philosophical abstraction. He's very real. The realest thing I've ever met up with."

Their mother blew her horn out in front, and then came for a quick look at the baby.

"You're looking great," Jordan said to Terry. "And you really brought it off, Sis. I'm proud of you."

"We're planning the christening for a week from Sunday, unless there's a blizzard or something."

"So soon? Is it all right for him to go out?"

"Sure. Don't be such a worry-wart." She said to her mother, "My brothers are impressed."

"They should be," her mother said.

Thinking about it on the way home, Jordan was glad the christening would be soon. He wanted to be on his feet for it, and staying on his feet was more and more of an effort. Pat had told him he could sit, if necessary, but that didn't seem to him like the right thing. Young Jordan was going to be christened in proper style.

Twenty-Eighth

In the middle of the week the weather suddenly turned springlike. A warm wind blew gently over the city, and Jordan awakened to the sound of melting snow. He had always loved these early promises of spring, and the first thing he always did, if he possibly could, was to go down and look at Boulder Creek. He liked to watch it all year round, in fact, but especially when the slow push of black water made its way along a narrow route between jagged edges of ice, the first step toward the torrent that would race under the arched stone bridge when spring and fishing weather came.

He lay in bed listening to his mother's car go, and then the Opel. He felt desperately alone. But then he heard steps on the stairs, and Skipper rushed in, slightly spilling a tall glass of fresh-squeezed orange juice.

"For you, sire. Drink every drop. It makes your teeth gleam in the dark." He put it on the bureau. "Got to run." He galloped off down the stairs before Jordan could say anything.

Jordan listened to the slam of the back door and the faint squeak of Skipper's old bike. He was glad his mother was going to get the kid a new one for his birthday. He got up slowly and drank the orange juice. Skipper had even remembered to take out the seeds.

He debated whether to stay in his room or go downstairs. The family consensus was that he shouldn't tackle the stairs now unless someone was home, but he was impatient with that idea. He dressed awkwardly, having trouble with the sleeves, and having to bend his head down so he could reach his hair with the comb. By the time he was dressed, he was tired and disgusted. But he decided to go down anyway. In a little over an hour his mother would dash in between classes to fix his breakfast. He had tried to persuade her not to do that, but she insisted. She was afraid he wouldn't eat properly if she didn't come and supervise. They had had several little arguments about it, but he had lost. All this fuss to make sure a guy was eating properly and all that, when he'd be dead pretty soon, anyway. It was silly and somehow humiliating.

He went downstairs slowly, holding to the banister with both hands. His muscles didn't jerk any more. Unfortunately, he knew what that meant. In this disease the muscle reflexes were extreme at first, and then as the wasting process accelerated and the muscles atrophied, the exaggerated reflexes stopped. He was lucky in one way; he had not had as much trouble as Dr. Parkhurst had been afraid of with bulbar paralysis. His voice was hoarse and a lot weaker than it normally had been, but he had not had much problem with swallowing or breathing. Thanks for small favors, he thought grimly as he moved carefully down the stairs, hand over hand on the banister. When he got to the bottom, he sat down for a few minutes to pull himself together.

He walked across the kitchen floor with the short, stiff steps that he used now to keep himself going. He opened the back door. The sun was shining brightly, and the yard was a mess of slush and mud, crisscrossed by tire marks. It looked like spring, all right. A sparrow hopped around, looking for goodies. Jordan tried to remember when the meadowlarks showed up. He loved meadowlarks, not just because their song was so pretty but because they were such brash, cocky birds. They always seemed ready to give you a bit of an argument.

He pulled a chair into the patch of sunlight in the doorway and sat down. The steady *drip-drip* of snow from the roof was a pleasant sound. It was funny what associations did to one's reactions; a leaky faucet would make the same dripping sound, and it would drive him crazy.

His mother drove fast into the driveway at exactly 9:20 as usual, and rushed into the house. He could tell she didn't really approve of his being downstairs or of his sitting in the open air without a coat, but she said little about it. She had to hurry to get his bacon and eggs cooked so she could get back for her next class. He thought of Dr. Parkhurst's saying "Your mother works too hard." He had always thought that someday he and the other guys would give her a break.

When she was gone again, he wondered what to do. It was a pity to waste a day like this. It might be the only spring he'd get. That thought hurt so much he put it out of his mind as quickly as he could. He wanted to go down and look at the river, but there was no one to take him. Anyway, they were all so busy that no one would have time for such a wool-gathering thing on a weekday morning. But he did want very much to go. The more he thought about it, the more determined he was. If he took it very slowly . . . But it was more than a mile. He'd never make it.

He thought about Alex and Jenifer on their skiing honeymoon at Vail. People didn't know how lucky they were. He picked up his old hockey stick, turned it upside down, and tried walking with it as a cane, but twice across the kitchen was about all he could do.

A thought suddenly came to him: he would call a taxi! A wonderfully simple solution. He got out the phone book and found the number of a cab company. He had never used a taxi in his own town before. He listened to the crisp, metallic voice of the dispatcher as she repeated Jordan's address.

"Where do you want to go, sir?"

He hadn't prepared for that. "Well, down to the . . ." He couldn't say "Down to the bridge." She'd think he was crazy. "The corner of Pearl and Broadway." When they got to the bridge, he'd tell the driver he'd decided to get out there. After all, it was nobody's business but his own.

Sooner than he expected, the cab swerved into the drive in a shower of slush. To his surprise the driver was a woman, about fifty, a tough-looking woman with a bullet-shaped head and very short-cut, curly gray hair. She watched impatiently as he walked toward the cab, leaning on the handle end of the hockey stick.

"Goin' to play a little hockey?" she said as he got in clumsily. She kept her eyes on him in the mirror as he let himself down carefully onto the seat.

"No," he said. He didn't like her. Her scrutiny annoyed him.

"Where you goin'?"

"Down toward Pearl and Broadway." He paused as she swung the cab around. "Actually you can let me off at the bridge. I . . . uh . . . have to do some errands."

She sniffed. "Hardly worth the trip."

"It's worth it to me," he said coldly.

"Well, it's your money, buster, but it's my time."

He didn't answer. He felt angry all out of proportion to the provocation. What business was it of hers if he wanted a short ride in a taxi?

She drove fast, calling out insults to cars that got in her way. She skidded to a fast stop at the head of the bridge. "I can't park here so speed it up, buster."

The fact that he couldn't "speed it up" made him all the angrier. He got the door open and leaned the hockey stick outside onto the sidewalk, but it took him several minutes to get out. All the time she muttered.

"How much?" He wished he had the nerve to literally throw the money at her. He was so enraged he could hardly keep his voice steady.

"Eighty cents."

Eighty cents for one mile. Pretty good money. But he didn't say anything. He counted out the change and gave it to her. No tip.

She gave him a malevolent glare. "You college kids better learn how to carry your booze." She pulled away from the curb so fast, she almost hit a passing car, but it was she who indignantly blew her horn.

What a type! He leaned against the cold stones of the bridge, trying to cool off. She thought he was drunk. But since when did taxi drivers take on the morals of their passengers? Oh, forget it, he told himself. Don't let it spoil what you came for. It's probably a lousy life, driving a taxi. But he didn't really believe that, and it did nothing to make him feel forgiving.

He leaned his elbows on the bridge and looked down at the river. Yes, it was the way he thought it would be, that kind of cautious little stream of dark water in the middle, the ice piled up and white, like rock salt, along the banks, the black branches of the overhanging trees. It would freeze over when normal winter weather came back, but then in late March or April it would open again and pretty soon the water would come rushing and frothing down from the glacier in the mountains, and it would be almost time to go fishing.

He began to cry. He kept his face down toward the creek so the few passersby wouldn't notice him. Anyway, people often stopped and stared into Boulder Creek; no one would think it was odd. The warm wind rumpled his hair, but there was still a touch of chill at the back of the wind when it blew strongly enough. He had worn only a denim jacket that was too big for him now that he had lost weight. He tucked the hockey stick under his arm and leaned still further toward the water, and wept.

Finally he pulled himself together. Stupid way to carry on. He wiped his wet face with his handkerchief. Nobody had said he wouldn't live to see the spring. He could even go fishing, maybe, if the guys went trolling in the boat. No more stream fishing, of course . . . no more . . . He forced himself to stop thinking. He straightened up and blew his nose and began to wonder how he was going to get home.

When he had had the idea of the taxi, he had intended to ask the driver to come back for him in half an hour — but not that old witch. He leaned with his back to the bridge, thinking about it. Tony was in the library; Alex was in Vail; his mother had a class; Skip was in school; Em was on campus somewhere. If he could get across the street to the tobacco store, he could call the other cab company. There was quite a bit of traffic. It would be tricky to negotiate the street at his rate of speed.

As he stood there feeling a little panicky, a driver of a Ford passed him, slammed on his brakes, and backed up, causing considerable havoc in the traffic behind him. It was Nick.

Nick rolled down the window, ignoring the horn-blaring, and said, "What you doin'?"

Jordan was so glad to see him, he broke into a broad grin. "Can you give me a lift home?"

"Sure." Nick opened the door on the passenger side and Jordan made his slow way to the car, leaning on the hockey stick. He had not seen Nick for a couple of weeks, and he knew from the look of shock in Nick's face that he had changed. He had stopped looking at himself in the mirror except when he had to, because he hated the thin, white, haggard face that looked back at him. Everyone who knew him now knew of course that he was seriously ill, but no one talked to him about it. He supposed they had been warned off by the family. Even Nick had said nothing.

But now Nick said, "Are you all right? What the blazes are you doing standing here on the bridge?" He started up quickly when Jordan closed the door.

Jordan felt foolish, but decided he might as well be honest. "It seemed like spring. I wanted to look at the damned river." He laughed.

"Oh." Nick didn't laugh. "How'd you get there?"

"Took a cab." He told Nick about the driver.

"Oh, I know that old broad. She's famous for being nasty. She owns the company."

"Nick, am I keeping you from a class or anything?"

"No. I was just going over to feed the monkeys." Nick's lean, dark face was serious. When they reached Jordan's house, he didn't accept the invitation to come in for coffee, but he walked to the door with Jordan. "Listen, Jord, the next time you want to go anyplace, don't mess with a stupid taxi. Call me, you hear?"

"Sure, Nick. Thanks."

"I mean it. I'm not just talking."

"I know you do." Jordan tried to grin. "I wouldn't want to take you away from your monkeys."

"My monkeys can always wait. I mean it, guy, you call me, whatever you want. You hear me?"

"I hear you, Nick. Thanks a lot. Really, thanks." Jordan choked up and turned quickly away.

"I'll see you then. You watch yourself, buddy. Take care."

Jordan nodded.

Nick ran lightly down the walk to his car, but he didn't drive off until Jordan had gone into the house.

Cicero skidded across the kitchen floor and circled Jordan's legs.

"Watch it, will you? You'll trip me up." Jordan sat down heavily and threw his hockey stick across the floor with an angry fling, but his wrist didn't have the strength to send it more than a few feet. Cicero jumped away from it and then examined it curiously.

Jordan sat with his face in his hands. After a few minutes he got up and washed his face and heated up some coffee. He turned on the TV and watched a children's cartoon for a few minutes, thinking about young Jordan. Then he shut it off and lay down with Cicero beside him. He realized that he was very hungry. He waited for his mother to come home and fix lunch.

Twenty-Ninth

The day of the christening was also a sunny day, but there was a sharper chill in the wind and the puddles had crusted over. Jordan got ready early so he would have time to rest a while before they left for the church. He hoped he was going to be able to get through the ceremony without any problems. The night before he had had a brief choking spell, the first one. It had been frightening.

Alex and Jenifer were back from Vail looking happy and sunburned. All the family would be at the christening, of course, and Em had been asked to be godmother. The time was set for the end of the regular service, after the congregation had gone.

Tony got them to the church a little early. They sat in the car until the last of the congregation had left, and Pat waved a signal to them. Terry and Em arrived, Em holding young Jordan.

Skipper helped Jordan out of the car and kept a supporting hand under his elbow as they went up the flagstone walk to church.

Young Jordan looked bigger already and, Jordan thought, like a small cherub in his white christening dress. He looked at Jordan and then at the others, one by one, with impartial interest. Jordan sat down to save his strength until things were ready.

"Isn't he a love?" Em said.

"I think so." He had noticed with pleasure that Tony gave Em an approving look when she came in, in a new dress. He hoped something would come of that.

Pat came in, in his vestments. He stood by the font and explained the service briefly. In this kind of situation, it seemed to Jordan, Pat was at his best. He knew what he was talking about, and there were no strangers here he had to impress. He looked at Jordan. "Feel up to standing?"

"Sure." Jordan turned sideways in his chair and slowly levered himself to his feet. He shook his head when Alex started to help him. "I'm fine." He took the prayer book that Pat gave him, his responses marked.

They stood in a row, Terry with the baby in the center, Jordan on one side, Em on the other. The rest of the family stood facing them. Pat began the service in his measured, rather pleasant voice. After a minute Jordan put out his hand and steadied himself on the font. Pat gave him a quick little nod, as if to say that was all right. Jordan and Em read out their responses. Pat took the baby in his arms and dipped his fingers in the water of the font and sprinkled the baby's head. Young Jordan's eyes widened with surprise. When Pat made the sign of the cross on his forehead, young Jordan shut his eyes tight, wrinkled up his face, and screamed.

Jordan was alarmed. He had never seen the baby cry. But as Pat concluded the ceremony, he looked at Jordan and smiled. "That's a good sign. They say that means the devil's come out of him." He handed the baby back to Terry, and young Jordan instantly stopped crying.

Alex put his arm around Jordan and headed him out to the car, keeping him from slipping in the slushy walk. "You were a splendid godfather," he said. "Though I keep wishing that word didn't make me think of the Mafia."

"It all happened so fast," Jordan said. "I was just bracing myself to last through it, and it was over." As Alex helped him into the car, he said, "You'll keep an eye on the boy, won't you?"

"Don't worry, chum. I've got a big vested interest."

Before they left, Pat came out and said, "Jordan, I wanted to say I'm very proud that you're my son's godfather." His eyes, behind the glasses, were kind and warm. Of course, of course, Jordan thought, this is what Terry sees and she's right.

"An old heathen like me?" Jordan said.

"You're no heathen. You're a man who likes to make up his own mind about things. We don't all see life in the same way. I respect your attitudes." He grinned in a sudden, boyish way. "And Tony's, too, but don't tell him I said so." He patted Jordan's knee. "Get home and get some rest."

That night before he went to sleep, Jordan wrote a letter to his godson, with instructions on the envelope to Terry to save it for him until he was old enough.

DEAR JORDAN:

Today you were christened and I stood up as your godfather. In a way it's a bit of a fraud because I'm not a churchgoer, and anyway, I won't be on hand to do my duty by you. But you will be all right. You have three terrific uncles who will give you love, loyalty, and laughter, and probably now and then a bawling out. Your choice of a mother could not be improved upon. Your father and I aren't always on the same wavelength but he is a kind and honest man, a good man. You'll love your grandmother. And if you're ever back East, look up your grandfather. He's not all that bad. I like being your godfather, Jordie. It gives me a connection, something special. You're the closest I'll get to a child of my own. They'll tell you a nice bunch of lies about me; they always do that when a guy dies young, but don't fall for it. I might have turned into the biggest stuffed shirt in the U.S.A. — who knows. On the other hand, I might have been a Supreme Court Justice. You'll never know me, but I know you and I like you. I like the gleam in your eye and your toothless grin and the way you yell when you feel outraged. You'll do all right. But don't expect it to be easy. Life is a tough business. It can also be tremendous at times. And taking it all in all, I'm for it. The main thing is: use it. And now here's my own private benediction just for you: May the gods of the pine tree, the shooting star, the ice crystal, and the spider web all be good to you.

Love,

JORDAN

Thirtieth

Three weeks after the baby was born, Jordan collapsed on his way upstairs. He was put into bed in Tony's room. He remained conscious, but he kept losing track of time, and such a weariness overcame him, he could scarcely speak. Sometimes when he thought he had said something, no one had heard him.

His family was there, not always all at once but appearing and reappearing, his brothers, Terry, Pat. His mother seemed almost always to be there, sitting in a chair by the bed and holding his hand. He slept and woke and slept again. Dr. Parkhurst came and went, feeling for Jordan's pulse with his broad, competent fingers.

The weather turned wintry again. Jordan woke and heard the wind howling and moaning around the house, and saw the snow piled up on the windowpanes. A loose latch was clattering at one of the windows and the trapped wind sang an uncertain tune, like an amateur playing a recorder. Tony went to the window and secured the latch and the eerie tune stopped, but outside the house the wind boomed, and Jordan wondered if that was how the ocean sounded. He wanted to say, "I've never seen the ocean," but it didn't seem worth the effort.

He managed to say to Terry, "How's the baby?" and she took his hand and said, "He's fine. He's showing signs of a sense of humor."

He smiled. He wanted to hear more, but Dr. Parkhurst came and gave him a pill, and Terry went out of the room. Cicero ran into the room and jumped onto the bed. Tony started to take him out, but Dr. Parkhurst said, "Let him stay if Jordan wants him," and Jordan nodded. Cicero curled up beside Jordan's knee, keeping his bright eyes on his face.

Time slipped and tilted and righted itself again. Only Tony and Skipper were in the room, standing by his bed. Skipper looked so unhappy, Jordan made an effort to speak to him.

"Sport . . . Keep your eye . . ." He had to stop for a breath. ". . . on those stars . . ."

Skipper started to speak but instead he burst into tears. Tony put his arms around Skipper and held his head against his chest.

"It's all right, Skip, it's all right." He looked at Jordan. "I'd better take him out . . ."

"No," Jordan said. He waited a minute to get his breath. "He's been so good . . ."

"I know," Tony said.

Skipper got a handkerchief from his pocket and mopped his face. He managed to stop crying but his voice shook. "I'm sorry. I didn't mean to do that . . ."

Jordan lifted his hand as far as he could, and Skipper took it in his.

"Don't worry, Jordie, I'm not going to be a baby. I'll cheer them up, like you said. I've got a flock of jokes all lined up . . ."

Jordan squeezed his hand. "Furred bird?"

"Furred bird and the whole bit. I've been practicing." He had himself under control now.

Jordan winked at him.

His mother came in. She glanced searchingly at Skipper, but she said nothing. She sat down in her chair and held Jordan's other hand. He noticed how tired and sad she looked. It was terrible to have to do this to these people. He had a moment of anger, but he was too tired to sustain it. He closed his eyes.

Terry had come in. He felt her cool hand on his forehead. Someone had taken Cicero away, and he could hear him whining softly outside in the hall.

Then Alex was there, and Jenifer came in for a moment, kissed him on the forehead, and went out again. Dr. Parkhurst again. It was getting dark. Someone turned on the bedside lamp. Jordan felt as if he were drifting. He closed his eyes. Now and then someone said something in a low voice but he no longer tried to hear. For a second panic swept him, and he said, "Wait! I'm not ready." But the words were only in his mind.

He felt his mother's hand brushing the hair back from his forehead. There were things he wanted to tell her, but he didn't have the strength now. He let his head fall sideways on the pillow. He was too tired to talk anymore.